T0148862

PENGUIN BOOKS

THE LAST GREAT LOVE SONG

Paul Callan was born in Dublin, Ireland. As a young man, he abandoned his first attempt at becoming a novelist in pursuit of a business career. He has since written five historical novels, all of which combine intricate storytelling with exotic settings. His first, *The Dulang Washer*, was longlisted for the IMPAC award in 2012. His most recent novel, *The Secrets of the Sakura Girls*, was published by Penguin Random House SEA in 2021. He lives between London and Kuala Lumpur.

OTHER BOOKS BY THE AUTHOR

The Secret of the Sakura Girls, published by Penguin Random House
SEA, 2021

The Last Great
Love Song

Paul Callan

PENGUIN BOOKS
An imprint of Penguin Random House

PENGUIN BOOKS

USA | Canada | UK | Ireland | Australia
New Zealand | India | South Africa | China | Southeast Asia

Penguin Books is part of the Penguin Random House group of companies
whose addresses can be found at global.penguinrandomhouse.com

Published by Penguin Random House SEA Pte Ltd
9, Changi South Street 3, Level 08-01,
Singapore 486361

First published in Penguin Books by Penguin Random House SEA 2023

Copyright © Paul Callan 2023

ISBN 9789815058871

Typeset in Garamond by MAP Systems, Bangalore, India

www.penguin.sg

To Alex

Contents

Part 1

Chapter 1

The *lamburi* tree is tall, tall
Its branches sweep the sky
My search is in vain, and o'er is all
Like a mate-lorn dove am I.

Two young women stood staring at one another, excitement filling their faces. In unison, as if the same thought had come to their minds simultaneously, they ran across the wooden floor to the open window and competed for the best view. That twenty-four-year-old Toh was a princess and seventeen-year-old Fatima was a slave, did not matter to either of them.

Clear is the moon, with stars agleam
The raven wastes in the paddy field
O my beloved, when false I seem
Open my breast, my heart is relieved.

'Oh, that voice,' Toh exclaimed. 'It is so beautiful. I wonder who taught him how to put the poem to song?'

Fatima gazed at her mistress, who smiled back at her before laughing gleefully. Toh's gums were black, as were her tongue and the inside of her cheeks, but her teeth were sparkling white. Fatima had become so accustomed to the sight that it no longer troubled her, but Toh hated her mouth and was self-conscious about it.

Toh stretched her arm over Fatima's shoulders and held her tightly. She was in high spirits at the prospect of sharing her bed with Fatima that night.

3

Toh's husband was off roaming the countryside, or so he claimed, and she was looking forward to getting a decent night's sleep.

'I think he's gone,' Fatima said, as the two girls strained over the windowsill and peered down into the darkness. Toh sighed gently, sharing her best friend's disappointment.

'What's he like?' Toh asked.

'Tall and attractive-looking, but I've never spoken to him.' A pause filled the stillness. 'But I haven't really spoken to many of the other slaves, either.'

Toh turned away from the window, rested against the wall, and scanned the palace bedroom. 'Do you mind that?'

'Not speaking to them? No, not especially. They seem to prefer it that way.'

'Is it because you're my slave?'

'Probably,' Fatima blurted out, unsure of herself.

Toh looked around the vast room. Months after moving in, she continued to marvel at the building. Previously, the palace had been sited on the flat planes of Fern Mountain, surrounded by a thick jungle. Now, it rested on a plateau mid-way up the mountain, with paddy fields that stretched in every direction. From its foundation to its gabled roof, the building was made entirely of wood. What confounded her the most was that dowels, rather than screws or nails, had been employed in the construction. Her brother, the Raja, had assured her that if struck by a strong gust of wind, like those common to the region's tropical climate, the palace would roll over rather than shatter into tiny pieces. 'Just like a bull elephant,' he had reassured her.

'Maybe I should invite Aashif to come here and sing for us?' Toh suggested.

'They say he's quite shy,' Fatima said.

'Perhaps not then.'

Toh grabbed Fatima's arm. 'Race you,' she said, and they both ran across the room to the huge bed they shared when her husband was away. In the opposite corner of the room, a much smaller bed was swathed in silk netting to protect Fatima from mosquitoes. Similar netting, but of a finer quality, was draped around the principal bed.

Before they settled down for the night, Toh gently drew the door open. Peeking along the corridor, she was reassured to find that the guard was fast asleep.

* * *

The next day, with the scorching sun beating down relentlessly, Toh and Fatima strolled around the perimeter of the palace and watched the men at work. The newly painted loadbearing stanchions acted as stilts. They raised the palace off the ground by a good fifteen feet to protect it from the horrendous floods that always followed the storms. The stilts also afforded security against wild animals, especially snakes, and created sufficient ventilation that cooled the floor and helped the walls and roof breathe.

In the middle of the opening, a wide flight of stairs led up to a trapdoor that provided access into the palace. At night, despite the doors being locked together, a fit and battle-hardened warrior would sleep on top of them for added security.

Every inch of the building's exterior had been painted with a thick, tar-like substance. Oriental designs in yellow, the royal colour, were beginning to cover the walls. By the time the workers finished, little of the black would be seen.

Despite the heat, Fatima wore a long-sleeved, green-and-gold-patterned silk blouse and a brown sarong. She repeatedly tugged at her left sleeve when it threatened to reveal the withered skin that ran all the way up her arm to her shoulder—the consequence of tipping a pot of boiling water over herself when she was younger.

They stopped to study the decorators as they painted. 'I hope my brother is pleased with the progress,' Toh said to Fatima softly, keeping her head low to ensure none of the workers could see her open mouth.

'It looks beautiful,' Fatima said. 'I could watch the decorators work for hours.'

'To think, it's 1825 and this building was only dismantled a few months ago. We are now approaching *Raya* and the holy month. By the time we get to Eid, it will all be finished.'

'It's as well that the kitchen is housed over there,' Fatima said, glancing across at the row of single-storey, whitewashed buildings with *attap* roofs that formed the servants' quarters. 'Can you imagine what would happen if there was a fire?' Fatima shuddered, touching her friend's arm.

'Come on,' the princess said. 'Let's go and see how the gardener and his men are progressing. Maybe you'll show me which one is Aashif.'

'His skin is as dark as the colour of the palace.'

Toh ignored her friend's description as they entered the gardens. Men swarmed all over the place, working in the flowerbeds, tending privy hedges, digging at the soil, or stabbing spear-like implements into the lawns. Toh was happy that, after the chaos of the previous months, healthy verdure had begun to form.

'I can't see him anywhere,' Fatima said peering at the scene before them.

'How many dark-skinned slaves do we have?'

'I don't think there are that many. I've only ever seen a few.' She paused. 'Oh, there he is,' she said, nodding towards a group of men working near the servants' quarters.

They made their way towards the whitewashed buildings but as soon as they got within calling distance, Aashif disappeared behind the quarters.

Toh came to a stop. 'Let's not bother him now,' she said, and they began retracing their steps. As they reached the palace, the sound of horses' hooves at the far side of the building told her that her brother had arrived. Without waiting for Fatima, she ran around to the front to find him dismounting from his horse. Accompanying him was his usual troop of two hundred men, who remained seated on their mounts as brother and sister embraced.

The Raja was a tall man in his mid-thirties. It was clear to Toh that his mop of black hair had not received attention in weeks. His face, while streaked with dirt after his recent journey, displayed many of the traits of youth, and his body demonstrated the firmness of a fierce warrior.

Toh took hold of his arm and directed him to the stairs. 'The men need to wash and eat,' he said. He stalled when Fatima approached, and his face brightened.

'Your Highness,' Fatima said, her voice friendly to the man who was more a father to her than a raja.

'You look well, Fatima,' he replied. 'Can you speak to Suraya in the kitchen and let her know we've returned? Ask her to prepare food for the men.'

Fatima was tempted to say that the noise of their arrival would no doubt have forewarned Suraya to commence cooking but nodded politely and turned away.

'Once you've done that, come back and join us,' he called after her. The Raja was fully aware that Fatima had long been his sister's confidant, and she was used to sharing in the siblings' discussions. 'Don't be long,' he added.

The Raja nodded to his men and they proceeded to dismount. He called one of his officers to him and gave instructions for the men to prepare to bed down for the night beneath the palace.

'You've done an excellent job, from what I can tell,' the Raja said, his eyes sharp as he glanced over his sister's shoulder at the building. 'From a distance, it looks as imposing as I hoped. Enough to ward off anyone thinking of attacking, and we know there are many who carry such a notion.'

'Would you like a tour of the grounds?'

He shook his head vigorously. 'Not now—later. First, I'd like to soak in a bath and then, eat. The men should do the same.'

They watched as the warriors gathered their possessions and selected places under the palace to billet. There was not a hint of rancour, these men held each other in such high regard that ill will never entered their thinking. They were a disciplined fighting unit and prepared to kill for each other without question—the Raja had attended to that.

When Fatima returned, the Raja embraced her openly, in full view of his men. He studied her small, heart-shaped angular face. She had the right proportions of nose and cheekbones, and full lips accentuated her beauty. He ruffled her short black hair playfully and looked into her penetrating black eyes. 'You understand that I'm making all my men jealous right now.'

With one arm around each woman, the Raja led them up the stairs and into the palace. A further flight of stairs led them to the throne room. On entering, the Raja stood alone and took in the imposing space where his throne stood on a stage at one end, ten feet off the floor. He turned to his sister, his expression full of pride. At times, he was unsure which of the two women was more attractive. He knew that Toh had a steely solitude hidden behind her large, black eyes. Unlike Fatima, she had long black hair that she allowed to cover her arresting face, though he could never tell if she let it fall as a gesture of coquettishness or to hide her ugly black mouth.

* * *

Bathed and refreshed, the Raja joined his sister and Fatima again. The three of them sat cross-legged on the floor supported by a variety of cushions of different colours, sizes, and materials. They ate the food prepared by Suraya, the old kitchen maid. An array of dishes sat between them: *gulai ikan masak tempoyak*, fish cooked in a spicy, durian sauce; *rendang ayam*, chicken marinated in a spicy paste; and a mix of blanched vegetables consisting of cassava shoots, wild fern shoots, and *jantung pisang*, the purple part of a banana blossom; and all with plentiful portions of rice. They ate with their right hands, scooping up a small helping of rice, mixing it into the sauce or paste and adding a portion of fish or chicken.

'Now that the palace is in a position where it can be better defended, you need to keep the guards on constant alert, sister. From here you have the ideal view of the tin mines below, meaning that any disturbance can be addressed speedily. The mines must be protected at all costs and before all other needs, it is where most of our income derives. Well, that and the rice fields that feed us all, including my army of warriors.'

Toh studied her brother's noble face and nodded eagerly, anxious to demonstrate her confidence.

'Above us, of course,' he continued, 'are the graves of the many warriors of the past. As we all know, they are defended by the *jinn* that none of us have ever seen. God help anyone who dares to attack from above.'

The Raja leant to one side, washed his hands vigorously in a bowl of water and then dried them using the hand cloth next to him. He studied the women closely, his mind seeming to journey to another realm as he addressed his sister. 'Tell me, where is that husband of yours?'

A heavy silence weighed over them, immediately placing Toh on edge. She let out a small breath and glanced at Fatima for support. Staring dumbly at her brother, she could only offer him a wan smile of embarrassment. 'He's up country,' she finally said quietly.

The Raja sighed with exasperation and bitterness entered his voice. 'I want him reined in, sister. Luckily for them, your first two husbands died. Otherwise, I might have taken a sword to them myself.'

Chapter 2

It was late in the afternoon, a time of day that Aashif had come to appreciate—for it was then that he worked with Hisham, the head gardener. This arrangement had been in place since the palace had been moved to its new position on the plateau.

Aashif had toiled away with the rest of the slaves through the day, the sun harsh on his eyes each time he pushed himself upright to ease the ache in his back. He was tall and lean and believed that he was around nineteen years old—Hisham had told him his age many years before, on the eve of Raya. Since then, although Raya came earlier each year, Aashif had been able to calculate when his birthday was. He stood up and used his hand to shade his eyes against the sun's glare as he studied the growing shadows. It would not be long before he could break away and join Hisham.

He looked at the developing shape of the gardens with pleasure. He had contributed to their evolution far more than the others because of the joy he found while working on the land. He loved it, he had told the others. He loved watching the plants he had seeded grow, and it was not unusual to find him watering them while others rested. His dedication had not gone unnoticed by the head gardener.

At last, he set down his hoe and went in search of Hisham. He did not want to be late, he knew how disciplined Hisham was and did not want to disappoint him. He was in awe of the man, who had been like a surrogate father to him. Aashif was haunted by the memory of the man he believed to be his true father, but he had never revealed his dreams to anyone, especially not Hisham.

Everything he knew about plants, trees, birds, and animals, he had learned from Hisham. He had such respect for the old man. As Aashif approached, he spotted the commander of the warriors walking away. Hisham had once been the head warrior and was rumoured to have been one of the old Raja's most ferocious fighters. After he had been badly wounded in a battle, the Raja had insisted that he take on the role of defending the palace and its lands. Hisham's love of gardening revealed itself—as time passed and his strength waned, he had come to enjoy his new role. Even now, he sometimes offered advice to the fighting men, many of whom he had helped train.

'Sir,' Aashif said, on reaching him.

'Good afternoon, Aashif. How has your day been?'

'Good, sir,' Aashif answered. Even if his day had not been a success, he would never have told Hisham.

'Did I spot one of the men taking a nap earlier?'

Aashif knew right away who Hisham was referring to—Feisal. 'He tripped over one of the flower boxes . . . and fell to the ground. He sprained his back . . . but he was up and working again soon,' he stammered.

Hisham allowed a smile to creep on to his face as he decided to let the matter rest. It would not please him for his prodigy to become known as someone who told tales on his workmates.

* * *

Hisham had reached a point in his life where he cherished the arrival of each new day. As a warrior for the Raja's late father, he had been a fit, nimble, and brutal fighter. He was taller than most of his fellow warriors, and he had earned his reputation as a man who was never to be crossed. His body might have shrunk, but he was still rumoured to be agile enough to be challenged to a physical contest. These days, his face was so weather-beaten that it belied the tales of a young and handsome man. The wrinkles on his face appeared to be fighting each other for dominance, but it did not bother him. His hair, which was now thin and grey, illustrated his maturing years, but his eyes remained as sharp as a hornbill's.

Since the palace had been relocated, one of Hisham's greatest pleasures had been taking Aashif under his wing and watching his planned successor develop. He studied Aashif and cast his mind back to all those years ago, to the day a frightened little boy had arrived, accompanied by a band of slaves. He had been a striking little fellow with dark, glowing skin that became the talk of the palace. To this day, Hisham couldn't fathom how the boy took to him—but it had remained that way ever since. He broke free of his thoughts to inspect the ongoing works, pondering over whether he might have been better off guiding Aashif towards a trade, rather than becoming a gardener. However, the young man had shown such dedication to the plants and trees that he doubted he could have been able to prise him away.

'What would you have me do today, sir?'

'Before we start, let me show you something.'

Aashif followed the old man as they stepped into the copse of trees nearby, strolling across the freshly cut tidy *rumput* grass, before arriving at a wall of *lalang*, a coarse, knee-high grass of a different shade. 'There,' Hisham said, waving at a flower within the mass of lalang. The crown of the plant had a puckered, cone-shaped appearance and was pale pink. Beneath its crown, leaves of a similar colour were spreading outwards.

Aashif bent low to gain a better view.

'Be careful young man. What have I told you? Never approach any plant unless you know its origin.'

Aashif glanced over at Hisham, his face overcome by self-doubt.

'That is yet another of the *bunga hantu*, also known as ghost flowers. As I have explained to you before, such flowers are believed to have been planted and cultivated by *hantu* spirits. Some of them are often used in medicines but others are highly poisonous and can cause blindness and deafness.'

'What should we do?'

'We should leave it alone. Let the others know where the flower is, I will do the same.'

'Do you know how to turn it into medicine?'

'No—that is a skill for the *Bomohs* and the medicine men.'

'They say that there is a Bomoh further up the mountain, near the graves of the warriors.'

'That is true, but only members of the royal family are granted access to him.'

'Is he not a ghost?'

'Some say he is, while others say he is a spirit who is able to conjure up all sorts of magic spells. You want to avoid Bomohs, and you should certainly make sure you don't offend them.' Hisham held his index finger to his lips and gestured to Aashif, nodding in the direction of the lalang.

Aashif fell silent when he noticed the lalang moving. He stood frozen at the sight of a long blue coral snake, with a red head and tail. It was one of the most venomous snakes in the region. The two men watched it slither away, wondering what had disturbed the animal. 'It must have been a rat,' Hisham said.

They stepped away cautiously and returned to the task of tending the orderly rows of red hibiscus flowers that Aashif had painstakingly watered each day, for weeks on end.

'We need to remove the new weeds in the beds,' Hisham said, looking up through the branches of the nearby trees at the bright blue of the late-afternoon sky. Without further ado, they each picked up a hoe from the stack of garden implements nearby and began the task of tilling the soil, stooping intermittently to gather up weeds.

Later that day, Aashif broke away and watched the sun going down behind the trees as evening fell. He loved to end his days by listening to Hisham talk about his pilgrimage to Mecca. There was little he hadn't already asked him about the topic, but he knew Hisham took as much pleasure in telling the tale as Aashif did listening to it. 'Sir,' Aashif began. 'Can I ask you something? Last week I witnessed the Raja and his warriors arriving, and I have been asking myself ever since why people like me aren't warriors.'

Hisham was puzzled. 'I used to be a warrior before I became the head gardener.'

'I don't mean gardeners,' Aashif said, suddenly emotional. 'I mean people like me—with my dark skin.'

Hisham was struck by the thought that Aashif had been waiting for the opportunity to raise this matter. He stared at his young assistant sharply, struggling for an answer. 'You come from Africa, lad. You need to be born in these lands to be allowed to fight for the Raja.'

'Why?'

Hisham swallowed. 'That's the way it is.'

'If I was in Africa, could I be a warrior there?'

'I suppose so, but you would also need to be a believer.'

'But I am. You taught me how. I say my prayers every time I hear the calling.'

Before Hisham had a chance to respond, Aashif continued. 'I have been thinking for a while that, maybe, I should do as you once did and make my pilgrimage to Mecca. What do you think?'

Hisham understood, for the first time, the impact of his teachings on the young man's mind. In one sense, he was proud of having encouraged Aashif's belief and yet, he also knew the time was approaching when Aashif would receive the calling to make the long journey to the Holy Land.

'You said that Africa is much closer to Mecca than here.'

'True. Mecca is above Africa on the map, remember. From here, you would have to make a long journey by land and across vast open seas.'

'And would I come across warriors from Africa at Mecca, too?'

'Certainly, you would come across many types of people there.'

'Including Malay warriors?'

Hisham quietly nodded his head.

'And do they also have rajas in Africa?'

'I see no reason why not.'

Aashif stretched his arms above his head. 'So, I could go to Mecca and then journey to Africa? Who knows, I might even become a warrior and discover where I come from.'

Aashif desperately wanted to add: 'And find my father.' Unknown to Hisham, Aashif longed to embrace his father. This was the man who had fought like a tiger, to stop the two from being separated, when Aashif was a small child. He could not recall his mother, but his father's wild and contorted face was before him now, as he bellowed, threatened, and roared until he was clubbed to the ground. The two had been forced apart at the slave market, where his father was sold to an Arab trader. Even now, he was able to cast his mind back to the memory of a large group of men—led by some pale-skinned men carrying guns—who had stormed into their village and captured whoever they chose. The haunting dream held him hostage again and again: his father slowly rose to his feet and grappled at the empty space between them, while tears soaked into Aashif's face. When the distance between them grew, Aashif cried soundlessly—promising that he would return one day to find his father. The bond between Aashif and Hisham had grown so strong that it was no longer possible for Aashif to talk to the old man about these hopes and dreams; it would have caused him too much pain.

'It's time to get back,' Hisham declared, taking in the darkening sky. Aashif was disappointed, he wanted to carry on talking and seek the old man's advice on his growing frustrations at being treated differently from everybody else. Why was he nearly always the last to eat and then expected to collect everyone's banana-leaf plate? He shrugged. Another time, perhaps.

Chapter 3

Princess Toh sat on the window seat, contemplating the mountains in front of her that stretched out all the way to the sea. She had never journeyed across them, nor had she ever been told of anyone doing so. As a small girl, she had visited the sea with her brother, but had little memory of the experience. The scorching sun was already up, and Toh dreaded the trip ahead of her.

In the courtyard, Anwar was waiting for her. He was a loyal and trusted man. It had often been said that he was the only warrior still fighting who might have been able to hold his own, in combat, against Hisham in his prime.

Fatima was unhappy as she departed Toh's chamber to wave her mistress off. She would have preferred to accompany Toh, but was not allowed to meet the Bomoh. Neither was Anwar. Instead, he would have wait within sight of the Bomoh's cave, and his presence nearby would be a comfort for Toh. As she was responsible for guarding the Raja's property, the princess knew that her visit had to be a short one: She would be away for less than a day.

'I could always join you and wait by Anwar's side,' Fatima had offered.

'No, it is best that you remain here. You can tell my husband that I've gone to visit one of the villages—if he ever returns, that is.' Her brother's angry criticism of her husband dominated Toh's mood. As she recalled the Raja's heated words, she continued to puzzle over his warning that this man should never sit on the throne. Should her brother learn of his long bouts of rage, she doubted her husband would ever want to return to the palace.

Her first two husbands had been cruel to the Raja's subjects, and the Raja had punished them severely. No one other than Fatima and the Bomoh knew that her first husband had lost his temper and struck a savage blow to her face.

Toh had sought the Bomoh's advice following the incident. Soon after that, when her husband attempted to assault her again, he had become paralysed and died days later. During her second marriage, she had to constantly reprimand her husband for treating the servants disrespectfully. During a particularly violent argument, he had accidentally scratched her with his fingernails. She had visited the Bomoh at once and her husband was subsequently struck down with a virulent itch, that brought about a speedy death. As it was, the memories of both her husbands had faded into insignificance. While she did not want more death on her hands, she could not continue in her present relationship without some help and guidance.

As Fatima knew only too well, what disturbed Toh the most was being in public and having to reveal her mouth to anyone. Anwar, however, was a man of considerable discretion and never stared into her face.

'By the time I get there, it will be blazing hot, and I'll be all sticky and sweaty,' Toh groaned.

Fatima laughed, 'Then I shall have a nice bath ready for your return.'

For an instant, Toh allowed her mind to wander back to the day that her father had first handed Fatima over to her, swaddled in a blanket. She had never imagined that the little bundle would become her closest friend and confidant one day.

* * *

Toh had stored her memories of her previous husbands somewhere in the back of her mind, but setting off on the journey brought her back to events that made her question why she had been such a bad judge of men.

'Ready, Princess?' Anwar addressed her formally, from up on his horse.

Toh nodded, flicked a loose strand of hair from her face and nudged her horse forward. The moment they stepped out beyond the shadows of the palace, the sun struck them and Toh was soon dabbing her face. She was dressed in a tight outfit made of brown cotton, as loose-fitted garments were more likely to become entangled in the thick foliage of the jungle. Anwar was dressed for battle. On his head, he wore a conical tin helmet, while his upper body was covered in a dark, leather jerkin. Two long iron *kris* daggers crossed his back, their handles jutting beyond his shoulders.

The instant they entered the jungle, her ears were filled by a cacophony of hisses and caws and the calls of gibbons and birds. The burning heat of the sun was replaced by a thick, muggy humidity that made her gulp for air. Towering *merbau* trees, wide-spread flame trees, palm trees, pine trees, birches, and *taman* trees—the extended branches were trapped together so densely that it was impossible to see anything beyond the patchwork of leaves that surrounded them.

Toh looked at Anwar who was ahead of her, the muscles on his arms prominent as he bent to avoid a cluster of thick, entwined branches. She gripped the reins and stooped, pulling the head of her horse down and causing beads of sweat to drip into her eyes. Though she was desperate to wipe them away, all she could do was blink and pray that her horse would find its way forward.

During her struggle against the thickest of the branches, Toh found herself remembering Fatima's expression when they had set off, and her promise to have a bath ready for Toh on her return. Had it not been for the severity of her husband's misconduct, she might have shouted to Anwar to turn back right then.

She was jolted from a stupor of confusing thoughts when she glanced ahead and became aware that the ground was rising sharply. Anwar raised his hand, slowed his horse and dismounted. He had no need to pass on instructions to Toh; it was clear to both of them that the rest of their journey would be made on foot. To ward off snakes, Anwar got his horse to stomp its hooves—a process he would repeat regularly as they climbed, the vibrations warning snakes to stay hidden. Hemmed in by trees, the princess began to feel trepidatious at the thought that she would soon meet the Bomoh again.

Her body was gasping as the climb began to take its toll. Despair, at the prospect of being in the Bomoh's presence once more, threatened to unhinge her. She hated the man and his stupid rhymes—typical of how Bomohs communicated with their callers—but most of all, she feared his ugliness. At the end of their climb, she gave Anwar a small bow and passed the reins of her horse to him, her stomach heaving. An unnerving silence came over the forest. As she pressed on alone, the only sound she could hear was the thumping of her heart.

The scene ahead disgusted her. In the side of the mountain was a dark opening, the entrance to the Bomoh's cave. As she approached, she stood rigid at the sight of a large rat scurrying across the ground. She tried to gather herself and keep on going when a second rat scampered after the first. The hairs on her arms and the back of her neck stiffened. Somehow, she managed to trap a scream in her throat and avoid calling for Anwar. She waited a moment to compose herself, drew up some hidden courage, took a deep breath, and walked on.

She stared into the darkness, desperately trying to hold on to her nerve. She called out but there was no response. Breathing hard, she edged forward and was shocked by the sudden noise of flapping wings—bats. She nervously prayed that none of them would land on her head.

Enraged at the disturbance, a handful of bats broke free of the colony hanging from the roof and flapped about, screeching. All she could do was stay still, close her eyes, and pray that the whole colony would not take flight. She held her ground and waited for calm to descend, but her senses were overcome by the nauseating smell of *guano*, bat droppings. She peered into the cave, trying to spot the Bomoh, but she was met by a blackness that reminded her of her mouth.

Her nostrils twitched when she picked up the scent of smoke, though she could not find evidence of a fire. Then, when the bats had settled down, she heard a shuffling sound. 'It's me, Princess Toh,' she called out and finally, she spotted a small light from smouldering embers on one side of the cave. The light grew and she was able to recognize the lumbering figure of the Bomoh, his huge silhouette bent over the coals. Her attention was drawn to a slight movement, and she saw the Bomoh, clad in a loose, pale *baju melayu*, waving a sleeve over the fire and causing flames to leap up at him.

Toh held her breath as she glanced around the cave. Above her head was a row of human skulls, covered in spiderwebs. Mesmerized, she followed a spider working its way toward a neighbouring skull. She didn't want to stay in this vile place for a moment longer than she had to.

The Bomoh impatiently waved to indicate that Toh should join him by the fire. The dirt floor was covered by a wicker mat, and she could feel her feet sink into the ground under her weight as she gingerly moved across the cave to join him. When she reached the fire, a stool covered in a grey layer of dust was waiting for her, and she sat on it. All she wanted to do was relay the problem caused by her husband, collect a potion, and leave.

The Bomoh, a huge expanse of a man, raised his head and Toh saw that his eyes were closed. She studied his cracked, withered face, with the texture of dry leaves. It occurred to her that no time seemed to have passed since her first visit to him, four years ago. She knew that it was best not to hurry him, so she sat still and waited for him to come to life. After a pause, he opened his eyes and fixed her with a fierce glare.

He prised his lips apart using his fat tongue and opened his mouth as if to speak but stopped himself and rolled his open hands at her, indicating that she should first explain the purpose of her visit. Transfixed by the sight of his toothless gums, Toh squinted. 'The problem is my husband,' she began.

A physical urgency made Toh want to convey her problem and leave as quickly as possible, but his hard, cruel eyes seemed to penetrate her deepest thoughts, and she struggled for words. She forced free a nervous breath and eventually began. 'He has not been violent to me, unlike my first two husbands. But every time we argue, he screams at me so loud that the whole palace can hear him. If I say anything he disagrees with, he takes it as a personal slight and his ranting begins. He will go on and on until I respond, and then he screams at me as loud as he can. I'm sure he does it deliberately, to embarrass me. Although he has not attacked me, he often comes rushing at me, threatening to do so. He is the same with the servants. The Raja does not know anything of his behaviour, but I fear he will soon learn of it from one of the staff. My slave, Fatima, has witnessed many such arguments and is frightened of him. She is the only person I can talk to about it but if he ever overheard us, I am certain he would attack her. And I do not ever want that to happen.' Toh pressed her lips together, fearing she had revealed more than she intended. Finally, she spoke, 'I want him stopped, but I don't want him to die.' She was met by another ferocious glare and all she could do was sit still and wait.

After a pause, the Bomoh slapped his thighs with his huge hands and left them resting there. At last, he pushed himself up, and Toh watched him trudge to an area of the cave beyond the fire. She could not see what he was doing, but it sounded like he was preparing a concoction for her. She listened to the clunk of clay pots followed by the sound of stoppers popping open, all the while clenching her hands tightly, fearing that every animal in the cave was looking at her. She listened to the racket of stones grinding together and could tell that he was mixing a medicine that would help stop the arguments. He came back to her and stood over her. Awkwardly, Toh rose to her feet and he passed her a small bottle containing a paste with a pinkish hue. He spoke in a rough, croaky voice when he said,

'Scream no more the lamburi may hear
For a price be paid by another unnear.'

Then he began to chant.

Chapter 4

The previous night, Hisham had instructed Aashif to join him in the morning, to shear the hedges surrounding the courtyard and tidy up the flowerbeds. It was the same morning that Anwar and Toh had set out together. Both men had been working when Anwar rode into the yard and they stopped what they were doing. Anwar had given Hisham a polite nod and Hisham had returned the gesture, though he refrained from engaging in conversation, as he was aware that Anwar was on royal duty.

Anwar's attire prompted Hisham to reflect on how hot he used to get when he wore his armour—but pride overcame any such discomfort. The old man watched as the princess hurried into the yard and mounted her horse, before the two set off in the direction of the mountains.

'Where's our young princess heading in such a hurry?' Hisham asked. There was affection in his voice, for he remembered her as a tiny girl. He knew that she was not the witch that many of the workforce called her. She had earned the title because of her black mouth. When he caught Aashif staring, he laughed at his own foolishness. 'She is a beautiful young woman, had it not been for her mouth she would never have been called a witch.' He paused. 'It is wrong of me to ignore the others when they speak of her in that way—I must put a stop to it.

'If she ever knew that she was called a witch, it would break her heart. In her young life she has had to endure the death of two husbands and from what we know of her third husband, he does not seem to make her happy at all.'

'What happened to her first husband?'

'He was a healthy young man, and many thought him deserving of a princess, but he was violent to her.'

'He was a fine-looking gentleman,' Aashif said. 'It's hard to imagine him being cruel to anyone.'

'We never know what happens behind closed doors. And if we do, we often wish that we didn't.' There was a tremor in the old man's voice at the memory of the princess's distress at the death of her first husband.

'How could anyone be cruel to Princess Toh?'

Hisham sighed, as if he was carrying the burdens of the princess on his shoulders.

'And her second husband?'

'He was a very different man, but also disrespectful to the princess and the people.'

Hisham recalled Toh's struggle to leave her childhood behind and enter womanhood. Never did he imagine that so much sadness would befall her. Thank God for Fatima, he thought, as he had so many times before.

Hisham's eyes narrowed. 'It is hard to believe, but her second husband was worse than her first. He was an older man and had little regard for others.'

The gardener sighed. 'It still haunts me that there was nothing I could do to defend one of the slaves working in this yard—and with the princess present, too.' The tremor was still in his voice as he continued, 'The slave, who was perhaps your age, had been ordered by the husband to take the reins of his horse. The lad was terrified and snatched at the strap—causing the horse to rear up and unsaddle the husband who fell heavily to the ground.' Hisham allowed a laugh to escape at the memory. 'I remember watching as the man slowly picked himself up from the ground before turning on the young slave and lashing him with a whip. Had Princess Toh not screamed for him to stop, he would have killed the boy.'

Aashif was stunned into silence.

'Following that incident, it was discovered that the husband was cruel to all the slaves in the palace, and that he would constantly berate the princess over trivial matters.'

Hisham's eyes were angry. 'It took that young man a long time to recover and who can blame him for rejoicing in the husband's death.' The old man sneered bitterly.

The two men stood quietly and Hisham gave him a small shrug before picking up a rake and resuming work.

Aashif couldn't clear his mind of the image of the defenceless boy being whipped. 'What happened to the slave?' he asked.

'He was afraid for his life and ran away.'

A wind picked up suddenly, disturbing Hisham's pile of leaves.

Aashif gasped. 'Did they catch him?'

'No, never. When the Raja learned of the slave's ordeal, he ordered that he was to be treated kindly—if he was ever found.'

An expression of relief appeared on Aashif's face. 'So nobody knows what happened to him.'

'Nobody. He probably died in the jungle somewhere,' Hisham said sadly. 'The souls of many grief-stricken slaves haunt these lands.'

The voice of his father was in Aashif's head and he couldn't clear the sound from in his mind. It was then that he considered for the first time, what would become of him when he was an old man. What future was there for a slave in a land that would remain foreign to him?

'Come,' Hisham said, scooping up as many of the leaves as he could. 'Let's get this lot to the fire.'

Aashif gathered his pile of leaves in his arms and followed Hisham.

* * *

It was as the two men were making their way back to the courtyard that Aashif spoke. 'Sir, why can't I be a free man? And the others too.'

Hisham had long been dreading this day and found Aashif's question more challenging than he had ever envisaged. 'When I was training to be a young warrior, I learned that slavery found a foothold in these lands over a thousand years ago. In those days there were more wars, not only here but in many neighbouring lands too. Slaves have never fought in any of the wars, but instead make up for the warriors' absence.'

'The people who captured us slaves went all the way to Africa. Couldn't they have captured more slaves from here?'

'They do, though dark-skinned slaves, like you, are usually bought in the Holy Land, in Jeddah.'

Aashif stopped in his tracks. 'I've been to the Holy Land, to Mecca?'

'Yes and no, lad. You have been to the Holy Land, but not Mecca. Malays on pilgrimage usually buy slaves of your skin colour from the Arab merchants.'

'Then I was very close to Mecca?'

'Yes, for a short time. The story has it that your ship's captain sailed to China but went first to Malaya and then went south.'

In the distance, Aashif could see Fatima talking to one of the guards. 'And the women?'

'They are local slaves, carried from the land where they were born.'

'But what about their parents?'

'In some places where a chief rules supreme, he can force the parents to surrender their child.'

Aashif was momentarily speechless. 'So how many slaves are there?'

Hisham dropped his eyes. 'In these parts, three thousand or so.'

Aashif was dumbstruck. 'And Fatima?'

'Hers is a sad tale. Her father died before she was born. Her mother went into labour when her village was under siege by enemies of the late Raja—the shock of the attack brought on Fatima's birth. Her mother pleaded for one of the female village elders to hide Fatima, but she was killed soon after giving birth. According to the elder, who survived the assault, somehow, Fatima slept through everything and was found on a riverbank in upper Perak, swaddled in a thick green blanket. The colour of the blanket had saved her life.'

'She must have been terribly frightened.'

'She wore a beaming smile.'

Aashif was startled. 'You were there when she was found?'

Tenderness clouded the old man's face and he spoke softly, 'With the help of the village elder, I was the one who found her.'

Aashif stared at Hisham with a look of surprise and admiration, and the old man gave him a rueful smile. 'I took her immediately to the Raja. He accepted the baby and asked me what I thought should be done with her—I was in charge of his warriors at the time. I knew that Princess Toh was an intelligent girl who had been brought up to respect all people, slaves included, so I suggested to him that Princess Toh could learn how to care for a young child, and he agreed.'

Aashif gazed towards the palace, as Fatima set out in their direction.

* * *

The prospect of meeting Fatima in Hisham's company set Aashif's pulse racing. Whenever they had met, other people had always been present and they had never spoken.

'I didn't know her story,' Aashif said.

'She never told you?'

'I've never spoken to her.' A surge of emotion gripped him at the thought of Fatima as a vulnerable baby being discovered by the man who now stood next to him.

Hisham sounded surprised. 'Then you have been denied the pleasure of a delightful and caring young woman.'

Aashif detected the strength of Hisham's pride. 'So I have been told,' he said.

The nearer Fatima came, the more Aashif doubted whether she would talk to him directly. Whenever he had been in her presence before, the opportunity to talk to her had never arisen. He had once offered her a polite nod, but she had turned away before his gesture and he feared that she thought him aloof. Unease mounted in him, but then a smile heightened Fatima's flawless, dewy complexion and he was awestruck by her confident manner.

'Hello, Uncle.'

Aashif was rendered numb by anxiety over his stammer, until she turned to him with a smile and tugged at her sleeve. 'Hello, Aashif,' she said.

Aashif's mouth was dry and his mind was filled by the thought of Fatima as a baby, swaddled in a green blanket. Enthralled by her calm voice, he stuttered, 'Hello,' relieved that he was able to speak.

'The gardens are magnificent, Uncle Hisham.'

Aashif couldn't drag his eyes away from her. Instead, he imagined her father fighting to the death to prevent his daughter becoming a slave. He had a vision of his soul in the afterlife, battling any obstacle to protect her.

'A lot of credit goes to this young man here.'

Aashif was embarrassed and feared that at any moment, the skin on his face would peel away, such was the heat in his cheeks.

'Then thank *you*, Aashif.'

Aashif struggled to say something meaningful.

'I have to meet Suraya and mustn't keep her waiting,' she said, before sidestepping them both and heading towards the kitchen.

Chapter 5

Anwar had noticed Princess Toh's face darken as she approached the entrance to the cave. He had nodded at her encouragingly. It had been the same every time she visited the Bomoh. At one point, he caught sight of two enormous rats scuttling around her and understood her hesitancy.

Anwar was accustomed to such creatures, having learned to live among them as a small boy. Under the guidance of his father, he had become a master tracker who could camouflage himself in any terrain. When the late Raja had been told of his skill, he had arranged for the boy to train in the art of war and learn how to search out the enemy and avoid ambushes.

One of Anwar's fondest pastimes was looking after his horses. His father was respected in the community because of the three horses he kept, and the task of tending to them fell on Anwar's shoulders. He stood now, caressing one of their manes. As a loyal warrior of the royal household, he had raced through the jungle the previous morning to meet the Raja and tell him about Princess Toh's planned visit to the Bomoh. Following the death of her first two husbands, he was under strict orders to report such events. The Raja was keen to discourage rumours spreading among his men that their princess was stoking the Bomoh's powers. Anwar had ridden his horse for most of the day and was keen to get the animal back to the stables.

The air was thick as Princess Toh disappeared into the cave, and a sinister silence fell over the area. Anwar raised his head as a rank smell entered his nostrils. The sky was bereft of birds and he stared into the jungle looking for signs of life, only to be met by dark shadows. He was relieved that Princess

Toh was inside; he expected she would have become agitated in such an uneasy atmosphere.

He kept a close eye on the entrance, withdrew his daggers, and prepared to charge into the cave. He recalled the first time that the princess had visited the Bomoh and her scream that had caused him to dash inside. Much to the outrage of the Bomoh, who had decapitated a bat and sprinkled blood over the princess to chase away demons. He had growled at them both and warned Princess Toh that if she ever permitted Anwar to enter his cave again, he would no longer assist her. He reminded her that she was permitted an audience only because of his own late father's decision to entertain princesses of the royal family.

When Toh emerged, she wore a distant expression. Anwar stayed quiet and gave her time to collect herself.

'Thank you, Anwar.'

'Princess,' Anwar responded and nodded respectfully, trying hard to hide his scepticism.

Annoyed that she had to reduce herself to a humble beggar in the presence of the Bomoh whenever she had matrimonial issues, she took her horse's reins from Anwar and mounted the animal. 'What an unpleasant man,' she said, her voice strained.

Anwar recalled his only meeting with the Bomoh; had it not been for the presence of the princess, he might have ended the Bomoh's life there and then. The thought of having to listen to that man berate him was still galling. He allowed the memory to wash over him as he mounted his horse and nudged the animal forward.

'Let us be away from here as quickly as we can,' Toh said to Anwar as he passed her.

Anwar noticed that Princess Toh's eyes were squeezed shut and it reminded him how much he cherished the young woman. The day the old Raja had presented Fatima, then a tiny baby, to the young princess was still vivid in his mind. Toh had been on the verge of tears, and squeezed her eyes closed to trap them in. Little did she realize that her father's intention had been to prevent Toh from suffering the loneliness that had blighted her early life. Toh's mother had died the day she was born, as had Fatima's. Since that day, Anwar had taken on the role of protecting the two girls whenever he was on duty, and when he was absent, he was still tasked with overseeing their protection.

They entered the jungle as the late-afternoon sun fell through the trees and Anwar calculated that they would be home before nightfall.

* * *

Princess Toh struggled to concentrate on Anwar's route through the trees, her judgement clouded by the Bomoh's parting words. What could his stupid rhyme mean? She had ignored his call for her to remain while he conducted a ritual, fear driving her from the cave.

She was certain 'scream no more the lamburi may hear' was a reference to her husband, but 'a price be paid by another unnear' terrified her. She stiffened at the screech of a gibbon and called out to Anwar, who had disappeared ahead. The sound of his horse whinnying calmed her and she encouraged hers to speed up. She was badgered by the thought that she ought to turn back and sit through the Bomoh's dreadful incantation. Toh was fearful that if she did not return, her husband might become the victim of the Bomoh's words. She called to Anwar to halt but the caw of a hornbill drowned out her voice. She decided to keep a close watch on her husband instead and return to the Bomoh only if it became necessary.

* * *

The Bomoh was enraged by Princess Toh's departure, but believed that the spell would work because he had commenced the ritual while she was in his sight. He continued murmuring the chant, while poking an incense stick into the fire and allowing the smoke to purify the cave.

* * *

Satisfied that the coast was clear, the Raja stepped out from the dark. He was captivated by the Bomoh, he watched as the huge man waddled from one side of the cave to the other and listened to him reciting the words required to draw the spirit he sought into the cave.

'How long is this going to take?' asked the Raja, sitting in the stool previously occupied by Toh. 'I need to be away before the sky darkens.'

The Bomoh lifted his head. He stared at the Raja, flapped his arms against the disturbance and stamped his feet, all the while continuing his chant. The Raja sighed and gave a small shrug before nodding for the Bomoh to continue.

Shadows from the flames leapt on the walls, and the fire lit up the Bomoh's big, pallid, well-worn face. The Raja pictured his sister sitting before this ugly man and disclosing her husband's intimate antics. He was glad to be before the Bomoh and not the husband, there was no telling what he would have done to the man.

While the Bomoh continued his incantation, the Raja reflected on his sister's bad luck with the men she married. Her first two husbands had been chiefs of vast lands and there had been joy at uniting their peoples, though his sister had suffered for the peace brought by both marriages. He was glad that the Bomoh had released her from their torment by ensuring the death of each husband through his sorcery.

The past faded from the Raja's thoughts when the Bomoh brought proceedings to a close by sitting next to him. The Raja sat bolt upright until silence descended and the Bomoh gave him a nod. Whether a result of the long journey or Princess Toh's account of her husband's behaviour, venom had infused his voice. 'Is this the first time my sister has consulted you over the conduct of her husband?' he asked.

The Bomoh peered at the Raja blankly and gave an abrupt nod. The Raja sighed. The image of a man assaulting a defenceless woman burned inside him and it took all his self-control to remain composed.

'Tell me, Bomoh, what does your message mean?'

A tense silence descended and the Raja accepted the inappropriateness of his question. He brushed it aside and spoke again. 'I understand that you only speak to my sister in couplets, is that correct?'

The Bomoh drew a sign in the air before answering. 'It is necessary,' he croaked.

The Raja was thankful he had arranged to be present, for otherwise he might never have learned of the wretchedness of his sister's situation. Her voice, as she told the Bomoh of her plight, had tugged at his heartstrings and he vowed to bring her misery to an end.

'Couplets?' The Raja asked again.

'Your father and mine agreed many years ago that we would offer our service to the women in the royal family, but that we would not be familiar towards them,' the Bomoh answered.

'Will she understand your message? And will her husband die?'

'You heard her instructions to me,' he barked.

'Then will he suffer?'

'He'll sour in his age.'

'What in hell is that supposed to mean?' the Raja demanded angrily.

The Bomoh glowered at him and deliberately stoked the Raja's irritation by prolonging the silence. Eventually, he spoke bitterly, 'Every time he shouts at Princess Toh, he will suffer serious discomfort. Meanwhile, you should remind her of my oft-repeated words: my powers must not be abused, especially those of shapeshifting, lest she remains alive but shrivels slowly from an elephant to an ant.'

'You're telling me not to kill him?' the Raja said, staring at the Bomoh for elucidation.

The Bomoh continued to glower at the Raja and eventually gave another abrupt nod.

'You have come to visit me but a few times, and have never had cause to consult me. You will, however, be aware from your father's teachings, as much as I am from mine, that the price of saving one life is that of another.' There was indignation in his eyes.

The Raja slowly rose to his feet. The Bomoh followed and the two men left the cave together. 'Where are your warriors?' the Bomoh asked affably, as if they were now in a civilized world.

'They are hidden in the jungle,' the Raja replied.

The Bomoh scanned the leaden sky. 'Do not go over the mountain, Your Majesty. Dusk is the time when the jinn become active. Such spirits can easily send a hail of knives and spears down on their enemies.'

Confused by the Bomoh's attempt at courtesy, the Raja turned and stormed off.

Chapter 6

Fatima entered the kitchen and strolled up to Suraya, who was stirring a huge pot of vegetable soup. The old woman broke away and drew her into a warm embrace. She had an easy disposition and Fatima loved to spend time with her.

Suraya always seemed happy, and Fatima thought of her as the mother she never had.

'Have you eaten?'

'Much earlier this morning,' Fatima said, trying hard to hide her worry.

Suraya looked at her through narrowed eyes. 'What's troubling you, dear?'

'Princess Toh has gone to visit the Bomoh, and he always unsettles her.'

'The Bomoh?'

'He sounds like such a dreadful man, Auntie. Princess Toh says he's terrible to her.'

'Come,' Suraya said, holding Fatima's hand and leading her to the huge wooden table that dominated the room. 'Sit there,' she said, gesturing to a wooden bench. She hurried back to the stove, returned with a bowl of soup, and sat beside the young slave. At the centre of the table was a tall tin jug of water, and a collection of tin cups. She filled a cup as Fatima quietly slurped her soup.

Eager to share, Fatima spoke, 'Princess Toh says he's a big man. She says he's missing all his teeth and hair.'

An uneasy look appeared on Suraya's face and her lips curled. Fatima glanced around and spoke softly, 'She only goes there when she's having problems with her marriage.' She shivered. 'Her visits always upset me. I know how frightened she gets when she goes there.' Fatima paused to take more soup and then continued, relieved to be sharing her concerns. 'She only visits him because she's so desperate to halt her husband's abuse.'

Suraya stared into her cup, as if a message was floating in it and she was trying to unravel its meaning.

When Fatima had finished the soup, she beamed the cheerful smile Suraya was so accustomed to seeing. 'Thank you, Auntie, that was delicious.'

'Where are you going, young lady?' the old woman asked when Fatima stood up.

'To wash my bowl.'

'Stay right where you are,' Suraya instructed. Fatima returned to her seat and noticed that Suraya's dark eyes were alive and energized. 'Princess Toh only has you, Fatima. And thanks to you, she has learned to accept her lot without complaint. Overseeing the protection of the palace, the lands, the mines, and the people is a heavy burden, and she needs the Bomoh to guide her in her personal affairs.' She observed Fatima keenly to judge her reaction, before continuing, 'Peace hasn't always reigned in these lands, but thanks to the late Raja, the wars that plagued our people are now largely confined to areas far away from here. Before you were born, a greedy family from a neighbouring state tried to establish their own kingdom here. Their chief gathered many men and proclaimed that he was our new leader.'

Fatima sat wide-eyed as she listened to what Suraya was saying, while the fire crackled.

'What he was really after were the tin mines—and he enjoyed the mines' revenue for a long time.' Suraya took a sip of water as Fatima waited, eager to hear more.

'A few years ago, the Raja's father raised an army and defeated the chief and his men, but only after many of our young men lost their lives. And so, the weight on Princess Toh's shoulders to keep us all safe is an enormous one.' Suraya took time to reflect and when she spoke again her voice lacked its usual energy. 'You, my dear, are a tremendous asset to the princess, for you are the only person to whom she can reveal her true feelings. And for that, we are all grateful to you.' Fatima dropped her gaze, unsure of what to say, but Suraya broke the silence that followed. 'You will have another bowl of soup.'

'Auntie, I couldn't.'

Suraya rose, stretched across the table, collected the water jug, and refilled Fatima's cup. The old woman winked at Fatima and patted her on the thigh.

Fatima decided to change the subject and turned to Suraya, 'Auntie, how long has Aashif been here?'

The old woman's face lit up. 'Why do you ask?'

Fatima had in mind that she would pass on as much information as she could about Aashif's singing to Princess Toh on her return. 'He sings beautifully.'

Suraya studied the young woman intently. 'We love getting him to sing,' she said. 'When did you hear him?'

'We've heard him a couple of times at night.'

'We?' asked Suraya, confused.

'Princess Toh and I.'

'Where?' A quizzical look formed on Suraya's face.

'Outside our bedroom window.'

'What?' Suraya gasped.

Fatima was mystified. 'Is anything wrong?' she asked.

'Does he know you can hear him?'

Fatima shrugged. 'Probably not—we're quite high up.'

'Aashif is a very shy young man.'

'Who taught him to convert that poem into a song that he sings so beautifully?'

'I did. When I was a young woman, my father used to sing it to me and he taught me to sing it, too. He used to call it "The Last Great Love Song". You are correct that Aashif has a glorious voice, but it takes all our effort to convince him to sing. I should warn him that he's being listened to.'

Fatima spoke earnestly. 'Please don't, Auntie. A peace comes over Princess Toh whenever she hears him.' Suraya nodded, and she smiled to herself.

* * *

Fatima had agreed to accompany Suraya to the slaves' quarters to deliver some soup to a female slave who was recovering from a fever.

'Will she be all right?' Fatima asked.

'She's over the worst.' Suraya bent low to collect a spoon from a drawer; in doing so, the pendant around her neck dangled in mid-air.

'Is that pendant heavy, Auntie?'

Suraya rose, shaking her head. 'I've been wearing it for many years,' she said, her voice faint. For years, it had been a deep secret. That Fatima should ask about it so innocently, freed her to discuss it but she remained determined to say nothing of its source.

'Feel the weight of it,' Suraya said, offering it to Fatima to hold.

Fatima had long decided it was ugly and was surprised by its weight, which to her mind merely added to its ugliness.

The pendant was shaped like a starfruit, its colour tarnished into a dirty bronze. 'It is an amulet that was given to me many years ago. It is said that the five points represent the footprint of King Solomon.'

Fatima held it in her hand, trying to imagine it hanging around her slender neck.

'It is a defence against demons,' Suraya said, as if overwhelmed by weariness.

Fatima let go of the pendant and Suraya stuffed it back under her blouse. 'Come,' she said, 'let us get this soup to the patient.'

The air outside was still as the two women strolled along the path. Beside them was a row of whitewashed buildings, their roofs covered in thatch made of palm fronds. On the opposite side, beyond a large patch of grassland, were several buildings that housed the warriors who defended the community, and the members of the royal household who served the palace and oversaw its lands.

Opposite the kitchen, some twenty feet across a clearing of grassland was a building that housed the female quarters, beyond that was a storeroom and the male quarters. Fatima followed Suraya into the female barracks, where there were around a hundred beds against each wall, all covered in the same drab bedspreads. Slung across the poles stretching overhead were garments of every colour, while at the foot of the beds were the slaves' personal belongings. Spread about the room were series of citronella plants, whose fragrance helped guard against mosquitoes. As the women became aware of Suraya and Fatima, their silence slowly filled the room. Like Fatima, every woman wore her hair short—no female slave was allowed to wear her hair in the long style favoured by free women.

'I've never been in here before,' Fatima said softly.

'Fatima,' a voice called. 'Where's your sweetheart, the Raja?'

A snigger ran round the room and the girl blushed.

'Yes, shouldn't you be in the palace, tidying his bedroom for him?' another slave called out.

Suraya left Fatima and went further into the room to attend to the sick slave and a handful of the women strolled up to Fatima. By the time they reached her, she was perfectly composed.

'He is so manly and attractive. What's he like?'

Fatima managed to suppress a smile, as her loyalty to the Raja preserved her silence and strengthened her will.

'What's his bed like? Is it comfortable?'

Fatima's big eyes were bright when she spoke. 'I've never been inside his chamber. I'm not allowed.'

The women suddenly became hostile. 'I don't believe you,' one of them said harshly.

Fatima was determined. 'It's true,' she insisted.

'What's true?' Suraya asked softly as she joined Fatima again.

'We were asking Fatima about her duties,' one of the women said. Fatima nodded delicately.

'Ladies,' Suraya said, 'be sure that someone returns the bowl to the kitchen.' She turned to Fatima. 'Let's go,' she said, and Fatima followed Suraya out.

Fatima was sad at the hostile atmosphere among some of the women. When she caught Suraya studying her, she grimaced.

'As you may suppose,' Suraya said, 'they are good women, but they become defensive when their privacy is invaded.'

'I've never really questioned it before, but seeing all the women together like that made me wonder why we must be slaves. Why can't we be allowed to grow our hair long, and live freely like the people in the villages, on the farms, and at the markets?'

'I'm not a slave,' Suraya said.

'But your hair?'

'In recent years I've taken to cutting it short.' She stared into Fatima's eyes. 'The system of slavery has been present in our land for centuries. It is part of the economic fibre of our country. The arrangement arose through the *abdi* slaves, who have been bought and the *orang berhutang*, the slaves who fell into debt. The system is against the teachings of God, but nothing has been done to stop it. Over the years, it has become a part of our way of life.'

Chapter 7

As the late afternoon call to prayer sounded, Aashif was busy in the vegetable allotments. He had a special spot in the woods where he prayed while he was working, and he strolled towards the trees, full of purpose. Time stood still for Aashif when he had to renew his relationship with God. As always, he carried a small wooden pail of water to perform his ablutions, along with his prayer mat. When he had arrived as a small boy fourteen years ago, he had possessed a red, tattered mat, but this new one had been given to him by Hisham.

He unfurled his mat and placed it carefully on the ground, bracing himself for the wave of anguish that washed over him as he pictured the bazaar Hisham had described. Row upon row of canopy-covered shops occupied by bartering stallholders drifted across his mind, while children darted hither and thither. His ears were filled with wild, excited noises. Men in white baju melayu and women wearing *tudung*, the headscarf of believers, vied for space as they made purchases. Aashif had never been to such an event—the images in his head were all the result of Hisham's descriptions. As he often did at such moments, he thought about his father and asked God to give him a sign that it was time to go in search of him. He calmly ended his prayers and set about rolling up his mat.

He was returning to his work when he saw dark clouds rising on the horizon. He hurried back to the allotments. A crowd of women had gathered around three large piles of vegetables and had kept two wicker baskets ready, one of which was nearly as tall as him. He ignored the women's banter and stood next to the baskets, allowing them to strap the larger of the two across his shoulders. They carefully placed potatoes, tomatoes and fresh green *petai* into each one. He hoisted the load against his back to make sure it was properly balanced and comfortable enough to carry.

'You'll bruise the potatoes, Aashif,' one of the women complained. 'And then Suraya will expect us to work in the rain to pick fresh ones.'

'Sorry,' he muttered.

Fearful that the rain would arrive as he was carrying the baskets to the kitchen, he kicked off his wooden sandals. 'Please tie them to the handles. I'll have better grip with my feet bare.'

He edged closer to the smaller basket, tested its weight, and was relieved to find that it was light enough to lift.

'Do you want us to call one of the other men to help you?'

Aashif had undertaken this task many times before and knew he could manage alone. Anyway, he did not want the women to think he lacked strength.

There was a flash of lightning followed by the roar of thunder. Aashif doubted he would complete the walk in time to avoid wading through mud.

'Hurry up,' a voice barked at him, and he set off, full of resolve.

* * *

Aashif had trundled forward, lost in his own world but careful not to disturb the weight on his back, when a jovial voice boomed out his name.

'Aashif. Do you want some help?'

He turned slowly to find Hazri, a giant of a warrior, approaching along with a younger man he did not recognize. Aashif had once seen Hazri fight against Anwar in a friendly bout. Despite his size he had been no match for Anwar, but he was capable of inflicting brutal damage on most opponents. As he neared, Aashif could see the kindness in his face.

'Come,' Hazri offered, 'let us help you with those baskets.'

Hazri introduced his colleague. 'This young fellow here is Haron, a trainee in our attachment from one of the local villages.'

Haron blinked, took a deep breath, and offered the smallest of nods. Aashif placed Haron at sixteen or seventeen. He noticed the sour look on the lad's face, and judged him to be arrogant and surly.

'This is one man you should take care of, Haron. If Aashif had his way, he'd be one of us.'

Aashif stared at the metal badge on Haron's belt that showed he was an employee of the royal household. Such items were not normally displayed publicly. Aashif found anger and resentment gnawing away at him.

'Haron, help me get this basket off Aashif's back,' Hazri was saying, as heavy drops of rain struck the ground and turned the grey soil into mud. The angry clouds above thickened.

'No, it's fine. I've got it nicely balanced.'

Haron's eyebrows rose when Aashif suggested that they could help him by carrying the smaller basket. In that split second, Aashif noticed Haron staring at him with contempt and wondered whether Haron would have offered to help had he been alone. Many of the other guards were as affable as Hazri, but he was sure that Haron was not such a person.

The wind picked up and the rain suddenly came down in great swells.

'Let's get cover,' Hazri shouted, and the two guards rushed towards a small hut by the entrance to the allotments, carrying the smaller basket of vegetables. Aashif struggled to keep up with them and practically fell into the hut, fighting against the weight of the wet vegetables. Both guards looked at him seriously.

'Let's get this off his back,' Hazri said firmly to Haron.

The two guards stepped forward and Aashif cautioned, 'Please, be careful of the prayer mat that's wedged between the basket and my back.'

Haron faltered. Staring straight at Aashif, he spoke, 'You should have wrapped it up to protect it against the weather.'

The words impacted Aashif so forcefully that he felt himself stumble. He desperately wanted to say that if he were in their position, he would have taken the mat and sheltered it from the rain straight away. He clamped his lips shut but burned to tell Haron that it was one thing to be a free man with a badge and another to be a compassionate one.

'This is a mighty weight,' Hazri said to Aashif, as the two guards struggled to remove the basket from his shoulders. 'How often do you carry this sort of load?'

'Most days.'

'You must be as fit as us warriors,' Hazri responded, grinning.

* * *

Aashif was soaking wet by the time he entered the hot kitchen. The female slaves sat on benches surrounding the principal table, others were clustered on wooden stools in an area by the stove, while yet more sat around the great sink beyond the main table. He gave a stiff bow to those who caught his eye and smiled wryly to others. He knew all the women—most were maid-slaves, while the remainder were nurses, and all of them were dedicated to their roles in the commune. Had it not been for the storm he would have avoided them, but he had arrived at the kitchen during their afternoon break.

He dropped the smaller of the two baskets where he stood, then hurried outside to collect the larger one where Hazri and Haron had brought it in and left it.

Suraya came up to him. 'You're drenched. Take that shirt off and I'll dry it by the stove.'

As he drew his shirt over his head, he heard one of the slaves say dryly, 'We are lucky—many of us could have landed up as *gundek* slaves, concubines and mistresses of the chiefs, or the Raja himself.'

'I might like that,' a voice chimed in, to much laughter.

'None of us would want to be a gundek, the lives of such slaves are a misery,' someone replied.

'The Raja, his father, and those before him refused to keep gundek slaves, so we should think ourselves lucky.'

Aashif had overheard the same conversation so many times and was surprised that the women were never tired of it.

'Maybe you'd have liked us all to be gundek slaves, Aashif?' Hanizah teased.

A desperate expression formed on Aashif's face and tension overcame him. He looked to Suraya, unsure how to respond.

Suraya glared at the slave who had spoken, her dark eyes full of contempt. This was her kitchen, and nobody had the right to misbehave here. Her voice was angry. 'I'll have no such nonsense in my kitchen, young woman. Leave Aashif alone.'

The atmosphere stiffened and Hanizah cowered in her seat, aware that she had spoken out of turn. The awkward silence was broken when the woman who had begun the conversation said, 'How fortunate we are to be under the Raja's command. If gundek slaves are not beautiful they are forced to prostitute themselves, and their earnings are handed over to their masters. I am grateful to the Raja, who has always been fair to us.'

Suraya clapped loudly. 'Come, ladies. I need some help with these vegetables.'

Aashif was still trying to gather his thoughts when the slave sought to redeem herself by being one of the first to assist. She smiled as she passed Aashif, and he gave her a shy bow. He watched as the baskets were unloaded, before picking them up and taking them to the cupboard to be stored.

He was stacking the vegetables on to shelves when Suraya marched up to him, accompanied by a woman carrying a stool. 'Here,' she said, handing him a garment. 'Sit yourself there and have something to eat while your shirt dries.'

'Thank you, Auntie,' he said, as he spotted Fatima entering the kitchen. His face brightened at the sight of her, and he tried to tidy his appearance— combing his fingers through his thick black hair and wriggling into the shirt Suraya had given him. His heart raced as he struggled to find any words he might say to her, before she made her way towards Suraya by the stove.

'There's one lucky slave,' Hanizah called. The room waited to hear what she had to say next, when another woman at the far end of the table called out. 'How's the witch, Fatima?'

Aashif was unable to discern Fatima's reaction because she was no longer in his line of sight.

'Don't be cruel, you know perfectly well that she is not a witch,' Fatima answered firmly.

'Tell that to some of the guards,' another voice called.

Fatima twisted around to face Hanizah. 'It is God's will how we appear, and it is not his will to create witches,' she replied calmly. She strolled towards Suraya and noticing Aashif sitting alone, gave him a tender smile. In turn, Aashif dropped his gaze awkwardly. The embarrassing moment was broken when Suraya called to her.

'Aashif knows all the guards, he'll tell you what they say about Princess Toh,' Hanizah continued.

Fatima turned to face Aashif, and his mouth went dry. His agitation increased further when Fatima made a beeline towards him. Her allure seemed to have suddenly disappeared and he struggled to free his tongue, which had fastened itself to the roof of his mouth. Out of the corner of his eye, he noticed Suraya approaching him with a plate of food.

Chapter 8

The circular shack was at the bottom of a hill, surrounded by dense jungle. It was an appropriate venue for the events to come, the man decided, and it was exactly as the village chief had described it.

He viewed the scene below and reflected on his decision, taking in every minute detail to ensure that nothing escaped his attention. The carpet of trees held him spellbound until he noticed the fast-flowing Perak river cleaving the landscape. The recent downpour had left it full to the banks.

The fresh scent of wet leaves seemed to act as a portent for the day ahead. He looked back at the shack. It was surrounded by thick lalang but he had been assured that the entrance was clear. The building leant towards the river and looked like it would collapse if struck by a strong gust. And yet, for all that, its bamboo walls and thick attap roof had withstood many tropical storms in its time.

The wet leaves glimmered under the hot sun, as the man slithered over the ground and began his descent. Shadows intermittently fell across the forest when thick clouds blocked the sun, but that did nothing to dampen his fervour.

When he was halfway down, he stopped and shouted, his voice echoing across the treetops. He stood waiting, his eyes stinging—he did not want to rush the next few minutes. He wanted to be able to recall them whenever the desire presented itself. The fulfilment of all that had dominated his thinking this past week, or more, was finally at hand.

He stopped by the shack and waited for his heart to slow down. Once he had regained control of his breath, he stepped up to the door and remained there for several minutes. It was when his patience was close to running out that he heard a sound inside. He pondered whether to crash through the door, irritated at the slowness of his actions. But he wanted composure, complete and utter calmness.

As he allowed himself to breathe freely, intuition told him that he would never visit this place again. Was he relaxed enough to remember everything that had happened so far, and would he remember all that was to come?

He removed the key from a small pouch strung across his chest, quietly freed the spring in the lock, and returned it to the pouch. He pushed against the door, and it made an annoying creaking sound—the element of surprise was gone. He had imagined himself standing in front of the young slave before she became aware of his presence.

The bottom half of his face was covered by a black mask, the colour of which matched his baju melayu.

He closed the door behind him and acclimatized himself to his surroundings. The air was so hot that he momentarily faltered. Across the floor, hunched into a ball, was the sixteen-year-old slave, her face between her knees. He could almost touch the fear emanating from her.

He rested his back against the door and waited for her to notice him. When his presence failed to provoke a response, he guffawed until she lifted her face to look at him. He fixed his eyes on her and gasped at her beauty. Her face was prettier than the chief had described it. Her nose was small, her cheekbones were sharp, her frightened eyes were pitch black, her lips were full, and her hair was cut in the style that was customary among all slaves. She dropped her head, and he beckoned her to raise it up again. When she failed to react, he addressed her firmly, 'Lift your head up.'

To his delight, she did as he asked.

'What is your name?'

'Hariati,' she answered softly. Her nervousness added to his pleasure.

Satisfied that she was watching him, he took his metal badge from his pouch, strolled across to her and held it in front of her face. 'What is this?'

'I don't know,' she replied.

'This grants me the permission to be present here today. Do you understand that?' he asked, his heart pounding.

She stared at him, confused.

'Nod your head,'

She did as he commanded, and he stepped back to the door, still staring at her. When she allowed her head to drop, he ordered her to keep it up.

'Are you a slave?'

She nodded.

'What sort of slave?'

'Gundek.'

He nodded slowly and purposefully, realizing what a wretched individual she was.

'How long have you been a gundek slave?'

'Only from today.'

This news, coupled with the tears spilling down her cheeks, delighted him. The chief had told him nothing of this. He took a long time to gather himself. 'It does me well to hear what you say,' he said at last, his mask hiding a lascivious smile.

'Why are you a gundek slave?' He wanted to know why it was that a girl this pretty was not one of the chief's concubines. He wondered, for a moment, if he should help her before he reminded himself that she was simply a mere slave.

'Stand up.'

When she failed to respond, he barked at her, 'Stand up now.'

Clumsily, she forced herself to her feet, before nearly tumbling back to the ground.

'Walk from side to side.'

He waited for her to speak until he realized that her lips were quivering, and he waved at her impatiently to amble around.

She reeled under the weight of his glare and walked back and forth. She was a waif of a girl. The expectancy that had drugged his mind all week was at fever pitch as he imagined how she would appear naked.

'Do you know why you are here?'

She blinked at him and shook her head, terror in her eyes.

'Do you know what is to happen to you?'

She shook her head again. Little did she realize that the tears soaking her cheeks were stoking his urges.

'You are to be punished, correct?'

She failed to reply. Her fear grew as his irritation became evident in the harshness of his voice. 'Go and sit where you were and stop that noise.'

Conscious of the power he had over her, he was content to wait until she had ceased to cry.

'What were you before you were a gundek slave?'

She hesitated, before speaking faintly. 'I was a *dayang-dayang*.'

Things were not going as he had foreseen, and the roar of the river was beginning to aggravate him. 'Speak up—I can't hear you,' he said unpleasantly as he strained his ears. 'That damned river,' he sighed.

She dared to glance up at him, and he fixed his eyes on her. 'So, you were one of the housekeepers?'

She looked at him and nodded, clearly terrified.

'What other duties did you perform?' he demanded, his lust welling up again.

He scrutinized her and caught her eyes darting around.

'Answer me,' he snapped.

He listened as she took a deep breath, before speaking in a broken voice. 'Cooking. Collecting firewood. Washing my master's clothes. Weaving. Harvesting the rice.'

He was aware that as a gundek slave she was obliged to prostitute herself in order to provide for herself. As he inspected her, he cherished the role of a captor. He could ask her anything he wanted and know that she had no choice but to answer.

'Now,' he said, 'how has your role as a gundek brought you here today?'

She sniffled, and he knew instantly that another bout of tears was coming. He shouted at her to stop crying, but that merely added to her distress. He waited until she had settled down and repeated his question.

'I locked myself in,' she said.

'What?'

'I locked myself in my master's chamber to keep him away from me. I was frightened because he wanted me in his bed.'

'And you locked yourself in his chamber without him? For how long?'

'All night.'

'Why?'

She lowered her voice and cast her eyes downwards. 'He is a cruel man.'

He paused, and a thought suddenly struck him. 'Have you ever been with a man?'

She pursed her lips tight and shook her head.

'This is why you are here to be punished,' he said, his tone brittle. Not once had he ever imagined having to punish a girl who was untouched. He remained fixed to the spot as he contemplated how best to proceed.

'Have you been told what your punishment is to be?' he asked her eagerly, trying to catch his breath. He waited for a response, visualizing how she had guarded her fragility while waiting for him to arrive.

* * *

He called to mind the chief, an obese man who was prone to excessive perspiration, and shuddered at the thought of how he must have smelled. He had no such problem, as this slave would soon discover.

'Your master is extremely angry at your conduct,' he said. His growing urge tightened its grip on him, and he continued, 'I am to make you a woman.' He paused. 'Do you understand that?'

She did not answer him, but he observed that the light had gone out of her. He shrugged with indifference as she remained in a crouched position. He drew breath, his pounding heart reminding him that he had to fulfil the chief's instructions.

'Stand up and take off your clothes.'

A hopelessness entered her eyes, and she looked up at him pleadingly. 'Stand up,' he snapped. She shifted her body upwards, slumped to the ground again and anger rushed at him as fast as the river outside.

He noticed her staring wide-eyed at the entrance and smirked. Many slaves ran away, but more often than not, they were captured because no local villager would offer them refuge, for fear of reprisals. He was tempted to throw the door open and allow some fresh air in, but he had no desire to chase her through the jungle.

He walked across to her, slapped her scalp and growled. 'Stand up.'

His breathing quickened as he withdrew his knife. She raised her eyes and leapt to her feet, pressing her body against the wall. He stepped back, pointed the dagger at her and spoke menacingly, 'Remove your clothes.' He waved the weapon up and down in front of her face until she bent down low and took hold of the hem of her baju.

Chapter 9

The waves are white on the Kataun shore
And day and night they beat
The garden has white blossoms o'er
But only one do I think sweet.

It was early afternoon, and Aashif was in high spirits as he ambled along, humming his favourite song. He carried a fishing rod and net, slung over his right shoulder and a basket in his left hand, while in his right hand, he held his axe. Following many years of training, he was so skilled with the weapon that he could chop a mosquito in half while the insect was still in flight.

The air was fresh after the early morning storm, and he happily sang aloud to himself as he followed his usual path to the river. From the sound of the rushing water, he calculated that it would be at least another hour before the water would be sufficiently settled for him to fish. He would have to fill his basket in order to satisfy Suraya.

These trips into the jungle gave him the solitude he cherished; being alone in the trees held no fear for him. He was enjoying the tranquillity when he noticed a low-pitched mewling. He stopped and looked around the jungle but failed to spot anything untoward. He remained still, listening intently, but pressed on when he heard nothing further. He had brushed past a branch that was blocking his way when the sound returned. He stood still and held his breath. The rush of the river was constant in his ears, but he had the feeling that something unfamiliar lay ahead. He gripped his axe tightly and was preparing to face an attack when the sound returned once more.

He moved forward cautiously and stepped out of the jungle on to the open riverbank. He immediately noticed that the foliage had been disturbed and followed a track until he gasped out loud. Lying a few feet away was the naked body of a young girl, her hair cropped. He turned around sharply, expecting to be attacked, but the scene was completely still. As he peered back into the trees, his concentration was broken when the girl cried out. Unsure of his ground, he approached cautiously.

The girl opened her lips and he stooped to hear what she was trying to say. He dropped his equipment, grasped his weapon, and brought his ear close to her face. She seemed to be saying the same word over and over again, 'water'. He raised himself and glanced about urgently, desperately searching for a container of some kind. Spotting some elephant leaves in the foliage, he dashed to them. He ripped a leaf from the tree and tore it into a manageable size. He then rushed to the river, washed the leaf clean, and rolled it into a cone. After filling the leaf with as much water as possible, he scampered back to the girl.

'Water,' he said, bending over her. He held the point of the cone over her mouth and allowed the water to drip on to her lips.

He tried to keep his eyes focused on her face, but his attention kept drifting down to her body. She had two wounds, one below her ribcage on her left side and another between her legs.

Embarrassed by her nakedness, he wondered whether he should gather more leaves and cover her modesty. He continued to let water drip over her lips as he addressed her. 'What happened to you?'

Her ghostly expression scared him, and he was terrified at the thought that she might die in his presence. She turned her face away from him and spoke quietly, 'I was punished.'

'What for?'

'I refused to lie with my master,' she managed to whisper.

He watched as her eyes flooded with tears. 'I'm not leaving you,' he said, trying to reassure her. 'We need to get you into the shade.' He followed the trail of disturbed foliage, from behind the trees to the shack where the girl had been assaulted.

'Please don't hurt me.'

Shocked, he dropped down beside her again and took her hand. 'I'm not going to hurt you. I need to cover you and make you safe.'

'He'll come back,' she said, her voice shaking.

'Who will?'

'The man with the badge, who punished me.'

'What badge?'

'He showed me his badge,' she said, her voice fading.

In response to the fright on her face, an immeasurable rage charged through him like a wild animal. He rushed to the undergrowth, tore two large elephant leaves, and spread them across her body. He knelt back down next to her and explained as calmly as he could that he was going to pick her up and take her to the shack.

Her eyes bulged and darted about, petrified. 'Don't take me back in there,' she wailed. 'He'll be waiting.'

Realizing that the assailant could be hiding in the shack, Aashif sprang to his feet and charged into the place, but it was empty. He ran back to the girl, dropped down beside her, and told her that there was nobody there. 'Will you be all right if I lift you?'

Tears ran down her cheeks as he gently raised her off the ground, surprised at how light she was. She groaned, and he responded instinctively, 'Sorry—I'll make you as safe and as comfortable as I can.'

As he carried her over the uneven ground, he felt a hot dampness on his arm that he guessed was her blood. He implored Allah to help him save the life of this innocent girl, as she slumped her head against his chest. He was scared by her silence. Don't let her die, he repeated to himself as he carried her into the shack and carefully laid her on the ground.

There were fresh tears in her eyes when he spoke in a low but steady voice. 'First, I'm going to make you safe here, and then, I'm going to run and get help.'

He raced outside and grabbed the sturdiest branch he could from a tree trunk, before hacking at the end and turning it into a spike. He hammered his axe into the soil to loosen it, then drove the spike into the broken soil until it stood upright. In barely a minute he had gathered several more branches. He rested them on the ground and went back inside. 'I'm going to leave you for a short while, to get help. I won't be long. I'm going to jam some branches against the door, you'll be safe until I get back.' Outside, he wedged the branches between the doorway and the upright branch, securing the entrance.

* * *

Time was against him, the sun would soon dip behind the mountains, and he had to return with help before darkness fell. He crashed through the jungle like a man possessed as he fought back his anger at the thought of the injured girl, terror all over her face.

'Why?' he yelled to himself as the image of the girl drifted in and out of his mind. 'She's only a slave.' He was burning with rage that someone could be so cruel to such a defenceless girl—and all for refusing to lie with some man. Would this have happened if she hadn't been a slave? He vented his fury at any obstacle standing in his path, smashing his way forward with the force of a charging elephant.

The sounds of her sobs were magnified in his brain, and he wished he was running towards her, so he could take her in his arms and make her feel safe.

'Why?' He screamed again, at the top of his voice. He shuddered at the memory of her pleading for him not to hurt her, yet he ploughed on. As he pictured the blood seeping from her, he swung his axe and hacked his way forward, sweat streaming down his face.

His mind was close to exploding when light burst through the trees. Gasping for breath, he ran into the open and crossed the paddy fields until he reached the palace. 'Hisham,' he bellowed, sprinting across the courtyard. He spotted two guards strolling towards him. 'Where's Hisham?'

Startled, one of the guards pointed to the far side of the palace. Aashif sprinted around the building to find Hisham in conversation with Anwar.

In a garbled clamour he told them what had happened, the turbulence of the situation causing him to stammer.

Anwar's eyes narrowed. 'And you left her there alone?' he asked sourly.

Dumbstruck, Aashif could only stare at him before turning to Hisham for support.

His face grim, he desperately pleaded, 'I didn't know what else to do. She needs help—now.'

Anwar met Aashif's eyes with a stony-faced glare, and Aashif turned back to Hisham. 'Please, sir, we must go now. We must save her. I promised.'

Paralysed by their lack of action, he shouted at both men, 'Please. She'll die. And it'll be dark soon.' Aashif's voice constricted from the sound of his own pleas.

Finally, Hisham spoke. 'Go to Suraya, tell her what you've told us, and ask her to give you what you'll need. And bring a woman back here who can tend to the girl. Now run.'

More terrified than he had ever been before, he sprinted to the kitchen and found Suraya in the company of several female slaves. He told Suraya what had happened, stammering as he spoke. 'We have to go now.' He watched as she dashed between cupboards, pulling whatever might be needed before thrusting some things at one of the women standing next to Aashif and ordering her to go with him.

* * *

Anwar, two guards, and the slave woman accompanied Aashif to the riverbank in silence. The light was failing as they reached, and Aashif accepted that they were going to have to spend the night in the shack. It would be too dangerous to return in the dark, especially with the wounded girl. He was gripped by disgust over what had happened to the girl as he approached the shack. He removed the branches, fearful of waking her. His shirt was sticking to his back with perspiration as he cleared the last branch away and prised the door open.

Anwar sighed, before ordering his men to gather up dry wood for a fire and as many twigs as they could, for torches. He led Aashif inside, ordering the slave to wait by the entrance.

'Hello,' Aashif whispered as he bent down next to the girl, unable to tell if she was asleep. They waited until one of the guards entered, carrying a flaming torch. Anwar took it from him and brought the light to the girl's face. The two elephant leaves had slipped from her body, and her eyes were bright but still. Aashif's heart pounded in his chest, the weight of her plight was so overpowering that tears welled up inside him.

Anwar brushed past Aashif and checked that the girl was dead. 'Fetch the baju from the slave. I don't want her to see the girl's body in this state,' he told the guard. He directed the light over the girl, identifying the wound in her side and noticing a thick patch of dried blood between her legs. 'Someone will pay for this,' he growled.

Anwar laid the baju over the girl's body and guessed that she had died recently—her body was still warm. Repulsion clung to him at the thought of someone doing such a brutal thing and, he clenched his teeth as he recalled the death of his baby sister in another unforgivable circumstance.

Chapter 10

Tension in the kitchen was high as the staff waited for news of Aashif's return. The word of the assault on the young slave girl had been spread by those who were present when he charged into the kitchen seeking Suraya's help.

'The Raja will be enraged when the news reaches him,' Suraya said. 'He may be the leader of these lands, but some of the local chiefs think they are a law unto themselves.'

Hanizah was seated amongst a small group of women and grumbled to them. 'It is time the Raja dealt properly with those chiefs and stopped them from abusing us.'

'Enough of that, Hanizah. If he ever learned that you talk about him like that, he would probably take action against you.'

'Well, let him take action against the chiefs.'

One of Suraya's many roles was to report disharmony among the slaves, and she was contemplating how to handle Hanizah when Fatima entered.

'Any news, Fatima?'

Fatima shook her head. 'Nothing yet. They still haven't returned.'

'The last time something like this happened, the chief was enslaved,' one of the women said. 'I hope this time, the punishment is even more severe.'

Fatima strolled up to Suraya. 'The breakfast?'

Each morning at this time, Fatima arrived to collect breakfast for Princess Toh. Suraya's eyes were far away, and Fatima recognized that she was preoccupied.

'I hope Aashif is all right—he gets flustered when he is placed under stress,' Suraya said. 'He's a strong young man, but his stammer comes on when he feels under pressure. The other day, he tried to deny that the guards talk about the princess the way Hanizah claimed, and he couldn't get the words out.'

Fatima scanned Suraya's face and realized that she had a warm spot for Aashif.

Suraya exhaled loudly and clapped her hands. 'Back to work everybody.'

Fatima and Suraya waited for the kitchen to empty as the slaves noisily left the room. Once they were alone, they began to prepare a meal of *nasi lemak*, a fragrant coconut rice with boiled eggs, nuts, anchovies, cucumber, and a spicy sambal sauce.

'I don't know Aashif well,' Fatima said as she helped to prepare the ingredients. 'Our paths had never crossed until a few days ago. I'd seen him around before that, of course, but we'd never had anything to say to one another.'

'He's a fine man with a heart of gold. He can be a daydreamer at times, but he's loyal and trusting. I clearly remember the day he arrived here. He was a frightened little boy, with the most beautiful face. When he wasn't crying, he lit the whole place up.'

'You're fond of him, aren't you?'

Suraya answered proudly, her face brightening. 'He's like a son to me, as you are a daughter,' she said, taking Fatima's hand.

* * *

'Sit down, I'll make us some tea.'

'Did you ever have children?' Fatima asked as Suraya set about making the tea.

Startled by her question, Suraya wished she could answer honestly. She was desperate to reveal the secrets eating away at her but managed to retain a calm countenance. She offered Fatima a rueful smile while she considered how to tell her how empty her life had been. Fatima's piercing eyes fixed on her, and she smiled uneasily.

'There was a man once,' she began. It took her a while to make sense of the questions festering within her. Embarrassed by the silence, Fatima sat and watched Suraya closely and let out a tender laugh. 'What was he like?' she asked, holding the cup of tea Suraya had made for her.

Suraya thought about how much she should divulge.

'He was a nice man,' she said, her tone subdued.

Noticing Fatima's disappointed expression, she added, 'He was a man of true intentions.'

'Was he local?'

'He is still alive. And yes, he is a local man.' She snatched her drink and covered her face as best she could, fearing that she might blush.

'Was he a warrior?'

'Of sorts.' She could tell that Fatima was not satisfied by her answer. 'His role entailed a great many responsibilities. You asked what he was like,' she went on, determined to appease Fatima. 'Well, he was tall, proud of his fine head of hair, and most attractive.'

'He was also a lucky man.'

'Lucky, in what way?' Suraya was puzzled.

'Because he knew you, of course.'

Suraya stroked Fatima's cheek. 'He would have liked you—he always had an eye for a pretty face.'

There was a sudden commotion by the entrance to the kitchen as two male slaves carried in the day's vegetables. The two women waited until they were alone again, and then Fatima spoke, 'Auntie, can I ask you something?'

Wary of what the young girl was going to say, Suraya nodded. 'Go ahead.'

'What happened?'

'Well, he was a loyal man who had many responsibilities, one of which weighed particularly heavy on him. He struggled to balance everything that was going on in his life for quite a while. At the time I was a mere kitchen maid, perhaps a year older than you. A decision had to be made that was for the best for everyone.' She slapped the table and rose calmly. 'Come, help me put the vegetables away.'

With that, Suraya ended the conversation.

* * *

It took Suraya and Fatima a while to put the vegetables away. They were struggling to wedge the cupboard doors closed when Aashif walked in. He was rubbing his eyes, and they noticed that his features were tightly drawn.

'Hello, Auntie.'

'Aashif, what's happened? And how's the girl?'

Aashif's eyes welled up with tears. 'She died,' he managed, surrendering to his distress. Suraya threw her hand over her mouth, and Fatima was unable to speak. The women glanced at each other and hurried to him.

'What dreadful news,' Suraya said, ushering Aashif to the table.

Fatima offered him a woeful smile.

'It was terrible,' he said, unable to manage more words.

'Sit here,' Suraya said, taking him by the arm and sitting him next to the entrance, where there was a cool draught.

'Have you eaten? You must be hungry.' Without letting him respond, she hurried to the stove and began filling bowls with food.

Fatima gazed at Aashif as he wiped his eyes. She noticed how strong his hands were. 'I'm sorry,' she said softly. Aashif looked back at her dolefully.

'Here, eat this,' Suraya said, passing the food across the table and sitting opposite him.

'What happened, Aashif?'

Aashif attempted to answer, but his lips quivered violently, and he broke down, overcome by sorrow. Instinct prompted Fatima to rest her hand on his arm and she left it there while his breathing settled.

He slowly regained control and shivered as he recalled the sight of the slave's body. 'She was dead when we got there. She had such beautiful, innocent eyes, Auntie. How could anybody be so cruel?'

He was trying to untangle his emotions when Fatima spoke softly. 'Where is she now—her body?'

He was silent for a while and then replied with a dry voice, his throat choked with wretchedness. 'When we got back, Anwar and his men took her away.'

Suraya nodded towards the food and watched, as he finally scooped up a portion of rice mixed with the sauce.

'Does anybody know which village she came from?' Suraya asked.

'Anwar says he'll find out, as well as whoever did this to her.' He turned to Fatima, but her eyes were far away.

'Anwar is a determined man, I'm sure he'll do as he says,' Suraya said.

'I wish I hadn't left her there on her own.'

'What else could you have done?' Suraya asked firmly. 'Had you stayed, you'd be asking why you didn't go for help.'

'I should have stayed, Auntie. She must have been so scared on her own. I can still see the terror in her eyes when she told me how scared she was that the man who had brutalized her would come back.'

He turned to Fatima, and her face grew hot as his gaze held hers.

'Thank you for being here and listening to me.'

In the tragedy of the moment, Fatima was overwhelmed by her emotions and felt as if her heart was being stolen from her.

* * *

Tormented, Aashif was unable to finish the food Suraya had served him. He rose, thanked her profusely, and excused himself, explaining that he had to report to Hisham. He bowed and hurried from the kitchen.

Suraya glanced at Fatima and noticed a new light shining through the girl. She said nothing, but realizing that Fatima had become enthralled with Aashif, recalled an earlier time in her life. 'He is greatly troubled, I pray Allah helps him,' she eventually said, while clearing away the table.

'Auntie, how long has Aashif had difficulty speaking?' Fatima asked.

Suraya lifted her head and stared at her. 'For as long as I can remember, there have been times when he's got flustered. But Hisham tells me that his speech has got much better recently.'

'I hope he's going to be all right.'

'Aashif is a tenacious young man. Hisham is very wise, and I've no doubt that Aashif will go a long way under his continued guidance.'

Fatima sat upright, alert to her duties. 'I'd better get back before Princess Toh sends for me.' She thanked Suraya, gathered her tray, and rushed out of the kitchen.

Suraya reflected on a troubling morning and resolved to do something to curtail Hanizah's disobedience. She was compelled to report misconduct in any of the slaves, and to fail in this duty would be an offence punishable by dismissal.

Chapter 11

'She's dead,' Fatima began.

'Dead?' Toh exclaimed.

'Her body was still warm when Aashif and Anwar reached her. They think she was about sixteen, maybe even younger.' Fatima choked with sorrow as she imagined the distress Aashif must have gone through.

'Was she raped?'

Fatima nodded. 'Anwar examined her and believes so. Aashif said that there was a lot of blood that had dried by the time they got there.' Her voice was weary.

Toh was perplexed. 'Dry? I don't understand.'

'When Aashif found her yesterday morning, she was still bleeding.'

'Didn't he do anything to stop it before he went for help?'

'He didn't know what to do, so he made her safe and ran for help.'

Strands of hair fell across Toh's face, she brushed them aside and stared at her hands. 'Fatima, my brother is going to be outraged when he hears about this. He'd rather punish his own men than the slaves.' She stared into the distance. 'You know how disgusted he is by the way chiefs abuse their slaves. He has always been keen that I don't abuse the power he's bestowed upon me. He'll want to know everything, from what I've done to discover who did this dreadful act to who the victim's chief was.'

Fatima nodded again, unable to offer any words of comfort.

'Where is Aashif now?' Toh asked.

'He went to report to Hisham.' Fatima could picture Aashif standing before Hisham, tripping over his words, and she almost wept at the thought.

Her voice was cautious. 'He's awfully shy. I've only recently begun speaking to him, and he stammers quite a lot.'

'I'm going to have to talk to him.'

Fatima hoped she would be present when Toh spoke to Aashif, to offer him support.

'Did Aashif say anything about finding any sort of weapon in the shack?'

Fatima shook her head. 'I think he was too concerned to get help to think about anything else. When he ran back here, he explained to Hisham and Anwar that the girl was naked.' Fatima paused and took a deep breath. 'He'd looked around the shack for her baju but couldn't find it.'

'I'll speak to Anwar and Hisham, and then I'll talk to Aashif,' Toh decided.

Fatima wished that she had chased after Aashif when he left the kitchen and extracted as much information as necessary for Toh. Then she could have avoided having to make Aashif explain everything to the princess.

Toh was serious. 'My brother will definitely want to speak to him. He'll want to talk to Anwar and Hisham, too.'

Fatima felt uneasy but masked her feelings and puckered her lips in acceptance of Aashif's fate.

'You know my brother will be thorough, Fatima.'

* * *

Toh was bewildered by the recent events. She was alarmed that the girl might have been a victim of the Bomoh's sorcery. 'Ever since you told me of the girl's assault, I've been greatly concerned.'

Fatima gasped and stared at Toh, fearful of what the princess would say next.

'Every time I return from visiting that dreadful man, I'm left feeling grave with apprehension. I remember returning after consulting him about the conduct of my first husband, convinced that something unpleasant was going to happen. As you know, he was an appalling man, but I would have much preferred that he had been banished from these lands forever. After my complaint against my second husband brought the same result, I insisted that my present husband should not die. Now I'm beginning to wonder if it would have been better to not have interfered in the Bomoh's spell at all—after all, he knows best. Oh, why did I ever get married, Fatima?'

There was pity in Fatima's reply. 'You weren't to know what your three husbands would be like.'

Toh pushed the hair from her eyes and gazed at Fatima thoughtfully. '"Scream no more the lamburi may hear." I've been repeating his words in my mind ever since I got back.'

'That's the tree, isn't it?' Fatima asked, looking at Toh with her eyes narrowed. 'The ones so tall that they scratch the sky.'

Toh nodded. 'I think the Bomoh was saying that if my husband screams so loudly, the sky spirits will hear him.'

Energized by speaking openly of the Bomoh's words, Toh confessed, 'It's the other words that upset me most.'

The princess's disturbed expression sent a rush of disquiet through Fatima, who hated listening to tales of the Bomoh.

'"For a price must be paid by another unnear"—that's what he said.'

Fatima threw her hands to her face and struggled to breathe. 'The girl?'

Toh shuddered and nodded, her eyes closed. In the silence that followed, Fatima wondered if it was chance that Aashif had fallen upon the girl in such harrowing circumstances or if it was rather some sort of portent of events to come. She peered at Toh uneasily, mortified that Aashif could be embroiled in Toh's affairs in some strange way. An image of him, singing in his lilting voice beneath their bedroom window, came to her.

'Maybe I should go back and talk to the Bomoh, to find out what his spell is intended to achieve,' Toh said.

'No,' Fatima replied, suddenly agitated. 'Then he might cast a spell on someone else.'

Toh stared at Fatima and continued, in a tight, troubled voice, 'Fatima, I don't want any of this spoken about to anyone else. I would not be surprised if the slaves are unsettled by what has happened, and the Raja would be angry if he learned there was restlessness within the community. Meanwhile, I will speak to Anwar, Hisham, and Suraya to make sure that discipline is maintained.'

* * *

Toh gazed out the window of the throne room. The grey sky matched her mood. Her stomach lurched at the thought of being trapped alone in a bleak, weather-beaten shack in the jungle, waiting to die. Even the smell was in her nostrils.

The only consolation she had left against the image in her mind was the thought of Anwar identifying the killer. She wanted the man dragged before the Raja. She floundered as she tried to visualize how she would have coped under such horrendous circumstances. She wandered to the window, hoping to spot Fatima, Anwar, Hisham, and saw Suraya approaching.

Remembering how the Bomoh had danced around his cave chanting, was driving her mad. She berated herself for fleeing—none of this might have happened had she remained there. Maybe, the girl would still be alive today. She clenched her fists and tried to think of something to sooth her nerves, but she could only bring to mind the ugly and suggestive glances that the Bomoh had cast in her direction.

After Toh had told the Bomoh about her second husband's behaviour, she had focused her attention on the rolls of flesh around his neck as his malevolent growl echoed through his cave. She had cowered in a fear that was probably similar to the tragic slave's emotions before she died. Toh blinked fiercely, blotting out the image until it disappeared from her mind.

In the distance, she spotted Fatima leaving the kitchen alone, her head bent low. Toh kept watching, expecting one of the others to join her. From Fatima's manner, Toh guessed that she was vexed by the savagery that her fellow slave had suffered. And yet, when she returned from collecting breakfast, there was a softness in her cheeks that Toh couldn't account for.

Toh loved Fatima's face, but her expression appeared to have become unreadable overnight. She concluded that Fatima was saddened by something other than the cruelty inflicted on the young slave, some hidden burden, and she could tell, even from this distance, that Fatima was discontent. Toh dismissed the thought when she noticed Suraya chasing after her and Hisham meeting up with them both.

As the three neared the palace, Toh recalled how her husband had screamed at her before he had set off for the countryside. 'We have to keep a watch on the people for the Raja,' he always insisted, before disappearing for days or even weeks at a time. Her disappointment at her husband's behaviour was wearing her down—if only she could get him to stop ranting and raving.

* * *

As the sun broke through the clouds, Dato Hamidi Hossain was pleased that it would not rain after all. He gazed at Suzanariahin revelling in the title of Dato, which had been bestowed upon him following his marriage to Princess Toh.

Dato Hamidi and Suzanariahin hadn't seen each another since his wedding, two years ago. Now, Suzanariahin stood naked and beamed down at him mischievously. So rambunctious was his mood that he would have happily made love to her in the rain.

Suzanariahin was plumper than she had been, and he liked that there was more of her to please him. She had painted her lips the colour of rubies and he liked that too. Suzanariahin was malleable in her youth. Two years ago, on the night before he was wedded, she had lost her maidenhead to him and had been pined for him ever since.

'Get down here,' he commanded.

Her cheeky expression hardened his eyes, and he remembered how much she enjoyed it when he spanked her bottom. But at that moment, he wanted his own pleasure first.

'Now,' he demanded.

Suzanariahin laughed coquettishly. She bent low and nudged closer to him so that she could share the baju he was lying on.

His stomach growled and he laughed, taking hold of her hand and placing it on his manhood, gasping as the tips of her fingers fuelled his desire. He raised himself, rolled across her body and prepared to enjoy the gratification awaiting him.

Once he was spent, he fell away from her, laying back on the ground and counting the passing clouds, jealous of their freedom.

Chapter 12

In the male dormitory, over a hundred beds flanked the walls. Aashif had never been inside the female barracks but, he had been assured by those men who had that their quarters were tidier than the women's. Similar counterpanes covered the beds, while a greater number of citronella plants were spread throughout the accommodation to fend off mosquitos. The argument went that because more men worked in the open air, they were more vulnerable to mosquito infestations.

In the doorway, a large number of men were deep in discussion. The single topic dominating their conversation was the slave's death and the brutal way in which her life had ended.

One of the senior slaves spoke up. 'The Raja will be up in arms when he learns what has happened.'

'What's Princess Toh doing?' another of the senior slaves asked angrily.

All eyes turned to Aashif. 'All I know is what I've told you,' he said. 'According to Hisham, Anwar set out to report the events to the Raja after their meeting with the princess.'

'The princess should send a party of armed guards into the jungle and scour the place for him now, starting at the shack you spoke of,' one slave said menacingly.

The vast majority of the group stood by, listening grimly, too frightened to express views that might be reported back to Princess Toh. They knew that to openly criticize the royal family could result in banishment.

'When the murderer is found, he will be blindfolded and taken deep into the jungle, where his arms and legs will be slashed to draw the attention of animals. If he was a slave, he will be left unarmed to fend for himself,' growled the original speaker. 'If he is a free man, he will be left with a kris.'

Another of the senior slaves spoke angrily. 'If the princess is not going to protect our women, we will.' His remark was met with murmurs of assent.

Aashif was wandering back to his bed when Osmin, the most unpopular of all the guards, strolled in, accompanied by the new guard, Haron. 'What's going on here?' Osmin demanded to know.

Aashif continued to his bed, before dropping to the floor and checking that his most prized possession was safe. Cut into the underside of his bed, and covered with a strip of wood, was a hiding place that contained a tiny pouch of soil from his village in Africa. His father had passed it to him with the words 'one day you must return this'.

It was while he was sprawled flat on his stomach on the floor, out of sight of anyone coming, that Osmin and Haron approached.

'You want to keep a careful eye on them,' Osmin was saying, when he stopped mid-sentence. 'Show me that,' he snapped.

'What?'

'Your badge—if the Raja ever sees it in this condition, you'll be in trouble. Keep it clean and polish it every day.' A short pause followed. 'What's this stain on it?'

'Blood, I was helping my mother on my day off and cut myself.'

'Get it cleaned.'

'Yes, sir.'

Aashif slid out from under the bed and pushed himself up.

'What are you doing there?' Osmin snarled, and all Aashif could do was stare dumbly. He stood still and stammered, 'I . . . I . . . was checking under my bed, sir.'

Haron stood next to Osmin, wearing a vacant expression that turned venomous—it reaffirmed Aashif's instinct that he would have to avoid Haron's hostility.

* * *

Aashif lay on his bed and stared up at the roof. There must have been an element of fate that caused him to overhear Osmin and Haron's conversation, but he couldn't fathom what it meant. He had long been used to the meanness in Osmin's face, but he was troubled by Haron's attitude towards him. He decided to say nothing about the guards' conversation and drove the incident from his mind, instead turning his attention to Fatima—when he recalled her broad smile, his heart soared. His musings were interrupted when Reza and Faiz, the slaves on either side of his bed, approached.

'What did Osmin want?' Faiz asked.

'I was looking under my bed for something, and he wanted to know what I was doing on the floor.'

Reza sat down on his bed.

'Things are getting heated back there,' Reza said. 'It's just as well Osmin left, or he'd have been able to hear everything.'

'It's the older ones who are getting really upset.'

'You can't blame them.'

'That witch Princess Toh had better act quickly,' Faiz said.

'Why?' Aashif interrupted. 'Hisham says that although Princess Toh is in charge, Anwar is the person making the decisions in the Raja's absence. If anybody needs to act it is him, not the princess.' Aashif knew he was making himself vulnerable to criticism by defending Princess Toh, but he had seen enough injustice to take a stand.

Heated voices travelled along the dormitory, and Aashif wished that he had not been the bearer of the news of the slave's death. He had been hounded for information the whole day and needed a break.

Reza and Faiz were silent until Reza eventually spoke. 'Thank God it wasn't me who found the girl.'

'Yes—Aashif, you'll probably be questioned by the Raja.'

Aashif hadn't imagined the possibility of meeting the Raja and was alarmed at the prospect.

'Have you met him before?' Reza asked as he began dressing.

'No,' Aashif replied.

A large crowd of men was heading towards Aashif, and he was relieved when they peeled off to their own beds.

'I'm hungry—are you ready?' Reza asked Faiz.

Aashif sat forward. 'I'll come and join you.'

'Sorry, but we've got a couple of personal issues to discuss,' Faiz said, glancing meaningfully at Reza.

'Yes, we've been planning it all day,' Reza said.

Aashif didn't know where to look. Faiz stood in the aisle and gave Aashif a shallow nod before he hurried off with Reza. Aashif was left alone, and his thoughts drifted back to Fatima.

* * *

Aashif waited well into the evening before going to get something to eat from the kitchen.

'You're late tonight,' Suraya said, noticing the despondency in his eyes.

He mumbled that he had been resting and glanced around the room. Reza and Faiz were seated at the head of the large table, enjoying some loud badinage with a group of men. The women were sitting around the smaller tables. He scanned the room and caught sight of an arm waving at him. To his surprise and delight, it was Hisham—he would not have to eat alone.

When Aashif joined his mentor at the opposite end of the table, Reza and Faiz were in his line of vision. He avoided Faiz's glances and concentrated on Hisham. It dawned on him that the other members of the household staff and guards were also present.

'You don't usually eat with us,' Aashif said.

'You'll often find me here if you arrive at this late hour,' Hisham said before nodding towards the other end of the table. 'Aren't they Reza and Faiz?' he asked, watching the men looking across at Aashif.

'Yes,' Aashif said. 'I offered to join them earlier. They told me they wanted to discuss a private matter, but it doesn't seem to have been *that* private.'

'Is everything all right?' Hisham asked.

'I'm not sure.' He brushed aside the thoughts of Reza and Faiz discussing disharmony among the men. 'They are upset at the death of the young girl.'

Hisham frowned and he pressed Aashif. 'Tell me more.'

Aashif looked around surreptitiously and lowered his voice. 'The men are saying that Princess Toh should be taking action. They want her to send armed guards to the shack where I found the girl, to search the area for any clues that might lead to her attacker.' When he noticed Faiz staring at him, his expression hardened.

Suraya appeared with a tray of food. 'You must be starving,' she said to Aashif, placing a banana leaf on the table and piling it with rice, chicken, and vegetables. 'That should sustain you, young man,' she said cheerfully.

Between mouthfuls, Aashif mumbled to Hisham. 'That guard Osmin puts everyone on edge. The moment he entered our dormitory, the men stopped talking. I don't know what he's been telling the new guard, Haron, but he seems to have taken a distinct dislike to me.' Aashif said nothing about Osmin checking Haron's badge, content for now to lay down a marker against the new guard.

'As I told you, Osmin is being watched closely. I'll pass on word of your disquiet over young Haron and arrange for him to be watched, too.'

A noisy commotion erupted, as Reza, Faiz, and the rest of their group prepared to leave.

'I know who I'm going to befriend tonight,' Faiz said, to jeers of laughter. It was usually around this time that the male slaves joined the girls in the female quarters. The guards turned a blind eye to such goings on, especially as many of them also regarded the hospitality of the girls as a perk of the job.

'Join me for a stroll,' Hisham said.

Aashif quickly finished his food and stood. Both men wandered outside— the moon had swelled, and they watched as the others danced towards the women's quarters in high spirits.

As they ambled along, Aashif asked his elder the question that was worrying him. 'Sir, will the Raja want to question me?'

'It's likely that he will, yes.'

As they sauntered along aimlessly, Hisham eventually said, 'Wouldn't you prefer to join the others in the women's quarters?'

'I've never been inside.'

Hisham stopped short. 'Why not?'

Aashif shrugged. 'I hope to meet a woman who does not flaunt herself publicly—maybe, once I've been to Mecca.'

'You're determined to get there, aren't you?'

'Yes, I must do my Haj.'

They resumed their stroll. 'Do you have any particular woman in mind?' Hisham asked.

'No, sir.'

They fell silent, until Hisham spoke. 'Tell me, what did the men have to say about Princess Toh?'

'They are blaming her for not doing anything. I told them that Anwar made all the decisions for her.'

Hisham stopped again and stared at Aashif as if assessing him. 'I have a task that I want you to perform. Anwar is concerned that the slaves are restless. A situation like this could easily get out of hand, and he needs to know if their disgruntlement is anything more serious. The last thing he wants is a rebellion, especially with the Raja and so many warriors away. The instant any of the men or women stir up trouble, I want you to come and tell me.'

Chapter 13

The following morning, Toh found that her mind was ambushed by images of the dead girl. There was a tense knot in her stomach, and she admitted to Fatima that she did not know what to do. 'I've been reliving my experiences with the Bomoh. I can't understand why that dreadful man must speak to me in those ridiculous rhymes.'

Toh's long hair kept brushing her face. Fatima watched her cast it off with a throw of the head and wondered what it would feel like to have such long hair.

Toh continued despondently. 'My first husband died after punching me and my second, after scratching me.' She sighed, 'Do I have the power to cause the death of another? Could I provoke someone into assaulting me, knowing that they would die?' She paced back and forth, agitated.

Fatima stared at Toh, aware that her mistress wanted reassurance that she would not be able to give. All she could think to say was, 'Anwar will know what to do. We should wait and hear what he says.'

'It was my father who insisted that I yield to the Bomoh's advice, and my brother said the same thing when he became the Raja.'

Desperate to unburden herself, Toh repeated the Bomoh's words. 'He said, "For a price must be paid by another unnear." Surely, he can't have meant that the young slave had to die in order for his spell to work? After all, I told him that I did not want the Dato to die.' She continued sadly. 'The thought that I may have contributed in some way to that poor girl's death is haunting me—I've had no sleep since we heard the news.'

Fatima stared at Toh. 'They say Bomohs have all the power. It is the Bomoh who should be thinking like this, not you.'

'But now I must worry how the Dato will react if he has to explain his movements to the Raja—he will probably get angry. I don't know why he insists on travelling around the countryside checking on the people, when he doesn't know what to look for.' She left her thoughts unfinished as she snatched her slave's hand. 'Oh Fatima, I wish I knew what to do.'

Fatima tried as hard as she could to mask her disdain at the Dato's behaviour.

Toh went on, 'I know he upsets you when he shouts. All I want the Bomoh to do is to stop him from screaming at me.'

Toh frantically tried to recall what the Bomoh had said to her during her first two visits to his cave, in a desperate search for a clue. 'As much as I despise the man, I have to go to see him again. I must know if he was, in any way, responsible for that young girl's death,' she said.

Fatima turned her thoughts to Aashif and her heart sank when she thought about what he must be going through—having tried to help the girl only to discover her dead body. Dreadful scenes kept blurring into each other as she battled to make sense of the pictures in her head. One minute, Aashif was desperately trying to comfort the slave girl, and the next, he was running through the jungle in a mad dash to get help. Then he was gasping for breath as he struggled to explain what was happening. These images caused her to question Toh's concerns for Aashif, as she remembered the purity of his beautiful singing voice. Her recent dreams of slavery, freedom, relationships, and families took over her thoughts and she tried to make sense of it all. Unable to look Toh in the eye, she gloomily pictured Aashif standing before the Raja and being interrogated. She had to be present, she told herself, and she had to let Aashif know that she would support him. But how could she reassure him without arousing his anxiety? Suraya was the one person who could tell her what to do.

'Shall I go and fetch breakfast?'

'I don't think I can eat.'

'You must keep your strength up.'

Lost in her own world, Toh finally nodded her assent. Fatima hurried from the room and dashed down the stairs. She stopped abruptly at the bottom—she did not want to miss sighting Aashif. As she walked towards the kitchen, her eyes were darting all over the place, but she failed to spot him.

Suraya was by herself when Fatima entered. Fatima hurried straight up to her. 'Have you seen Aashif, Auntie?' she asked urgently.

'He was in here earlier for his breakfast. What's the matter?'

Fatima had not slept well, and Suraya noticed the dark circles around her eyes. 'Sit down,' she said, pouring out a mug of water for each of them. 'Now,' she said, 'what's happening?'

Fatima explained her concerns. 'Toh is not up to questioning Aashif. Anyway, she says Anwar and Hisham have told her all that she needs to know.

'I'm worried for him, Auntie. The Raja will want to question him. Will he be able to cope, do you think? With his stammer, I mean.'

'You like him, don't you?' Suraya asked.

Fatima blushed deeply.

'Well, I can tell he likes you too.'

Fatima's eyes opened wide. 'But we've hardly spoke to one another.'

'Sometimes words can be such a nuisance.'

'But how do you know?' Fatima said, her heart racing.

'I've seen the way he looks at you. I may be an old woman, but I am not a stupid one,' Suraya said with a smile. The old lady patted Fatima's cheek. 'He and Hisham are in the jungle. They'll be back this afternoon. You can catch him then.'

The conversation was not at all what Fatima had envisaged, but as she made her way back to the palace, she was impatient to see Aashif.

* * *

When Fatima spotted Aashif in the distance, a great burst of excitement exploded inside her. He was working with Hisham, and she wondered how she might speak to him alone. Her dilemma was solved when she reached the area of the gardens where the two men were working. They were some distance apart, and she came upon Hisham first. Aashif, who was busy tilling the soil, didn't notice her arrival.

'It is a pleasant surprise to find you out here, Fatima. How are you?'

'I'm well, Uncle, thank you.'

Hisham caught her glancing towards Aashif. 'You've come to talk to Aashif?' he asked, tactfully.

'Could I?' she asked shyly.

'You can,' he said, trying not to smile.

Suraya's words were at the forefront of her mind as Fatima reached Aashif. 'Hello, Aashif,' she said. 'How are you?'

Aashif turned sharply.

She was captivated by a vitality she had only now woken up to, when she took in his strong-featured face and large, dark eyes. She noticed him snatching a glance in Hisham's direction. 'I asked Uncle if it was all right to come and talk to you.'

'I . . . I'm fine.' Aashif stammered.

She feared saying something idiotic and felt her stomach clench. 'I've been trying to meet you all day.'

'Has . . . something happened? Have I . . . done something wrong?'

'No. I've been so worried about you after your dreadful ordeal, that I had to check that you were all right.' Alarmed that she had frightened him; she ached to embrace him but accepted that such a gesture would be indecorous.

'I keep seeing the dead girl's face and remembering her pleading for help.'

They stood, gazing at one another in silence.

Unsure of what to do, she plunged straight in. 'Can I confide in you? Ever since the girl was killed, I've been having horrible dreams about being a slave. Do you ever get such dreams?'

Wide-eyed and speechless, Aashif nodded.

Fatima had to remind herself that she had wanted to talk to him about the Raja. 'You're aware that Anwar has gone to report to the Raja.' She watched as he got more anxious and continued. 'The Raja will want to talk to you. I wanted to tell you that I shall do everything I can to be present when you meet him.'

'What . . . will he ask me . . . do you know?'

'I imagine he'll want to know everything that you know. But you mustn't worry—I'll be there to support you.'

The pair fell silent once more until Aashif spoke again. 'I won't . . . I . . . I might not be able to . . . speak to him.'

Aashif's struggle to talk went straight to Fatima's heart. 'If you see me tugging at my sleeve, it's because I don't like people looking at my arm. I burned it when I was little, and it embarrasses me. When the Raja talks to you, Princess Toh will be there, but she won't say anything. She hates to open her mouth because it's black inside. We all have our afflictions to overcome.'

In Fatima's quest to put Aashif's mind at ease, she decided to discuss their common predicament. She turned her face back to check if Hisham was out of earshot and lowered her voice. 'Please tell me about your dreams of being a slave.' When he didn't respond, she continued, 'I've been spoilt, Aashif. Until that poor girl was killed, I'm ashamed to admit I gave little attention to anything apart from my own day-to-day existence.'

'I want to visit Mecca, and from there, I want to go in search of my father and discover the land where I was born.'

The most striking aspect of what Aashif was saying was the lack of a stammer. It struck Fatima that his speech impediment only came to the fore when he was under stress.

'If I was free, like the guards, and like Hisham, Suraya, and the others, I would be able to fulfil my dreams. We all believe in the same God, so I don't understand why I can't do my Haj when free people can.'

Aashif's eyes were full of passion and Fatima's desire to embrace him was even stronger as she replied, 'I shall pray that you achieve your dreams.'

Part 2

Chapter 14

The Raja's intense hostility was new to Princess Toh and Fatima, neither of them had seen him in this mood before. He sat on his throne in deep thought, occasionally looking at them sternly, before he finally spoke. The three were alone and Toh and Fatima stood before him.

'A serious insurgency, many miles south of here, prevented me from returning sooner,' he said. 'But I do not drag two hundred men away from the front for my sole benefit. If I were to be killed, there would be terrible battles for the control of the mines.'

He drummed his fingers on his grand chair. 'Where's that husband of yours?'

Toh swallowed timidly. 'He's still up country.'

The Raja stared at his sister disdainfully, his eyes dark. 'He's been absent since my last visit. What does he do on his travels?'

Toh could only shrug her shoulders in reply.

The Raja continued, his voice sharp, 'Fatima, get across to the kitchen and fetch me some breakfast. Ask Suraya to feed the men as well, and fetch the slave, Aashif. Leave him downstairs while I eat, and then bring him up to me.'

Fatima bowed, before leaving the room.

Toh could sense that something unpleasant might be afoot, and she stared at her brother, who spoke sternly.

'I sent Fatima away so that we may talk in private. It is not my wish to embarrass you in front of her, but I have learned that your husband has not been treating you with respect.'

Toh's face went pale, as the Raja's features hardened into a penetrating glare. He had no desire to distress his sister any more than necessary, but her husband's indecorous conduct had angered him. 'The way he screams and shouts at you is undermining your authority among our people, and I cannot have that. Toh, you must put a stop to it.'

He noticed a sadness welling up in Toh's face and wanted to comfort her, but he also knew that he had to stand firm. 'While Fatima is away, let us address the murder of this young slave,' he continued. 'Father taught us to respect the slaves, and with good reason. Incidents such as the death of that young girl simply stoke unrest.'

Toh struggled to fight back her tears, determined to demonstrate her ability to control herself. 'I've already put matters in hand to address my husband's behaviour. And as for the death of the young slave, I've let it be known that the person responsible will pay dearly.'

'Good,' the Raja said, sitting back on his throne. 'Father always prioritized controlling the slaves, over their welfare. It hasn't yet happened under my reign, but every time a slave runs away, I have to take a warrior from the battlefield—we simply do not have enough slaves to cope. If the slaves ever took it upon themselves to revolt, we would be in dire trouble.' He paused. 'This is obviously a topic I would never discuss in Fatima's presence.'

* * *

Fatima dashed to the kitchen but was not initially able to enter, for two hundred boisterous warriors had crammed into the room and were sitting at every available table. She hurried up to Suraya, ignoring the men's stares. 'The Raja has ordered me to collect his breakfast and requests that you feed his warriors,' she said while struggling to catch her breath.

'Well, young lady, as you can see, the second of your orders is already being met. As for the first, if you give me a moment, I'll prepare his food. Stay next to me,' she said, glancing at the men as Fatima followed her to the stove. 'You can stoke the fire while I attend to his breakfast.'

Fatima struggled in vain to hide her dread. 'He also wants me to bring Aashif to him now. He wants to question him.'

Suraya grimaced. 'Then you'd better fetch Aashif. Bring him here and I'll talk to him before you take him to the palace.'

Outside, spots of rain were falling, and Fatima prayed that a storm was not on the way. She could not see Aashif anywhere, but she spotted Hisham working in the distance and called out to him. 'Uncle, have you seen Aashif? The Raja has called for him.'

'There he is,' Hisham said, as Aashif walked toward them. Fatima gave him a beguiling smile as he neared. 'The Raja has asked me to fetch you,' she said as calmly as she could. 'He wants to talk to you about the murdered slave.'

Aashif looked puzzled at first and Fatima watched as panic filled his eyes. 'When?' he stammered.

'Now.' Fatima noticed that his eyes were red and wondered if he'd been having difficulty sleeping. She put her hand on his arm. 'It'll be fine, I promise.'

'Of course, it will be,' Hisham interrupted. 'The Raja wants to hear first-hand what you know, Aashif, nothing more. He'll be determined to learn who killed that poor girl.'

'We had better go,' Fatima said. 'I need to stop off at the kitchen and collect the Raja's breakfast.'

Aashif glanced at Hisham who nodded at him before they set off at a brisk pace. 'You'll be fine,' Fatima said, trying to ignore the mounting tension.

'How do I address him?'

She looked at his careworn face. 'Everybody calls him Your Majesty, but you needn't worry about that. He doesn't stand on ceremony.'

'I . . . I'm worried . . . speaking . . . to him.'

Fatima remembered how angry the Raja had seemed, when he asked her to collect Aashif, and took his arm. 'Please don't worry.'

The atmosphere in the kitchen was far quieter than when Fatima had entered previously—the men were busy eating. Suraya passed the Raja's breakfast to Fatima.

'Aashif, remember what I've taught you,' the cook said, kindly. 'Take deep breaths and talk slowly.' She gave Fatima a friendly wink. 'Off you go.'

When they reached the stairs leading into the palace, Fatima signalled that they should stop. 'Wait here. I'll take the food up to the Raja and come back to fetch you as soon as I can.'

Fatima's heart raced as she saw the fright in Aashif's eyes. She wanted desperately to embrace him, but instead climbed the stairs, glancing back when she was halfway up. Their eyes met, both of them aware of the gravity of the situation.

* * *

When Fatima entered the throne room, she found the Raja pacing back and forth. As soon as he saw her, he walked to the table where Toh was seated.

'Aashif is waiting downstairs,' Fatima said meekly. 'Shall I go and fetch him?' she asked, setting the food down.

'Let me enjoy this first,' he said and began to eat his breakfast of nasi lemak.

When he had finished eating, the Raja spoke again, 'You can bring him to me now.'

It was clear from the man's expression that his mood had not changed; his eyes were still wild with rage. Fatima hurried along the corridor and down the stairs, reaching Aashif, slightly short of breath. 'He's ready for you now,' she said, wincing at his obvious nervousness before leading him to the throne room where the Raja was seated, waiting for them.

In a well-intentioned display of humility, Aashif walked forward carefully, stood to attention, and gave a long, stiff bow that left the Raja wondering if the slave would ever raise his head.

Still gripped by rage, the Raja spoke. 'What's your name?'

'Aashif, Your Majesty.' His voice was so quiet that Fatima and Toh had to strain to hear him.

'I've been told that you discovered the girl by the riverbank. Is that correct?'

Aashif's heart was racing. 'Yes, Your Majesty.'

'Speak up, lad—I can't hear you.

'Yes, Your Majesty,' Aashif shouted.

'Tell me what happened.'

'I . . . went . . . fishing.' Aashif stopped. It was as though he couldn't find the words. Fatima's heart sank, the urge to go to his aid almost overwhelming her.

The Raja sat forward. 'Let me ask you some questions, lad. You say you were fishing—correct?'

Aashif shook his head. 'No, Your Majesty,' he stammered. 'I didn't fish.'

'So, you went fishing but didn't fish?'

Aashif nodded. 'Yes, Your Majesty,' he said limply.

'Yes or no will suffice.'

'Yes.'

'Good. And when you found the girl, she was still alive?

'Yes,' Aashif answered.

'And she was naked?'

'Yes.'

'Tell me, was her baju anywhere?'

Aashif stared at the Raja but said nothing.

'I need an answer. Did you look for it?'

'I looked around the shack, but I couldn't find it,' he said quietly, before explaining that he had covered her in leaves.

'So, there was no sign of her baju anywhere?'

'No, sir.'

The Raja stared long and hard at him. 'I'm told that there was no cooking pot outside the hut, correct?' Throughout the jungle, similar huts—many on stilts and known as *pemburu pondok*, resting huts for hunters—often had sturdy cooking pots outside them. The Raja was familiar with such huts, having helped build a couple as a young boy.

'Yes, sir. Correct, sir.'

Aashif was nervously swaying on the spot and Fatima willed him to stand still.

'You know Anwar?' the Raja continued.

'Yes.'

'He tells me that the girl told you she was frightened of her attacker coming back. Is that true?'

Aashif nodded.

'Now think, lad. Did she say anything else?'

Aashif stiffened before suddenly standing upright. 'Only about the badge,' he stuttered.

'What about it?'

Fatima's stomach churned as Aashif struggled to explain how the girl had told him that the perpetrator had shown her his badge.

'A badge of identification, you mean—like our badge of authority?'

Aashif nodded again, and the Raja stiffened and finally snapped, 'And you told Anwar none of this?'

'He didn't ask me,' Aashif said, the panic clear in his eyes.

The Raja questioned Aashif about the badge again and again, his patience wearing thin. Fatima watched as Aashif seemed to wilt, worn down by the weight of the Raja's onslaught. She could never have imagined him being so cruel and desperately wanted to make him stop.

* * *

In the late afternoon, Anwar stood with the Raja in the courtyard in front of his company of warriors.

'Frankly, I don't have any reason to doubt the slave,' the Raja said. 'My guess is that he was hiding nothing. If we could only find that baju, it might help us identify her. Right now, all we can do is try to discover if any young female slave is missing.'

Anwar couldn't stop thinking about the badge, it seemed to suggest that the attacker was a member of the palace staff or one of the guards. Meanwhile, the Raja's gentle manner had abandoned him. 'Find out everyone's movements,' he said angrily. 'Except for the royal family, of course.' The two men locked eyes and the Raja continued coldly. 'You had better check on the slaves, too. Who knows, maybe someone was able to get hold of a badge and use it to deceive the girl. Finish off any duties you have here and begin your search of the shack as soon as possible. Take a handful of men to help you. I want the attacker identified—and punished.'

Anwar bowed, and the Raja stepped away, taking the reins of his horse from one of his warriors.

Chapter 15

Dato Hamidi Hossain wandered around the palace as if it was his own private quarters.

'There you are,' he said, entering the bedroom and finding Toh sitting in front of her dresser. Fatima stood over her, working a brush through the princess's hair. The women seemed frosty, but that was no more than he expected.

'The Raja left over an hour ago,' Toh said.

'So I've been told.'

'Where have you been?'

'You know perfectly well where I've been—I told you where I was going.'

Toh let out a contemptuous sigh.

'Hello, Fatima.'

Fatima nodded at Dato Hamidi, while making it clear that her loyalty lay with Toh.

Dato Hamidi was a man of average height and build. His hair was straight black and he had reasonable looks, though his features were thin. While he had little spirit, he could hold the palace in fear with his moods. As he watched the women intently, he gave a lustful grin. He stared at Fatima's reflection and her beautiful smile. It reminded him of Suzanariahin, and how she had spread her lips before placing them over his manhood. He couldn't remember what had caused Suzanariahin's high-pitched giggle, but the memory of it amused him.

He addressed Toh. 'I've had stern words with some of the farmers about their diminishing crops. I was hoping your brother would be here so that I could discuss the situation with him.'

'You know what the Raja told you before. We mustn't upset the farmers—their lives are difficult enough as it is.'

Dato Hamidi looked back at Fatima. The notion of enjoying the pleasure Fatima could offer him had passed his mind many times but until recently, it had been nothing more than a whimsical fancy. He now promised himself that he would pursue the possibility. He turned his attention away from the slave girl and to his marital duties, a thought that gave him no pleasure whatsoever.

'Where did your travels take you?' Toh asked.

'All over the countryside.' He glared at her. 'Why, has something happened while I've been away?'

'A young slave girl was brutally raped and murdered by the Perak river.'

To Toh's surprise, her husband furrowed his brow and spoke slowly, 'When did this happen?'

'Ten days ago.'

The couple was silent, until the Dato finally spoke, 'Why didn't you tell me this straight away? Is that why the Raja was here?'

'He came back as soon as he could to try and find the killer—you know how he protects his slaves. He has placed Anwar in charge.'

A stern, sceptical look came over Toh, and Dato Hamidi snapped, 'Are you trying to suggest that this murder has something to do with me?'

'Please don't shout. The Raja has warned you that if your screaming and shouting doesn't stop, there will be serious consequences.' She paused before adding, 'Right now, everyone is under suspicion.'

'What?' Dato Hamidi roared. 'I spend my life travelling around the country, ensuring that people are doing their duty to this family, and you think that somehow, I might have had something to do with this murder?'

Toh was used to her husband's behaviour and glanced up at Fatima.

'There's no point looking to Fatima for support,' he bellowed.

'It wasn't me that told the Raja how you behave—which means someone else did. And that same person is likely to tell him how you are behaving now.'

'Why did you ask where I've been when you knew I was up-country?' he demanded.

'Please be civil. You've been away for twelve days, and this is how you behave on your return.'

There was a long pause before Dato Hamidi spoke again, 'Tell me this: Why has the Raja left Anwar in charge of the enquiry? I'm a member of this family, why did he not appoint me?'

'You were not here.'

'And if I had been, would he have appointed me?'

'I don't know, but you would certainly be more likely to appease him if you were here.' She stared at the Dato, who shook his head.

'Have you eaten?' Toh asked, resigned to the fact that her husband was in another of his bad moods.

'I'll get some food later. Where's Anwar? Do you know what he's doing?'

'I've no idea. The Raja spoke to him barely an hour ago, so he won't have had time to do much.'

Dato Hamidi realized that the Raja had probably appointed Anwar because of the lack of respect the Raja had for him, his sister's husband, and a pinch of malice worked its way inside him. 'How did you learn of the killing?' he asked his wife angrily.

'One of the slaves, a young man, reported it.'

'What's his name? I should talk to him.'

'No.'

'What do you mean?' Dato Hamidi snarled. 'Tell me his name, or do I have to ask every slave until I find out who he is?'

'Stop screaming,' Toh said, glancing at Fatima.

Dato noticed that Fatima seemed to have become agitated, and it occurred to him that she might know the young man. Toh gave him a brutal stare, and a little quiver ran through him as his suspicion appeared to be confirmed. He wondered whether Fatima might be intimate with him. 'Fatima, I'll have some food now, if you don't mind.'

Toh nodded at Fatima, and Dato Hamidi watched as she elegantly left the room, her pert little bottom visible beneath her thin baju.

* * *

Toh entered the courtyard and greeted Anwar, who was waiting for her.

'Anwar, I am sorry to drag you away from your duties, but a troubling matter has arisen.' She reluctantly met his gaze. 'My husband is asleep after an exhausting journey. Unfortunately, for some reason, he thinks the Raja would have appointed him to lead the murder enquiry, had he been here. You and I both know that he lacks the necessary knowledge and experience. Please ensure you remain in charge—do not permit him to override you or question Aashif.'

Anwar smiled. 'The Raja has already given me the same instructions,' he said, offering Toh the reins of her horse.

The pair set off at a brisk pace and soon entered the jungle, where they were met by the usual hisses and caws, with dark shapes hiding in the thick foliage. By the time they reached the slope, Toh's agitation at the prospect of meeting the Bomoh again had reached fever pitch. She prayed that he had cleaned his abode and gotten rid of the bats, rats, and snakes.

When they reached the point where they were required to dismount, the forest was filled with a strange wind and a shuddering roar. Startled, they stared skywards. Though their vision was restricted by the dense trees, the sky that they could see was cloudless. Yet, thunder roared. Then, as if some great animal had caught its breath, the world fell silent and the whistles, tweets, warbles, and caws suddenly stopped.

The silence was broken by a piercing screech from above, like the noise uttered by a man before his death. Toh rushed to Anwar, who had drawn his daggers and was searching everywhere, watchful for an enemy. The silence resumed, broken now and then by the cries of birds.

'Hold on to your reins, princess. We must keep the animals calm.'

'Please don't walk away—stay by my side.'

Toh was terrified as they stepped into the clearing in front of the Bomoh's cave. The usual jungle sounds had returned.

'Go,' Anwar commanded, agitated by the strange atmosphere. Without further ado, Toh hurried into the cave to find the Bomoh waiting for her. He directed her to follow him and shuffled across to the fire, before gesturing for her to sit down next to him.

The princess began to tell the Bomoh what had happened since her last visit. 'All my life, my father and now my brother, have instilled in me the belief that you are here to serve me. Please, was the death of the young slave girl a part of your spell?'

The Bomoh's grumpiness was exacerbated by Toh's scruffiness. She could have at least made herself presentable, he grumbled to himself. He had been aware from the disturbances in the forest that someone was approaching. Only when he identified that it was Toh and Anwar, did he know who it was.

He fixed Toh with a troubled expression, annoyed that she had travelled all this way for reassurance with a matter that was out of his control. As they sat together, he contemplated her request. Toh's heavy breathing only added to his irritation.

He turned away from the fire's embers and stared at her mockingly, his nose flaring in anger, until she looked into his eyes and fell under his spell. He stood up slowly, fiercely warned her to stay still, and began to repeat his chant from her previous visit.

When he had finished his incantation, he made a fresh supply of the pink paste and thrust it at Toh, who snapped out from her stupor:

'While the dove has wings to flee the sky
Actions as yours cause the spell to die.'

Chapter 16

The little boy happily hopped and skipped ahead of his father, who was careful to keep his son within eyeshot. On reaching the riverbank, the boy lay on his stomach, stretched out an arm, and dipped his hand into the water to test the strength of the current. The flow was steady, and he watched as shoals of fish swam past. He rolled on to his side and waved at his father to hurry. When the man reached him, the boy sprang to his feet and watched as his father set up his fishing gear. Then, he snatched up his spear and began stabbing it into the water. He was euphoric when he caught a fish. His father joined him, and they had soon caught enough to sell to the villagers.

At midmorning, the father suggested they take a rest. The boy lay down and rested his head on his father's sturdy thigh. Before long, sleep drew him into his own world, the rhythm of his deep breathing bonding with his contentment.

The boy was jolted from his slumber by a cracking sound. He looked up at the face of his father, who was sitting bolt upright. 'Dada?'

The man leapt to his feet and picked up the boy. The pair headed back to their village. On entering a clearing, they encountered a gang of men— heavily armed with spears, knives, hammers, and scythes. They were quickly surrounded, and the boy watched in terror at the sight. A group of pale-skinned men seemed to be giving orders to their armed captors. Having been dragged through the village, they reached a large pool of water and human blood. Several women lay lifeless in it, their legs spread wide apart. One of them had had her breasts severed. They rounded a group of huts to find a huddle of men and boys. As they passed a tree in the centre of the village, they suddenly turned around. There, pinned to the trunk by a spear through her throat, was the boy's mother. She was trying desperately to speak. Tears were flowing slowly down her cheeks, and she blinked while gurgling noises came from her mouth.

The boy cried out, and the vultures which had been circling her soared into the sky. He snatched at his father's leg and moved his lips to speak, but no sound came out.

That night, along with other captives, the pair were led across the savannah. Chained together at the neck, they walked until their captors decided that they wanted to rest. If they were overheard whispering, they were beaten on the spot. They trekked for days on end, stopping only at the behest of their captors, and surviving on scraps of food and drips of water.

A few weeks into the journey, a tiger was spotted on high ground. The captives were rounded up, and one of the white men strolled among them and selected an elderly villager. The man was released from his chains and a new chain was locked around his neck, with the loose end held in place by a huge boulder. When they were satisfied that the villager could not escape, the pale-skinned men ordered the rest of the gang to proceed. Those who hesitated were lashed with a cane. Around half an hour later, they heard the yells of the old man as the animal devoured him. He had sated its appetite and allowed the rest of them to make their escape.

Aashif sat upright in his bed, screaming—and was met by two pillows flung at him from the opposite side of the dormitory. 'One of these days, that nightmare of yours is going to kill you.'

* * *

Hisham spotted Aashif approaching. 'Another bad night?'

The young man nodded sheepishly. Hisham had known for a long time that Aashif's sleep was regularly haunted by nightmares. He took him by the arm. 'Come, let's walk around the gardens and check that everything is in order.'

They inspected a row of pink and purple hibiscus and watched bees buzz from one flower to another.

'They're certainly getting their fill,' Hisham commented.

The pair was silent until Aashif spoke. 'The others are getting fed up because I constantly wake them up.'

'They'll all have nightmares of their own,' Hisham replied kindly.

'But they don't bother everyone by waking them up.'

'Perhaps, but that doesn't mean their dreams are less frightening than yours. I take it that the images were the same?'

'Yes.'

'What brought them on this time?'

'The Raja—he kept asking me the same questions, over and over again, and I had no idea what to say.'

'You could do no more than tell him what you know, and from what I hear, you did precisely that.'

'I don't think he believed me.'

'He did. I spoke to Anwar earlier this morning, and he told me that the Raja is convinced by your story. He's left Anwar in charge of finding out who did that terrible thing to the young girl, so I'm afraid you'll have to go through it all again with him.'

'I'd never spoken to the Raja before, sir. I couldn't get my words out with him, and I'm sure I'll be the same in front of Anwar.'

'If you'd like, I could speak to Anwar and arrange to be present when he talks to you?'

Aashif knew Hisham to be a tender-hearted man. 'I'd like that,' he said. 'I was embarrassed that Princess Toh was there, Fatima too. I thought her presence might have helped me, but I was ashamed of myself when my words wouldn't come out. The Raja kept on insisting that the girl's baju must have been around somewhere.'

'Well, Anwar tells me that if they can find her baju, it might help to identify who she was, which might lead to her killer.'

'Am I the only witness?'

'Not entirely. Have you forgotten the *semangat*, the spirit? Remember, how I told you that a person's soul may persist after death? According to the peasants in these parts, the souls live in the great trees in the jungle. Many of them will have witnessed everything. Remember that a violent death, where blood is spilled, leads to the creation of the *badi*, the bad spirit. The ghosts of the murdered are believed to be powerful and malicious. It would not surprise me if Anwar comes across the tree surrounded by elephant plants and finds it covered in nails to prevent its ghost from descending to the ground—another local superstition.'

Hisham turned to Aashif. 'Now, have you eaten anything this morning?'

Aashif's blank expression answered Hisham's question. 'Go and see Suraya—she'll make you some breakfast.'

'What about my work?'

'Take a bit of time off, and come and join me after lunch.'

* * *

'Shouldn't you be working?' Suraya asked when Aashif walked in.

'Hisham has allowed me some time off,' Aashif said.

'I didn't see you for breakfast,' she replied. She was worried about Aashif, having overheard some of the slaves talking about his spine-chilling cries. She had known for years about the nightmares that tormented him but had never raised the topic.

'Auntie, Uncle Hisham was telling me about the tree ghosts and jungle spirits. Do they really exist?'

'Why do you ask?'

'Can they ever be brought to life?'

'Well, many people believe they are alive.'

A look of misery came over Aashif's face and Suraya tried to comfort him. 'Let me get you some breakfast, and we can talk.'

She returned, carrying a banana leaf containing a portion of rice covered in a spicy sauce. They sat together at the head of the table.

'Why do the jungle spirits suddenly interest you?' Suraya asked.

'I'm the only person who knows first-hand what happened to that girl, and I was wondering if the spirits could tell us who killed her.'

Suraya shifted in her seat to make herself comfortable. 'Many of the trees in the forest have souls, and there are a great number of free spirits known as hantu or jinn. I have not seen any, but I know people who claim they have.'

She paused and wondered how far she should go, anxious about further disturbing this troubled young man.

'The hantu or jinn can even change their appearance or size, making themselves bigger or smaller. And have you ever heard of the *naiads*?'

Aashif shook his head and waited for Suraya to continue.

'Many years ago, someone I knew told me that the naiads were once brought here from a faraway land. They are female spirits who preside over bodies of water—wells, springs, rivers, and so on.'

At the mention of rivers, Aashif's attention was piqued.

'It could be that such spirits are found in the Perak river, near where you discovered the girl.'

The fog that had formed in Aashif's head evaporated when Fatima burst into the kitchen. 'Morning, Auntie,' she said.

The instant she saw Aashif, her features displayed a new warmth. 'Hello Aashif,' she said, joining them.

'Hello,' Aashif stuttered, his eyes fixed on his food.

Fatima sensed Aashif's mood and winked at Suraya. 'The Raja was impressed by you yesterday, Aashif,' she said sincerely. 'He said that he doubted he could meet someone who was more honest.'

Aashif turned to her sharply, and his heart leapt at the sight of her sparkling eyes.

Fatima took his arm. 'I'm sorry you have to go through it all again by talking to Anwar, but he won't be nearly as persistent.'

Suraya noticed Fatima's hand resting on Aashif's arm and sensed that their relationship was growing more personal. 'Aashif is hoping that if the jungle spirits make themselves known, they might point to the person who killed that poor girl.'

'Maybe the Bomoh could help,' Aashif suggested.

Fatima interjected, 'Princess Toh doesn't like him at all. He's told her lots of things about the spirits, but I doubt he would talk to anyone else.'

Suraya concurred, 'The Bomoh is there for the sole benefit of the royal family; he won't help anyone else.'

'Princess Toh says that according to the Bomoh, the trees are a jungle of illusions,' Fatima offered.

'Don't forget, there's also the *hantu dogok*, the ghosts that take the form of odd-shaped clouds and that are not a part of the jungle,' Suraya reminded them both.

'It was only a thought,' Aashif said, rubbing his face vigorously.

Chapter 17

Fatima lay in her bed and tried to fall sleep, but she found it hard to ignore the sounds that came from Toh's bed every time the princess or her husband moved.

She looked up at the netting over her bed and recalled her visit to the kitchen the previous week. She had been telling the truth when she had told Aashif that the Raja thought he was honest, but he had otherwise been far from impressed. 'He's so stupid that I doubt he has the intelligence to make up a story like that,' he had said. The chilling tone with which the Raja had spoken these words had rankled Fatima. She had never known him to be so hurtful.

She could understand the seriousness of the Raja's voice when he had begun to interrogate Aashif, but his questioning had gone on and on. She had been tempted to interrupt and bring Aashif's ordeal to a halt, but the Raja had been in such a frosty mood that she didn't dare.

She recalled how the Raja had snapped at Aashif; the scene had been threatening her peace of mind ever since. She rubbed the skin of her withered arm as she tried to fathom why he had been so savage. He was supposed to be caring towards his slaves, yet he treated Aashif so cruelly.

The young slave girl's death had stirred up a lot of emotions inside her brain. She was also a slave—would the Raja have treated her as severely if she'd been in Aashif's position? And anyway, why did she have to be a slave? Why did *anyone* have to be a slave? And why was she asking herself all these questions only now?

Why couldn't Toh brush her hair as they chatted? She was the same age as Toh had been when she had first gotten married. What chance was there of her ever marrying? Would Toh and the Raja ever allow it?

She was snatched from her reverie by the noises coming from Toh's bed and tried to block her ears, fearing more sounds would follow. Instead, she focused on Aashif's gentle ways and how he excited her.

She would have loved to discuss her feelings, but there was no one to whom she could turn. There was Toh, of course, but Fatima had not been able to mention it to her, so far. There was Suraya too, but the same alarm rang in her head when she thought about how she might broach the subject. Perhaps she could talk to one of the female slaves, but whom? After all, she had spent her whole life shielded from them. Why had Toh discouraged her from making friends? She loved Toh more than anyone else, but she would like to have other friends, too.

* * *

Dato Hamidi lay in bed, irritated by Toh's repetitive wheezing. He pictured Suzanariahin arching her body in expectation, and he smiled contentedly. Why had he not married that wild and beautiful woman? After all, she gave him more pleasure than Toh ever did. Granted, he would not be the Dato, but surely, he would have been far happier. On the other side of the room, the allure of Fatima's nubile body teased him. He was unaccustomed to sleeping in a room occupied by another beautiful female and could not stop thinking about the way she looked at him and held his gaze: how she made no effort to avoid him, and how she strolled around, the outline of her shapely bottom so visible beneath her baju. The impure desire he often felt for her wormed its way into his mind once more, and he lay there scheming.

When he heard Toh breathing steadily, he snuck out from the bed. Excitement surged through him as he dropped his feet to the floor. He took care not to disturb his wife. Aware of every squeak in the floorboards, he crept across the room to Fatima's small bed. He skulked up to her while pulling down the front of his night pants and stroking his erect penis. He bent low and stooped under the drapes surrounding Fatima's bed, before ogling at the shape of her body. He gazed at her small hand that lay restfully on top of the bed, before carefully tugging at the bedding beneath. Satisfied that she was asleep, he took hold of her wrist and placed her limp fingers on his erection.

Fatima's eyes shot open, and she blinked furiously, trying to clear her befuddlement.

'Shh,' Dato Hamidi said firmly. 'Be quiet.'

Fatima sprung up, shouting, 'What's happening? What are you doing? Get away from me.'

Dato Hamidi pulled his pants up as the drapes fell away. 'Get away from her,' Toh shouted, having been woken by the disturbance.

'What's happening? Where am I?' Dato Hamidi said, feigning disorientation. He covered his groin with his hands as Toh glared at him and feebly repeated that he did not understand what was happening. He turned to Fatima, making sure Toh could not see his face, and stared at her menacingly. 'Was I sleepwalking?' he asked, trembling.

A feverish fury charged through Toh as her husband continued to pretend to be confused. 'Get away from her,' she snarled.

Toh grabbed her husband by the arm and pulled him away. Shaken by fear, Fatima fell into Toh's arms and held her mistress tight as the princess stroked her neck. 'My sleepwalking,' Dato Hamidi said, 'it's happened again.'

His hangdog look warned Toh that a shouting match was building, but she didn't care—Fatima's comfort was her priority.

Dato Hamidi defended himself. 'It must have been all those teasing signs she's been giving me. They caused me to come to her bed when I was sleeping.'

Still holding Fatima, Toh turned to him, her eyes filled with hate. 'Look what you've done,' she growled. 'She's petrified.'

Toh turned back to Fatima, but as she did, Dato Hamidi stuck his tongue out at her, behind her back. Fatima noticed his action out of the corner of her eye and tightened her grip on Toh, who released Fatima and stepped back. 'What happened?'

'He stuck his tongue out at you.'

'You lying brat,' Dato Hamidi snarled, having quickly composed his face.

Toh swung round and stared at her husband angrily. Dato Hamidi tried to smile, but her glower rooted him to the spot. She gnashed her teeth at him. 'Tell me, when you were sleepwalking in the past, did you ever appear naked before one of your sisters or your mother and get them to place their hand on you?'

'How dare you. She's a stupid slave, and her taunting made me do it.' A smirk formed on his face when he sensed a moment of doubt in Toh's eyes.

'You disgust me.' Her eyes were almost popping out of their sockets as she sprayed his face with spittle. 'Well? Did you ever frighten your sisters like that? Or did your mother touch you, you filthy man?'

Dato Hamidi's face contorted with rage. 'Don't you dare say such things to me,' he said bitterly. 'She's just an ignorant slave. And why has she been sleeping in our bedroom, anyway?'

Toh stared at him. 'Let us see what my brother has to say when he hears of all this.'

'I don't care what he thinks,' Dato Hamidi screamed. 'I'll ask him why she's been sleeping in your bedroom ever since you married your first husband.'

'My previous husbands didn't ever abuse her.'

'How do you know?' he screeched. His rage renewed, he continued. 'She's a nasty, cunning liar.'

'I've known Fatima since I was a child and trust her with my life—and so does my brother,' Toh thundered.

'I wouldn't be surprised if this devious girl contributed to the death of your first two husbands. Well, she's not going to contribute to mine,' he replied.

The corners of Toh's mouth turned upwards in contempt. 'You vile man. There's no excuse for your filthy behaviour.'

'She's a liar,' he shrieked.

'I'm not going to let you embarrass me any more.'

'Liar,' he howled again, his voice echoing through the palace.

The room fell silent as Dato Hamidi grabbed at his own throat, before bringing his hands to his ears and desperately massaging the side of his head. He saw Toh's lips moving but couldn't hear a word. Fright was written all over his face as he pleaded with Toh for help while struggling to keep his balance.

* * *

'The Bomoh's words,' Fatima whispered. '"Scream no more."'

Toh gazed at her husband, who was now curled up in bed. 'How long will the spell last?' she wondered out loud and shuddered.

'He was lying, Toh. I've never seen a man's private parts before,' Fatima said, reeling from the shock of what had just happened.

Toh held Fatima's hand and looked into her face, aware of the girl's innocence. 'I know.'

Chapter 18

A week had passed since the Raja had ordered Anwar to search for the slave girl's murderer. He led a party of three along the path that bordered the paddy fields. He had brought Shafie, who was one of the guards who had been with him when they discovered the dead slave girl, as well as Osmin and Haron.

Anwar tried to blink away his tiredness as they rode. The memory of the dead girl's face kept haunting him and brought to his mind the image of his baby sister— she had been killed in a fire by a crazed neighbour, four years ago, and offered to some unknown god as a sacrifice. Anwar, who had been away fighting at the time, had made a promise to himself that he would avenge her death.

He allowed his mind to wander and remembered the sight of his sister looking at him with her big, black eyes. She would tease him mercilessly over his constant concern for her safety, whenever he was home—telling him that their neighbour, himself a father to seven children, would protect her. Alas, those seven children died in the same fire. His eyes burned with anger at the memory as he entered the jungle.

Despite his belief that Aashif's anguish over the girl's death was genuine, Anwar tried to keep an open mind over the possibility that the slave had been involved in the murder, remembering his misplaced trust in his former neighbour.

Inside the jungle, the blur of shadows between the close columns of trees kept him and his men alert. For the most part, the journey was free of trouble, but Anwar became increasingly vexed at having to listen to Osmin and Haron's conversations. Hearing Osmin talking about the slaves and their limited value increasingly riled him. Anwar had brought Haron with him to assess his capabilities in jungle terrain, but he had quickly realized that the trainee guard had a lot to learn.

When they reached the river, they dismounted. As Anwar surveyed the area, he overheard Osmin saying, 'Speak to the master.'

Anwar turned his head. 'What is it, Osmin?'

Osmin nodded at Haron, who spoke, 'I presume we're looking for someone, sir?'

'You presume nothing,' Anwar answered, getting angry. 'Now, get to the top of that slope and look for signs that anyone has been there recently—specifically, a discarded baju.'

The three warriors watched Haron as he scampered up the slope. 'I doubt he'll find anything,' Osmin said.

Anwar turned to him. 'From now on, you are responsible for that fool's welfare. Make sure he's safe and ensure that his inspection of the area is thorough.'

As he watched Osmin chase Haron up the slope, Anwar snarled at Shafie. 'I want that baju found. Come with me.' The pair reached the shack and stood outside it. 'Imagine throwing a baju as far from here as you can. Search the jungle thoroughly and see if you can find a garment anywhere. I'll do the same on this side.'

* * *

Hisham and Aashif were silent as they approached the jungle, the vast expanse of trees gently undulating across the landscape and stretching beyond the horizon.

Hisham noticed Aashif's gloom and decided to say nothing for the time being. The pair planned to pick as many durians as they could carry. Though many claimed the fruit smelled like hell, it tasted like heaven. Shaped like a pineapple but far larger and heavier, its thick skin was covered in spikes, which made it difficult to handle. The bulk of each fruit meant that the two men could only carry one basket each.

The moment they entered the forest, they were hit by an explosion of noise. Hisham glanced surreptitiously at his protégé and was met by a lost look. There was a pause until Aashif broke the silence. 'I was awoken early this morning by a terrible row coming from the palace.'

'Yes,' Hisham said, 'I heard it too.'

Aashif grimaced, before speaking again, 'I'm worried for Fatima.'

Hisham looked at his young friend and sensed the strength of his feelings for the girl. 'You are fond of her, are you not?'

'I still feel so embarrassed by my conduct in front of the Raja.'

'As I've said before, I'm sure you handled the situation well.'

'I wish Fatima hadn't been there. I couldn't stop stuttering.'

Hisham listened to Aashif recall his interrogation and guessed that he was avoiding replying to his question, concerning his feelings for Fatima.

'Goodness me,' Hisham said, breaking off slightly from their trail, 'is that not a beautiful sight?' Hidden behind a thicket of shrubbery was a bed of pink ghost flowers.

The two men bent forward to inspect the flowers, but Aashif was distracted. 'Dato Hamidi must be a horrible man, screaming the way he did. I hope he didn't upset Fatima.' When Hisham didn't respond he continued, 'Princess Toh's first two husbands didn't ever behave like that.'

The quiet was broken by a sudden high-pitched shriek, as if a troop of gibbons was in great distress. The two stood and stared at one another, stunned, before peering into the jungle to search for a clue as to what might have happened.

'Come,' Hisham said, a hint of urgency in his voice. 'Let's pick some durians and get back to the palace.'

They walked deeper into the jungle. 'What were you saying when we stopped to inspect the flowers?' Hisham asked.

'I was worried for Fatima and about the Raja's questions.'

'No, I mean when we were inspecting the flowers.'

'About Princess Toh's first two husbands, you mean?'

Before Hisham could say anything more, another bloodcurdling scream filled the forest, followed by silence. Hisham and Aashif remained still until the jungle came back to life. It was as if the forest had taken stock before resuming its normal routine.

They pressed further into the jungle, and Hisham reflected on Aashif's comment relating to Princess Toh's two husbands—when it happened again. This time, the noise was so threatening that Hisham winced and the hairs on his arms and the back of his neck stood on end.

* * *

Aashif and Hisham placed their baskets on the ground and gazed at the trees trying to spot anything untoward, but the scene was completely calm.

In the peace of the moment, Aashif couldn't stop thinking about what Mecca might be like were Fatima to accompany him. His love for her had swelled, and he dearly wanted to talk to Hisham about her. The memory of her taking his arm before he went to talk to the Raja occupied his mind. His feelings for her had grown but he feared telling her because of the concern he had that his words would come out in a rush. The only person he could confide in was standing next to him, but he had no idea how to broach the topic and what tone to adopt. He lived in the constant hope that he would one day defeat his stammer and express himself untroubled.

'You still haven't answered my question,' Hisham said playfully.

Aashif turned to him, puzzled.

'I asked if you're fond of Fatima.'

Aashif swallowed hard, daring himself to open up to Hisham. 'Yes,' he managed in a whisper. An image of Fatima's smile formed in his head, and his heart lurched at the tenderness in her eyes. 'I'm frightened for her, sir.'

While he waited for Hisham to respond, he recalled the times he had overheard his fellow slaves talking of their feelings for some girl or the other and realized that he did not know how to express his love for anyone other than his father.

'After what we all heard early this morning, you are right to be worried for her, but Princess Toh is a strong-willed young woman and will not let any harm come to Fatima,' Hisham said.

Though he was reassured by Hisham's words, Aashif remained unconvinced that Fatima was safe. 'I should visit her and check that she is all right,' he said.

Aashif could tell from the concern on Hisham's face that the disturbance in the jungle was playing on his mind. He was unable to give Aashif his full attention, which left the young slave feeling hopelessly lost. He mocked himself for ever dreaming of becoming a warrior when he couldn't even find the courage to check that Fatima was safe. He found solace in the knowledge that she seemed to be in control of her own mind, a quality in her that he admired greatly.

Hisham scooped up his basket of fruit. 'Let's get these to Suraya,' he said.

Aashif realized that his opportunity to discuss his feelings about Fatima had been lost and picked up his basket. When they reached their housing block, Hisham stopped outside the kitchen. 'I need to have a quiet word with Suraya. Can you take the fruit around the back and then join us?'

Inside, a few stragglers were lingering over their breakfast, but as soon as they spotted Hisham, they quickly finished and left.

'Can we have a quiet word?' he asked Suraya and they sat at the end of the table. A frown formed on Hisham's brow as he told Suraya about the noises that had emanated from the jungle.

Suraya froze and they sat still for a minute before Hisham continued.

'I've said nothing to Aashif, but I had the distinct sense of danger growing ever nearer—it was like a ghost was hurtling towards us.'

Suraya stroked her amulet, and Hisham stared at her and listened as she tried to control her ragged breathing.

'The Bomoh?'

'There are many spirits in the jungle,' she said gravely, before stretching across the table to pick up one of the tin mugs and fill it with water. Her heart was racing when she met Hisham's gaze, and she contemplated what to say to him.

Hisham glanced back over his shoulder and saw Aashif approaching them. 'We'll talk about this later,' he said before inviting Aashif to join them.

'Have you two had anything to eat?' Suraya asked, springing to her feet and returning with a tray of fish and rice. Under one arm, she held two banana leaves.

'Has Fatima been here for her breakfast?' Aashif asked.

'No, she hasn't,' Suraya replied. 'I take it that you both heard the fracas early this morning?'

Aashif grimaced. 'Yes, we did,' Hisham said quietly. 'Aashif is worried about Fatima's safety and would like to check on her.'

'In that case,' said Suraya. 'You can help me take breakfast to Princess Toh, the Dato and Fatima.'

Chapter 19

'I still can't hear anything,' Dato Hamidi said hysterically. He glowered at Fatima. 'This is all her fault,' he claimed, pointing at the girl.

Distraught, Fatima ran from the bedroom and sprinted along the corridor, past the stairs and into a storeroom, before slumping on to the floor and bursting into tears. Meanwhile, Suraya and Aashif were making their way across the courtyard towards the palace. A guard acknowledged Suraya and inspected Aashif coldly.

'He's carrying Fatima's breakfast,' Suraya said.

The guard nodded them through, and they climbed the stairs together. On the landing, a second guard wore a dour expression and Suraya raised an eyebrow at him. 'Breakfast for Princess Toh and Dato Hamidi. This one,' she said, nodding towards the tray in Aashif's hands, 'is Fatima's.'

'Fatima is hiding in the storeroom,' the guard whispered.

'Aashif, please take her breakfast to her. The storeroom is the last door at the end of the corridor.'

Aashif walked briskly along the passageway with the tray balanced in one hand and opened the door with the other. 'Fatima,' he called out softly.

Fatima was sitting on the floor, her arms wrapped round her knees. She gazed at Aashif in disbelief, drawing several gasps and trying to get to her feet.

'Stay there,' Aashif said, 'I've brought you some breakfast.'

'Aashif, you shouldn't be here.'

'Suraya brought me.'

Fatima's face changed. 'But you're not allowed,' she said in a hushed voice.

'I had to check that you were safe,' he said, passing the food to her. 'I was worried.'

'If the Dato finds you here, there'll be trouble,' she said, her voice shaking.

Aashif gazed into her face and gave her a shy smile. He desperately wanted to take her in his arms, but he didn't have the nerve. 'Please eat,' he said quietly.

Fatima's body eased. 'I don't think the Dato can hear us,' she said. 'He keeps shouting that he can't hear anything.'

Aashif tried to find the words that would comfort her and show his concern for her safety, but he could only ask her what happened. Fatima looked at him through moist eyes for a moment. Shame tugged at her, and she knew that she could not tell him what had happened with the Dato earlier that morning. Instead, she averted her gaze and concentrated on the tray of food.

As Aashif watched her chase the rice around the bowl, he was stunned by the sound of her sniffing and the sight of tears spilling down her cheeks. He was once more overcome by the urge to take her in his arms, but he remained unsure if that was the correct action. Instead, he lowered himself beside her. The sound of the raw, cruel voice of the Dato came to him, and he was struck with fear as he watched Fatima shudder. Twisting around to face her, he tried to offer some reassurance, 'Everything will be all right, I promise.'

In her distress, Fatima could only pick at her breakfast. Incensed, Aashif found himself wondering whether she would have suffered such abuse if she had been a free woman. He managed to hide his flash of anger from her when the memory of his own father being clubbed to the ground came to him. The image of the naked slave girl's body by the Perak river then filled his head and he glanced at Fatima, relieved that she was safe.

At the sound of footsteps approaching, Fatima stared at Aashif. They sprang to their feet silently. When the door opened, Suraya entered. 'There you are,' she said.

The couple steadied themselves and Suraya gave the young woman a smile of encouragement. 'How is she?' she asked Aashif.

'She's had a very unpleasant time,' Aashif said, gazing at Fatima.

'After the way that man has been screaming, he's likely to have damaged his throat,' Suraya said, her voice full of contempt.

'It was the Bomoh, Auntie. Toh says it's his fault.'

Suraya flinched and glared at Fatima. Before the girl could say any more, Suraya snapped at Aashif, 'Leave us and get back to your duties.'

Aashif stared at her, speechless. Without saying anything more, Suraya held the door open for him.

Closing it behind him, she spoke to Fatima, 'Now tell me, what do you mean, "the Bomoh's fault"?'

Fatima was bemused. 'Toh went to see the Bomoh twice,' she said, 'and he said that something would happen to Dato Hamidi if he didn't stop shouting.'

Suraya furrowed her brow. 'Tell me exactly what you know.'

Bothered by the change in Suraya's mood, Fatima told her everything she knew. When she came to describe the Dato's behaviour towards her, Fatima dropped her gaze. 'Dato Hamidi came to my bed and made me touch him.'

'What?' Suraya gasped and stared at the girl, open-mouthed.

'I woke up to find him leaning against my bed. He had no pants on and placed my hand on him. I shouted, and Toh rushed to my bedside.'

Suraya remained speechless as she tried to imagine what Fatima had gone through. She could see that the awfulness of Fatima's experience was causing her to be overwhelmed with embarrassment. As she scrutinized Fatima, a suspicion that the Bomoh was not only at the bottom of Toh and Fatima's distress, but that he was also the cause of the disturbance in the jungle that morning, took root.

She decided that Fatima needed to be taken away from the palace until she had collected herself. She took the breakfast utensils from Fatima and led her along the passageway. 'If Princess Toh asks after Fatima, can you tell her she is with me?' she asked the guard.

As the two women wandered across the courtyard, Suraya could tell from Fatima's face that she was suffering great unhappiness. She knew that a few choice words from her could instantly ease the girl's distress, but she was determined to keep her secret.

* * *

To his delight, Aashif found himself spending more time with Hisham and the pair were together in the kitchen when Suraya and Fatima entered the room. At Suraya's suggestion, Aashif and Fatima went for a stroll.

'You take care of her,' Suraya told him, 'and take your time.'

Whenever he could, Aashif displayed his gallantry by walking near the undergrowth, where danger might lurk. At one point, when Aashif stepped into the shrubbery to allow Fatima space, she rewarded him with a radiance that caused his heart to miss a beat.

'I've never met a Bomoh. What's Princess Toh's Bomoh like?' Aashif asked. A breeze had picked up, disturbing the foliage. Aashif had no real interest in the Bomoh—it was all he could think of to begin a conversation.

'I've never met him,' she said. 'Thank you for checking on me. You took a terrible risk. Had the Dato seen us together, I dread to think what might have happened.'

The heat rushed into Aashif's face. 'I'm sorry.'

'Please don't be—I'm glad you came.'

Her loyalty to Toh did not allow Fatima to criticize the Bomoh, but she said that the Dato was a horrible man. She took a deep breath. 'For all our lives, the princess and I have slept in the same room. When we are alone, we sleep together, but when the Dato is there, I have my own bed.' She stopped and stared at him earnestly, and he watched as she nervously tugged at the sleeve of her blouse. 'But last night, he came to my bed.'

Aashif was clearly horrified, and Fatima contemplated whether to continue her story, but decided that she must press forward. She turned her head away and continued, 'He had no pants on. I screamed and Toh came running, and that's when all the shouting started.' Her heart was pounding against her chest as she peered into Aashif's face, imagining how he might be judging her.

Aashif spoke quietly, as if he was in shock. 'I'm glad I visited you.'

They resumed their walk and after a lengthy pause Fatima spoke, 'I'm so worried for Princess Toh—he's such a vile man.' The memory of Toh's smile came to her and she felt overwhelmed by her absence from the princess's side.

'Is the Dato worried that the Raja will punish him for treating his sister badly?'

'He's never been this bad before.'

'I don't know if there's anything I can do because I'm not allowed into the palace. But if you ever need my help, get a message to me.'

From the day that Fatima had first met Aashif, she had sensed that he was sincere. They carried on walking until Aashif noticed that they had reached the trail that climbed up to the graveyard of the slain warriors.

* * *

Suraya and Hisham sat at the kitchen table that was nearest to the stove. Their sense of time had abandoned them, and Suraya made no effort to hide her uneasiness at the situation.

'I didn't get a chance to speak to Princess Toh on her own, but I did speak to Fatima,' she said quietly. 'She knows everything that's going on in the princess's life. Apparently, she recently visited the Bomoh twice. On her first visit, she ran from his cave before he had finished a chant—it may be that what's happening now is a warning that she should follow his instructions.'

Hisham was sceptical. 'My thoughts have been clouded since the incident in the jungle, and I've come to the conclusion that the animals were probably disturbed by a whirlwind.'

He took Suraya's hand and patted it affectionately. 'Let the past rest,' he said gently.

Chapter 20

As Dato Hamidi lay in bed and stared at the empty space where Fatima would have been, his face wore a rictus grin at one moment and a mask of self-pity, the next. The storeroom had been emptied and a bed had been set up for Fatima. He resolved to take her in that room if he had to.

Despite being preoccupied with plotting revenge on Fatima, he also feared he would never see Suzanariahin again. And even if he did see her, he would not be able to hear her sweet voice.

It had been a week since he lost his hearing. Watching the movement of people's lips and trying to fathom what they were saying made him so tired. For the most part, he couldn't work out if he was being mocked or if he was living in a world of sulky silence. Because of the loss of his hearing, all he could think about was what he might do to Fatima.

He had last set eyes on Suzanariahin when they had made love in the forest. Though he recalled her free spirit and pined to meet her again, there had been frequent occasions over the past week when his memory was occupied by the touch of Fatima's hand on his manhood. He was determined to experience that pleasure again —and much more besides.

In rational moments, he sought an explanation for the loss of his hearing. Desperate for a recovery, he rejected spicy food and hot drinks, believing that he should eliminate anything that might cause his throat discomfort.

He tried to engineer a situation where he could be alone with Fatima and had repeatedly apologized for his ungentlemanly conduct, insisting that it had occurred during one of his terrifying bouts of sleepwalking. As he lay in bed like a scheming crocodile, plotting when to strike at Fatima again, he smiled to

101

himself at his cunning. He climbed from his bed, aware that the tension inside him was at last beginning to abate.

He wandered across to the window and gazed outside, but the absence of bird sounds and jungle noises caused him to fall into melancholy. All the more reason to exact his revenge, he thought to himself.

He turned with a start to find Toh next to him and gave her a well-practised bow. Two days before, he had realized that there was little point in speaking to her because he never knew if she was answering him. Toh nodded, in what seemed to be a gesture of sympathy—it seemed to him that his plotting was beginning to pay off. He suppressed a smile at the thought.

Toh asked him if he was hungry, and he angrily pointed to his ears and made an exaggerated shrug. The princess, in turn, brought her fingers to her mouth, suggesting that he might like something to eat.

Toh's unexpected appearance convinced Dato Hamidi of the necessity of the action he had been contemplating, which would tell him whether anybody was within the immediate vicinity: He would install mirrors to forewarn him of the presence of others.

* * *

Toh sat on the edge of Fatima's bed and waited for her to wake. For the past week, she had been up for half the night checking on her friend. In their seventeen years together, Toh had never appreciated the soothing sound of Fatima's gentle snores as much as she did now.

She sat upright when Fatima stirred and was soon gazing into her eyes. 'Can't sleep?' Fatima whispered.

Toh was quiet for a moment before speaking softly, 'I think I should pay the Bomoh another visit and see what he suggests.'

Fatima stared at Toh, trying hard to conceal her doubt.

'As usual, he's fast asleep in there,' Toh said angrily. 'If I have to listen to his feeble apology once more, I'll scream.' The thought of his apologetic gesture made her shudder. She had no idea what her future held, but she was certain that listening to her husband's constant lies would not be part of it.

To lighten her mood, Toh asked about Aashif. Fatima's eyes flickered as she told Toh that she hadn't seen him since he brought her breakfast. 'I'd be frightened if he came again—in case the Dato saw him.'

'You're fond of him, aren't you?' Toh had been bursting to ask her this all week, but there hadn't been an appropriate time to mention it.

Fatima sat upright. 'Yes.'

Toh's face lit up and she embraced her friend. Recalling her recent bouts of crushing loneliness, she was keen to help Fatima. 'I would not object to him visiting you, but I fear the Dato's reaction.'

'According to Suraya, Aashif is a gentleman—and loyal to the household,' Fatima said.

'You don't need to assure me of that. I saw for myself what he was like when he went before the Raja. There was something so honest and gentle about him. And when he was stuttering over his words, I remembered his lovely singing voice. He obviously finds singing easier than speaking.'

They were silent for a moment until Toh spoke again, 'I'll ask the guard to stop Anwar this morning and get him to accompany me to the Bomoh. If I do go, you should stay with Suraya until I get back, I don't trust the Dato enough to leave you alone.'

Toh had been paying careful attention to her husband and was disgusted by how he stared at Fatima. She tried to make her presence known, to warn him to behave, but she felt lost in a morass of lies as she sought desperately to present an image of being in control.

* * *

Anwar set out at first light with Shafie, Osmin, and Haron, eager to continue the search for the identity of the murdered slave. Spurred on by the memory of his sister's death some years before, he remained determined to avenge the girl's brutal murder.

It was a grey morning and heavy mist blanketed the canopy of treetops. Anwar accepted that the jungle would be wet at this hour of the day. The men were still half-asleep, and Osmin's eyes drooped behind sulky eyelids as they approached the jungle. Anwar was unaware that, at that moment, one of the palace guards was searching for him on the orders of Princess Toh.

For the past two weeks, the troop had been traipsing across the countryside, asking in various villages whether any slave had gone missing. He knew that the three men were bored of sitting on horseback for mile upon mile, but he cared little for their discomfort—he was driven solely by the task of discovering where the girl had come from, hoping that it would lead them to her killer.

Anwar could hear the sound of running water in the distance. By his estimation, they were several miles north of where the slave's body had been found. He already knew that most of the villages were close to the river, where there was ample drinking water and fish. They broke free of the trees and looked down into a small dip where bamboo longhouses with attap roofs, in the traditional Malay style—and where families lived and slept together— stood perched on stilts.

Anwar gazed at the activity below. Chickens were scurrying around with children chasing after them, while women were hanging clothes on washing lines or draping them over bushes. The sight helped to relax his troubled mind as he guided his horse down the slope. Earlier, he had commanded Shafie to follow him into any village, but when he heard Osmin inform Haron of this he realized that the guard was good at eavesdropping. However, the truth was that Osmin was so inattentive at times that Anwar did not want him guarding his back.

As they entered the village, Anwar turned back towards Osmin and Haron, who were lagging behind. "What the hell do you think you're doing?" he snapped at them angrily.

Rays of sunlight forced themselves through the clouds as the men entered the *kampung*, only for storm clouds to loom overhead, seconds later. At the sight of the four riders, life in the village came to an abrupt halt and frightened faces stared at them.

The four dismounted and Anwar greeted an old woman warmly. Then all eyes turned at the booming voice of a huge man who came out of a large hut that dominated the centre of the kampung. 'What do you want?' he thundered, pumped up like a bull and mopping perspiration from his brow. A gathering of men appeared from nowhere and surrounded Anwar and his men, blocking their chance of retreat.

* * *

Anwar ordered his men to show their badges and draw their weapons, and the villagers fell away, with the chief arranging for the Raja's men to be fed and for their horses to be tended.

The chief claimed to have no knowledge of an absent slave but assured Anwar that he would send men to check the smaller villages that were dotted throughout the vicinity.

* * *

Anwar stood frustrated as he held the reins of his and Princess Toh's horses and watched as she approached the entrance to the Bomoh's cave. There would not be an opportunity to return to the kampung in the days ahead, though he reasoned that it would give the chief the time to check on all his slaves.

Toh entered the cave and a bat brushed against her neck. Letting out a screech, she shuddered violently and walked further inside. The rancid smell of bat droppings filled her nostrils, while the stifling warmth caused her to gag.

The Bomoh invited Toh to sit, and she struggled to mask her fear. As much as she could, she avoided looking into his gargoyle-like face and kept thinking about how soon she could escape.

In a thin voice that she hoped would draw sympathy, she told the Bomoh what had happened since her last visit. She was trying to explain that she did not know how to cope, when the Bomoh grew angry. In a fierce tone that grew louder, he said:

> 'As the raven waits on an abandoned road
> So, this Fatima must move to another abode.'

Chapter 21

Fatima and Aashif walked along the perimeter of the palace grounds, away from prying eyes. Aashif had been bubbling up with excitement all day, while Fatima stayed away from the palace at Princess Toh's behest.

'Suraya says you joined us when you were a little boy,' Fatima said.

'I was maybe five years old. I came with four others from my village.'

'Are they the other dark-skinned men?'

'Yes. There are five of us in the palace; all the other slaves are local.'

'What are your fellow villagers like?'

'All four are now married to local slave women. I don't have a lot to do with them. They're older than me and live with their wives in their village.'

'Tell me about your village.'

Aashif hesitated, before drawing in a deep breath and considering what to tell her. 'I don't remember much,' he lied, unwilling to discuss the memories that still haunted him. 'It was like the villages here—there were lots of little shacks with attap roofs. There was a river nearby and we used to go there to swim.'

Fatima was full of curiosity. 'I don't remember you as a little boy. I imagine you were frightened when you arrived here?'

The memory made him shudder. 'I was terrified,' he admitted. 'We had been travelling for weeks, and I'd cried the whole way. When we arrived, my innards were churning. We were standing around with some local slaves when Uncle Hisham smiled at me, ruffled my hair, gave me a hug, and lifted me into the air. From that moment, I began to feel safe.'

'You're fond of him, aren't you?'

'He's been in my life from the day I got here, and he's taught me everything I know.' He recalled the patience Hisham had shown in teaching him how to become a believer.

'He's always been warm to me,' Fatima said. 'While Princess Toh is like a big sister to me, Uncle Hisham and Auntie Suraya are the parents I never had. You could say I was spoilt in having two fathers—the Raja and Uncle Hisham.'

Fatima spotted a cluster of trumpet-like white flowers among the foliage, calmly swaying in the breeze. 'Aren't they beautiful?'

'Be careful,' Aashif said hastily. 'They are poisonous—Hisham told me.'

They walked on without speaking until Aashif asked, 'Is everything all right at the palace?'

Fatima sighed. 'The princess got back from seeing the Bomoh yesterday, and he upsets her so much. She's always quiet when she returns, but this time she's even quieter. She usually tells me what happened, but she's said nothing. I'm worried for her. She's under such stress because of that disgusting husband of hers. It can't be good for her to keep everything that happened with the Bomoh to herself.'

Aashif felt his heart thumping in his chest as he asked Fatima if she was safe in the palace.

'A bed has been set up for me in the storeroom.'

'The storeroom?'

'The room where you found me.'

'Are you safe in there?'

'It's cramped and there's no window, but at least I can lock the door. But I hate the way Dato Hamidi stares at me—he makes my skin crawl.'

Aashif was stony-faced. 'Are you able to keep out of his way?'

'Most of the time, yes.'

Aashif was enraged. Would a free woman be treated in this way? And if Dato Hamidi assaulted a free woman, would he be allowed to escape unpunished? For once, he found himself agreeing with the slaves who complained of the princess's lack of action.

'I cannot conceive what it must have been like to have found that poor girl dead.'

Aashif stared at her. His words crashed into each other in a desperate rush to escape his mouth. 'Please . . . can I tell you?'

'Do—I'd like to hear.'

At the sight of her kind expression, his words suddenly fell into place. He told her that he could not sleep at night, explaining that he had prayed to

God for a second chance to save the girl. 'You'll think I'm stupid, but at night, I try to imagine a smile on her beautiful face. If only I'd stayed,' he broke off, determined not to disclose that he cried into his pillow every night, at his failure to save her.

Fatima breathed in deeply. 'Will you tell me about your dreams of the time when you became a slave?'

They stopped for a moment before they resumed their walk. 'They're rather macabre,' Aashif said. 'More nightmares than dreams. Are you sure you want to hear them?'

Fatima grew sombre and nodded, before they waiting for him to continue.

'A group of pale-skinned men led a charge into our village. They captured the men and boys, as well as a few women and girls. They tied chains around our necks and led us away. My mother was pinned against a tree with a spear through her throat. The worst of it was that I couldn't call out to her. I tried and tried, but the words wouldn't come.'

Fatima gasped in shock.

'We were marched across strange lands for weeks on end. A number of men died on the way, along with all the women and girls, but we weren't allowed to bury them. Eventually, we reached a town by the sea, and that's when I was separated from my father.'

'What happened?' Fatima asked, her voice cracking.

'We were sold to different slave traders.'

'Oh, Aashif,' Fatima said, struggling to overcome her emotion.

Aashif grimaced. 'I'd love to find my father and to visit my mother's grave one day, but I fear I will never get the chance. What I hate about my life is my lack of freedom. A lot of people would say that we slaves are lucky to have a roof over our heads and food in our bellies, but I want to do my Haj, to roam the countryside, and to be regarded as a free man while looking after myself and my family.' He smiled. 'And yes, I want to have a family, with a free wife and free children. Those are the dreams that drive me on.' He wanted to tell her how much he hated being subservient to anyone, but he knew those dreams would only be achievable once he became a free man.

* * *

Anwar had set out at dawn with his men. Osmin and Haron had been talking incessantly all morning, and Anwar wondered if they were doing it deliberately to provoke him. He listened as Haron mocked a slave who had failed to carry a pile of logs to the kitchen, leaving a trail of wood in his wake.

'Why didn't you help him?' Osmin asked.

'It's not my role—I'm to train as a warrior. I watched over him and made sure he gathered them all up.'

Anwar was enraged and turned around to Shafie who rolled his eyes in disgust.

'Haron, get up here,' Anwar barked.

Haron rode jauntily up to Anwar. 'How old are you?' he asked.

'Seventeen.'

'Seventeen, what?' Anwar snapped, fixing him with a brutal stare.

'Seventeen, sir.'

'And how long have you been in training?' Anwar asked coldly.

'Ever since I joined, sir.'

Anwar stared into Haron's face, his eyes blazing. 'If I ever hear you mocking any of the slaves, I will personally take my sword to you. Do you understand?'

There was a tense silence. 'Yes, sir,' Haron said.

'Now, ride ahead and lead us back to the kampung.'

Haron's face went pale. 'But I don't know the way, sir.'

'But you came with us last time?'

'Yes, sir, but I can't remember how we got there.'

Anwar sighed. 'Then you had better remember quickly, or you may well find yourself on your own. Leave the same distance between you and me as there is between me and Shafie.'

Haron swallowed hard, seeing that the gap was at least fifteen yards.

'And make sure your horse stamps its hooves to warn snakes of our presence.'

The remainder of the journey took far longer because Haron kept slowing to check that the others were still behind him.

'Follow the noise of the river,' Anwar shouted. It had gone noon when Haron came to an abrupt halt and raised his arm. Anwar rode up to him and they gazed down at the kampung. When Shafie and Osmin had caught up, Anwar ordered Haron to lead them down.

Once they were down, Anwar commanded Haron to remain at the entrance to the kampung while he, Shafie, and Osmin rode into the village. As soon as they entered, they were surrounded by a pack of excited children.

The entire village came to a standstill and Anwar bowed to anyone who caught his eye.

As they approached the chief's home, the man wandered out on to the terrace, mopping his brow. Seconds later a young girl, no older than the slave girl who had been murdered, followed him out, pulling her baju into place.

Anwar dismounted from his horse and climbed the steps, nodding at the chief and addressing him without preamble. 'What news do you have for me?' He glanced at the young girl, who lowered her gaze.

The chief snorted, 'One of my slaves has gone missing.'

Anwar waited for him to continue.

The chief cleared his throat. 'A young girl—she disappeared a month or so ago, but I knew nothing about it.'

'As young as this girl, perhaps?' Anwar asked, glancing towards the girl who was by the chief's side.

'Yes.'

'Was she to be punished?'

'Punished? What for?'

Chapter 22

Toh quietly let herself into the storeroom. She eased herself on to Fatima's bed and listened to her friend's gentle wheezes, reminded of the comfort she had always gained when Fatima slept next to her. She looked at her friend's face, imagining what she was dreaming of and dreading what she was going to have to say to her. Ever since she had stepped out of the Bomoh's cave, she had been struggling over how to explain her decision to ask Fatima to move out of the palace.

She steeled herself when Fatima turned towards her, stretched out and opened her eyes.

'Good morning,' Toh whispered.

Dazed, Fatima stared at Toh. 'What time is it?' she asked softly while rubbing her eyes.

'Early. Everybody else is fast asleep.'

'Can't you sleep?'

'I've been awake all night.'

Fatima moved across the bed, leaving space for Toh to lie down beside her.

'You must be tired.'

Toh smothered a yawn and stretched her arms out. 'When he gets up, I'll be able to sleep.'

'Would you like me to go to the kitchen and fetch you something to eat?'

'It's too early for that.'

Fatima persisted, 'Are you sure?'

'I'm sure.'

'It's so quiet here—maybe we should have moved here long ago.'

'It might have been fun for a while,' Toh replied, 'but with such little room we would have found it difficult.'

'We'd certainly never have been able to have those pillow fights.'

'As I remember, you always won.'

Toh looked weary. 'I want to talk to you about something.' She took a deep breath. 'I've been observing the way the Dato has been watching you.'

Fatima stiffened.

'I keep going over that horrible scene in my head. I'm so worried that he might do something unpleasant again, particularly if I'm ever called away.'

'I'll make sure I'm never alone with him.'

Toh smiled and let out a sigh. 'I feel like such a failure. Three marriages by the age of twenty-four—I can imagine what everybody must think. And with all his screaming and shouting, they must wonder why I put up with it.'

'Everyone feels sorry for you, Toh.'

'But I don't want their sympathy. All I seek is their respect.'

'Nobody has ever spoken badly of you,' she said, failing to mention that many people called the princess a witch.

'I know they call me a witch.'

Fatima stared at Toh, aghast.

'If I can prove to them that the trust my brother has placed in me is deserved, they'll stop their name-calling.' Her bottom lip quivered. 'I visited the Bomoh hoping that his advice would counter my own thoughts, but he merely confirmed what I must do.'

She took hold of Fatima's hand and looked into her eyes. 'Fatima, I want you to move out of the palace.'

* * *

The news knocked Suraya sideways. She couldn't stop picturing an eleven-year-old Princess Toh taking a four-year-old Fatima by the hand and leading her around the gardens of the old palace. Fatima's plight drew tears to Suraya's eyes—she was shocked that Toh could neglect her responsibilities so easily, and the older woman battled to keep her anger in check.

'Her first two husbands sometimes looked at me crudely, but they never did anything to me. Auntie, please don't tell anyone that he made me touch him.'

'Of course, I won't.'

Suraya's heart bled at the sight of Fatima's misery. It was the first time in Fatima's seventeen years that Suraya had thought of her as a slave. A voice inside her head kept reminding her that this young woman was like a daughter to her—an unworldly young woman, so unsophisticated in her wants and needs.

'Where's Toh now?'

'Sleeping, I think.'

Suraya smacked her hands against the table and let out a sigh.

'It's so unfair, Auntie,' Fatima said. 'I might be a slave, but I did nothing wrong.'

All Suraya could do was place an arm across the girl's shoulders and draw her in. 'Where's that vile man now?' she asked.

Fatima hesitated. 'I don't know—I've no idea what he does all day.'

'And you're going to have to live and sleep with the rest of the slaves?'

When Fatima nodded, Suraya's heart sank.

'Has Princess Toh ever been inside the dormitory?' she asked.

'I don't think so.'

Suraya couldn't stop thinking about the barracks being visited at night by male slaves, guards, warriors, and even men from the local villages. At one end of the room were several empty beds, which were screened off to afford privacy to the female slaves who wanted to enjoy intimate time with such visitors. Suraya resolved to arrange for Fatima to sleep as far away from that area as possible, though she realized that there was nothing she could do about the noises. 'Do you know what goes on there during the night?'

Fatima nodded. 'It's so unfair, Auntie.'

'I'll talk to some of the women who sleep there and make sure you're comfortable and not bothered.'

'Thank you, Auntie.' Fatima blew out her cheeks. 'It's only since that poor slave girl died that I've begun to think about my situation. I never had any reason to question being a slave before, but then Aashif told me that he hates being a slave and is desperate to be free.'

'Aashif's a fine young man,' Suraya said. 'Now you'll be able to spend a lot more time together—in the evenings, before you retire, I mean.'

Fatima stared at Suraya. 'It was the Bomoh's doing, auntie. He told Toh that I had to move out of the palace. Toh said that she'd been thinking of asking me to move out, only for the Bomoh to confirm that my move was for the best.'

Suraya was speechless as she contemplated this news. 'It is troubling that the princess feels the need to visit him so often,' she said eventually.

'She only started going because of the problems with her husband. I hate him, Auntie,' Fatima said vehemently.

* * *

At the age of forty-one, Zainuddin was happy. The love of his life had borne him six children, and that morning, before he set out, his wife had told him that she was pregnant with a seventh child. He was so excited by the prospect that he wanted to tell the whole world. As he wended his way through the forest, he was preoccupied by the thought that an extra mouth to feed would mean more fish to catch. He was careful as he made his way through the thickets of shrubbery where snakes might be hidden, while looking skywards every now and then to check on the weather. He was startled by the sight of a single cloud chasing across the empty sky—it was thought to be an augury of discontent. Perhaps storm clouds were building. The world was completely silent. The whistle of insects, the bark of frogs, and the usual calls of hornbills and gibbons—nothing. It was as if the jungle was holding its breath.

Zainuddin stood still. A shiver ran down his spine and the hair on his arms stood on end like tiny needles. He turned sharply, expecting an attack from behind, when everything suddenly returned to normal. He shook his head, clearing his mind before panic could set in, and laughed at his stupidity. He had begun to move forward warily when a strange, sweet smell caused his nostrils to twitch and stopped him in his tracks. 'Hello? Who's there?' he called out, but all he could hear were the familiar sounds of the dense undergrowth.

Aware that he had to return home with enough food for his family, he pressed on but heard a strange whisper from somewhere behind him. He tensed, trying to shake off his nerves and keep on going.

As soon as he saw the river, the whispering sound returned. He shuddered, clutched his fishing gear, and rushed to the water's edge. Looking around him urgently, he peered into the trees. Something made him think he was not alone, and he shouted out, 'Who are you? What do you want?'

He stayed where he was on the riverbank until he was sure that he was alone. What was troubling him most were the thoughts that the sounds were not those of an animal and that he had been followed. He took several deep breaths as he made his way to the shack. He stepped inside and set about organizing his tackle before heading back to the river. But the moment he stepped outside, there was a high-pitched, piercing screech and he stiffened.

He looked around him frantically until he noticed something moving in the branches of a tree. He edged towards it bellowing, 'What do you want?' as a deep panic flooded through him.

Then he saw it. Seated high up on a sturdy branch was a figure with long unkempt hair, dressed in a grubby white baju. Its bloodshot eyes were wild, and it hissed at him threateningly. Zainuddin had never seen a *pontianak* before but knew from his grandfather that they were the vampiric spirits of women who died while pregnant. He was momentarily frozen to the spot as it gave a screeching laugh and dropped to a lower branch. Zainuddin threw his fishing rod at the trunk and ran away as quickly as he could. He tried to follow the path to the river but the pontianak hopped from tree to tree, screaming at Zainuddin as he stumbled, blind with terror. As he smashed through the jungle, his ears filled with the crazed shrieks, he called out to Allah.

Chapter 23

It was late morning by the time Anwar and his men trotted back into the courtyard of the palace. Their hosts had treated them like royalty—the chief had offered them four young women, but Anwar had declined. When his men had sulked, he'd asked them why they'd want to be entertained by women who had been soiled by the grotesque chief, and they had accepted his decision.

Anwar saw Hisham at the far end of the courtyard and wandered up to him.

'How was your trip?' Hisham asked.

'We've found out who the girl was. She was an orphan and enslaved to a chief in a kampung by the North Perak river.'

Hisham's brow furrowed. 'Is that not some distance from the place where she was found?'

'It is.'

'So, someone must have taken her there?'

'Correct,' Anwar answered. 'What's been happening here?'

'Young Fatima has been forced to move out of the palace.'

Anwar stared at Hisham in disbelief. 'Why?'

Hisham merely shrugged. 'We'll find out soon enough.'

'By the way, thanks for drawing Haron's behaviour to my attention. Osmin is clearly a bad influence on him. I'll soon have the pair of them sorted out.'

Anwar left Hisham and strolled into the palace. The guard at the foot of the stairs stood to attention as Anwar passed him and ascended the steps.

'Sir, the princess is in the throne room waiting for you,' the guard at the top of the stairs said.

'Your Highness,' Anwar said, as he entered the room.

'Any news?'

'We have identified the girl and know who her chief was. Her parents were long dead, although that is irrelevant since she was sold into slavery many years ago.'

Anwar was explaining that the kampung where she lived was some distance from where she was found, when Dato Hamidi entered. Toh glanced at her husband, and Anwar could sense her contempt for him. When the Dato walked out without acknowledging either of them, Toh forced an awkward smile and Anwar resumed his account of events.

'I have yet to identify the girl's killer, but I suspect that more than one person was involved. Someone must have taken her from her kampung to the shack where she was found.'

'Why do you say that?'

'She was taken several miles through the jungle, so whoever accompanied her had many opportunities to attack her. The fact that he didn't, suggests to me that she was left in the shack for someone else.'

'So, you'll continue your investigation?'

'Yes.'

As Anwar left Toh, his thoughts drifted back to memories of his baby sister. Though he sensed that the chief had been involved in the girl's murder, he had decided to keep his suspicion to himself until he discovered the facts.

* * *

Aashif was desperate to talk to Fatima. He had been working at the vegetable plot that day and was keen to talk to Hisham, in the hope that he might cast some light on what had happened to Fatima—it must have been something serious for her to move to the slaves' quarters. He also needed to face an issue that had been troubling him for several months—he wanted to leave the palace, but should he tell Hisham? Every time he saw his benefactor, he was confronted by the notion of the disappointment he would cause him. And yet, to leave without saying goodbye would be too painful to contemplate.

When the time came for him to join Hisham, he approached slowly, trying to get his thoughts straight. The old man was working near the rice fields, preparing the land for planting. As Aashif approached, he decided that it was not yet the right time to tell Hisham of his plans.

'Sir,' he began. 'Have you seen Fatima?'

'No, lad, I haven't.'

'You've heard that she's moved out of the palace?'

'Suraya told me,' the old man replied.

'Did she say why?'

'No—there were too many people around for us to talk, but I plan to ask her when we finish for the day.'

'I'm so worried for her,' Aashif mumbled, shy at revealing his feelings.

Hisham looked at Aashif as the young man bent down and picked up a fork, ready to take out his frustration on the soil.

'Everyone's saying that she was ordered to leave,' he said as he drove the tool into the ground. 'It's so unfair, Uncle.'

'What is?'

'The death of that girl, Fatima being harassed by the Dato, everything. That girl died because she wouldn't lie with her chief, and it could happen to any of the female slaves.'

'There's news of the girl,' Hisham said. 'According to Anwar, they know which kampung she came from. It was some distance from where you discovered her.'

'Does he know who killed her?'

'He didn't say, so I suspect not. But I imagine that it won't take too long to discover her killer—and it is believed that more than one person was involved.'

Aashif stared at Hisham, speechless.

'The distance between her kampung and the place where you found her means someone must have accompanied her. And whoever took her there could have attacked her long before reaching the shack, so it is thought that the murderer must have had an accomplice.'

* * *

Six men from Zainuddin's village, heavily armed and with the village chief among them, entered the palace grounds unannounced. The same grounds were constantly guarded by well-positioned warriors, often unseen to visitors and ready to attack unknown intruders.

'Surely you know better than to enter these grounds armed?' Anwar asked the chief. 'Are you trying to get yourselves killed? Leave your weapons with my men—they'll be returned to you when you depart.' All six surrendered their arms while Anwar continued, 'I'll join you as soon as I can. I have several tasks I must address first.' The chief and his entourage followed his directions and headed towards the kitchen.

The chief was a stumpy man whose warriors towered over him. Anwar had met him before, but he had encountered many chiefs in the past couple of weeks and could not recall their meeting. His village was nearest to the scene of the murder and the chief had indicated that he wanted to talk undisturbed. All Anwar knew was that there had been a dangerous disturbance in the jungle that required his assistance.

Two hours later, Anwar walked into the kitchen. The chief and his men were seated away from the main table, which gave them privacy.

'Apologies for my delay, chief, but I'm glad to see you have been well looked after,' he said, noticing the empty banana leaves on the table. 'Now, how can I help you?'

'Yesterday, one of my villagers returned half-crazed from a fishing trip. He is a fine fellow, or at least he was—happy with life, with six children and a seventh on the way. But he has transformed into a jabbering mess and his hair has turned white with fright. He had gone to fish close to where that female slave was found dead.'

Anwar sat upright, conscious that this might be vital evidence.

'The man, whose name is Zainuddin, said that as he neared the river, he experienced all manner of unusual happenings. One moment the jungle was noisy and the next it was completely silent. Then he heard clapping leaves and whispering voices.'

The chief shifted uncomfortably and when he spoke again, his voice was strained, 'He went into a shack to store some of his equipment, and when he stepped back outside, he was confronted by mocking, screeching, and laughter.'

The chief paused for breath.

'It was a pontianak, a female vampire.' He paused again. 'As you know, such fiends die when they're with child. So, it seems clear to me that whoever killed that poor slave must have impregnated her before she died. Either that, or perhaps she was already pregnant.'

The chief studied Anwar's face and was relieved that, far from scoffing at his tale, he looked solemn.

'The pontianak chased Zainuddin through the jungle until he got back to the kampung. Many of the other villagers, while they didn't witness the pontianak, heard its screeches. And now everyone's scared to leave their homes.'

The chief was flushed and short of breath. 'Sir, we need your help.'

* * *

'Being as fond of Fatima as you are, it is not surprising that you are worried about her,' Hisham said to Aashif. 'She's a worthy young lady, and I'm sure your presence gives her comfort.'

It had rained earlier in the day, and the sunlight was making the wet leaves sparkle and highlighting the splendour of the canopy of treetops beyond the rice fields. Aashif grasped the opportunity to talk about Fatima. 'The other day, I became so engrossed by her that I foolishly took us on to the path that leads towards the graveyard of the slain warriors.'

'Aashif,' Hisham snapped, 'that was irresponsible. Have I not told you about the history of those graves? Surely you understand how dangerous it can be to go near that area?'

'It was my mistake,' Aashif replied, feeling chastened.

'Was the recent incident in the jungle when we heard all that commotion not enough warning for you? Nobody in their right mind would go where you two went.'

Aashif was tempted to suggest to Hisham that they had been hallucinating when the incident occurred, but he managed to stop himself.

'Whatever's up there, it is worth remembering that the dead always make space for the living to join them.'

Chapter 24

After nearly fifty-five years of working in the kitchen, Suraya had no intention of putting her position in jeopardy. 'Your behaviour is unacceptable. Do I make myself clear?'

Hanizah's expression indicated that Suraya was getting through to her.

'You remember several months ago, when two women were fighting here in the kitchen?' she continued in the same menacing tone. 'To this day, I do not know who reported that incident, but I ended up taking an earful for not reporting it myself. If you think I'm going to ignore your misbehaviour, you are very much mistaken. It has been made clear to me that should I fail in my duties again; I will be dismissed. And I'm certainly not putting my job on the line for the likes of you.'

Suraya waited for her words to sink in and glared into Hanizah's face.

'I'm sorry,' Hanizah said, abashed.

Suraya was silent for a moment. 'Fatima will be moving out of the palace this evening, and I'm placing her in your care. You will set up a bed for her as far away from the entertainment area as possible. I'll bring her myself to check on the suitability of the arrangements you put in place, so don't let me down.'

'What's happened?'

'It's none of your business, but I'm placing her in your charge. Make sure she's not harassed by any of the others. If you fail me, you'll be sent to one of the outer kampungs, where life is brutal. And where, incidentally, you will not have me to protect you.'

For the rest of the day, Suraya was worried about Fatima's welfare. That Princess Toh could place her in such a situation was inexcusable. She was busy cleaning the cooking pots when Fatima strolled in with a small bundle of possessions.

'Hello, dear,' Suraya said, trying to hide her outrage. When she noticed the small bundle Fatima was carrying, her heart sank. 'Are these all the possessions you're bringing?'

'Yes,' Fatima said softly.

'Come,' Suraya said and put down the pot she was working on. She placed an arm across her surrogate daughter's shoulder and guided her outside. It was already dark, and the moon was out. 'Surely you have more belongings than that?' Suraya asked.

'Princess Toh wanted me to leave most of my possessions in the palace because I'll be there during the day.'

Suraya glanced at Fatima and thought to herself that it was fortunate that Dato Hamidi wasn't present—if he had been, there would have been no telling what she might have done to him.

The two wandered into the dormitory and Hanizah, standing by the door, greeted them. When the other slaves realized that Suraya and Fatima had entered, they fell silent.

'*Selamat patang*,' Hanizah said, wishing Fatima a good evening. Before Fatima could respond, Hanizah asked her how she was. Fatima stood fidgeting with the sleeve on her disfigured arm but returned Hanizah's smile, the light of the moon through the open door softening her expression.

* * *

Fatima had never visited the dormitory at night, and this was the first time she had seen it full. She felt everyone looking at her and nodded, bowed, or smiled at those with whom she made eye contact. She was taken aback when someone deep within the room shouted out to welcome her and found herself forcing back nervous tears.

'Let me show you to your bed,' Hanizah said, leading Fatima and Suraya to the last bed in one of the two rows. It was next to the rear wall, which meant she had only one neighbour.

Stunned by the cramped conditions, Fatima took in the reaction of each woman as she passed them, making a determined effort to be friendly. The deeper into the room she ventured, the more she realized that she was going to miss the palace.

Only when they arrived at her empty bed did the full impact of the cramped conditions strike Fatima. Her gaze settled on the screen at the far end of the dormitory and shuddered at the memory of Dato Hamidi standing naked before her. She was used to a peaceful, private setting and had no idea how she would be able to sleep in these conditions.

Suraya held her in a brief embrace before patting her cheek. 'I will leave you now, but Hanizah will take care of you if there's anything you need.' She turned to Hanizah, 'Where's your bed?'

'By the door.'

Fatima's heart pounded as she watched Suraya leave, and she was immediately attacked by loneliness. Racing through her mind was the thought of Aashif—she knew he would never abandon her in the way that Toh had. She wished she could tell him about her hopes and ambitions for her future.

Hanizah shook her from her reverie. 'I'll leave you to settle in.'

Before Fatima had thanked her, Hanizah had turned and was walking away. When the chatter between the women resumed, Fatima was stunned by the noise. Trying to occupy herself, she placed her bundle of possessions on her bed, withdrew her nightgown and stretched it out on the bed. She inspected her small dresser and stuffed the remainder of her effects inside. Glancing around, she realized that she would have to hang her clothes over the bed rest, as the woman nearby had done.

She sat and studied her hands, trying to appear casual, when her immediate neighbour spoke, 'Are you all right?'

Startled, Fatima looked up. 'I think so, thank you. It's all a bit strange but I'll soon settle in.'

'Different from what you're used to?'

'I suppose so, but it's nice to be among so many women,' she lied, keen to make a good impression.

The conversation came to an end and Fatima stretched out on the bed and stared up at the roof. The heavy air was overbearing, and she forced back tears of fear, anger, sadness, and pain. Why did Toh have to be so mean to her, after they'd spent their whole lives together? If she'd been a free woman, she would never have been cast out like this—and that man would never have dared to make her touch him. She shuddered at the memory and squeezed her eyes shut. She thought of Aashif again and understood why he so wanted to become a free man.

* * *

After a night of broken sleep, interrupted by the moans emanating from behind the screen at the far end of the dormitory, Fatima was exhausted. She watched the women rush off to the wash area in small groups. She was shy about being naked in front of others and wondered whether to go straight to the palace, but she did not know if Toh would welcome her at such an early hour. In the end, the girl in the neighbouring bed invited her to bathe, and the pair went together.

As soon as she walked into the washroom, she was met by more noise. Women were calling out to one another, mostly shouting for those standing under the water to hurry up. She felt panicked at the prospect of having to strip in front of all these women. She took deep breaths to steady herself, and when her turn came, she removed her baju, rushed to the far wall, and allowed the water to pour over her. While she rubbed soap on her body, she reflected on the privacy she was accustomed to. How could Toh put her through all this?

She dried herself and then discovered that her neighbour had left, so she returned to the dormitory alone. She sat on her bed and watched as the room slowly emptied. The other women were in a hurry to have breakfast before setting off for work. Fatima listened in to their conversations and learned that punishments were meted out to any woman who was late.

Eventually, she forced herself to get dressed and set off for the kitchen. The moment Suraya saw her, she rushed up to her.

'How are you?'

Fatima managed to reply that she was fine.

'How was it?'

'A bit noisy, but I'll get used to it.'

'Come, we'll eat breakfast together.'

'I'd better get over to the palace. Are the breakfasts ready?'

Suraya looked at her, surprised. 'Didn't Toh explain the new arrangement? One of the guards came earlier and collected them.'

Fatima shook her head. 'She hasn't said anything to me about what's going to happen.'

Fatima looked around at the other slaves.

'Oh, don't worry about them.'

But Fatima fretted that if Suraya treated her favourably, she would find it harder to fit in with the others. Despite the cook's efforts to coax Fatima into eating more food, she refused. Suraya eventually relented and allowed her to leave for the palace.

Fatima's mood brightened when she approached the palace steps and was greeted warmly by the guard. 'Good morning, Fatima; good to see you.'

She encountered the same benevolence at the top of the stairs, and she couldn't help but relax. When she stepped out into the hall, she turned at the sound of footsteps to find Toh racing toward her. Fatima's frown disintegrated and the two women fell into an embrace.

Toh took Fatima by the arm and led her to the throne room. 'How was it in the dormitory? Did they all look after you well? Did you sleep?'

'It was fun. They're nice women,' she said, trying to smile.

'I missed you.'

Fatima wanted to say that Toh should tell her vile husband to sleep in the dormitory with the male slaves, but she managed to bite her tongue. 'Did you sleep?' she asked instead.

'Hardly at all.'

'I slept a bit, but everyone was friendly, and the conditions are not as bad as I'd feared.' She paused and glanced around the room. 'Where is he?'

'He's taken two guards and left for the day.'

'Then I'll change my baju.'

'I moved your things into the storeroom to give you privacy.'

Startled by the permanence of the situation, Fatima replied coolly, 'I'll change now, in case he returns unexpectedly.'

'I'll come with you.'

Fatima felt a sudden need to be alone, but she was compelled to obey Toh's wishes. As the two women walked along the passage to the storeroom, Fatima repressed a desire to flee from the place. The memory of the Dato standing naked in front of her was tormenting her yet again.

In the storeroom, Fatima discovered that all her clothes had been laid out across the bed. She chose a green garment that she knew was Toh's favourite. 'I'll wear this,' she said, but Toh spoke at the same time. 'You don't normally wear that during the day.' Their words collided, and Fatima resolved to wear her garment of choice, despite Toh's objection.

Chapter 25

Next to the vegetable allotments, in the dense jungle, there was a small kampung that housed the married slaves. Along with some of the male slaves, Aashif was working to help clear some of the jungle—in order to expand the allotments. Suraya had advised that if more potatoes were grown it would reduce the pressure on the rice crop.

Among the group were Aashif's neighbours Faiz and Reza, and he couldn't help but notice their lax approach to the task at hand. Every time they swung their axe, they seemed to stop for a breather.

With the sun beating down on them, Aashif was glad to take a rest. He stood for several moments, allowing the cooling breeze to hit his face, but sweat covered his brow and he felt sombre. Unlike his neighbours, he was relieved to be able to throw himself into the assignment and rid himself of some of the rage he felt at the treatment of Fatima. As excited as he was at the prospect of seeing more of her, he was appalled that she had to witness the likes of Faiz and Reza visiting her dormitory at night. Worse still, was the thought that he was soon to add to her woes by telling her that he planned to leave. But how should he tell her?

A flash of anger raced through him when he caught Faiz staring at him and he took out his frustration on the tree he was working on, attacking it with such ferocity that he felled it with several brutal blows. He turned to find Faiz still staring at him with his mouth open.

Aashif's eyes were constantly alert for a glimpse of Fatima. He drifted off into his own world. Ever since his love for her had knocked him sideways, he had known that he would miss her when he left. Time and again, he contemplated abandoning his dreams, but he realized that doing so would betray the duty he had to his father's memory—he had to find out what happened to him. But the worst thing now was the plight Fatima found herself in. He had come to despise Faiz, Reza, and the other male slaves who visited the female dormitory. He resolved to ask Suraya to keep a watch on Fatima while he was away; he knew that he would return to claim her, no matter the risk. As much as he knew that he could not give up on his dream of finding his father, he could not abandon Fatima.

His life had become a quest for answers, but he was sure of one thing: He would fulfil his quest to be a free man.

* * *

At lunchtime, the men were glad to put down their tools. Faiz and Reza tried to get Aashif's attention, but he wasn't interested in talking to them. The conversation soon turned to the subject of women. One of the senior slaves said, 'I promised Mawar my best efforts tonight, but by the time we're finished for the day I'm going to be too exhausted.'

'Don't worry yourself—I'll take your place and see that she receives the pleasure she deserves,' another one called out to laughter.

'But she needs a man,' someone else replied.

The slaves fell silent as food took priority, and it was only after the men had finished eating, that Aashif's ears pricked up at the mention of Fatima's name.

'Now there's a real beauty.'

'What I wouldn't do to lie with her,' someone called out, only to be told that he would have to get in the queue.

When Aashif heard this, his face folded in fury. He identified the man who'd spoken last and looked right into him with his eyes wide open, hoping the speaker would notice that he was glowering at him.

'She's a snooty little brat if you ask me. The women say she struts around with little interest in any of them. She doesn't even have to work with them; she's living a cushy life at the palace.'

'Does anybody know why she's been banished from the palace at night?'

'Maybe Princess Toh's scared she'll entertain the Dato and she'll lose another husband.'

'Or maybe she's a spy sent to check on the women,' someone else suggested.

Aashif was holding himself steady when, to his surprise, someone in the crowd spoke up in Fatima's defence. 'You're being unfair. How would any of you like to have been brought up in the palace, with its luxuries and comforts, only to be suddenly cast out at night? It must be an enormous strain on her.'

'She still gets to enjoy her days; she doesn't have to work in the fields, and from what the women say, she spends her time in the palace with the princess.'

'She needs our support,' said another. 'After all, we've known her all our lives —let's show her our respect.'

'She's never even spoken to me,' someone else said dryly.

The conversation ended, and the men returned to work.

As hard as Aashif tried to shake off the thoughts of leaving Fatima behind, he could not stop worrying about her welfare. He considered warning the other men off her, but he knew that such an action would not benefit her at a time when he would not be around to protect her.

* * *

When Aashif joined Hisham, the extent of his exertions was clear from his sweat-soaked clothes. He was impressed with the progress Hisham had made with planting hedges around the rice fields. He had picked up a fork and was turning over the soil when Anwar approached the pair of them.

'A word with you, Hisham, if I may.'

Aashif began to move away.

'Stay, lad,' Anwar said.

Anwar's face darkened. 'I had a visit from a local chief and his men.'

Aashif was grave, 'You've found the murderer?'

'No, but we will soon enough.' He turned to Hisham, 'Have either of you gentlemen encountered any unusual disturbances in the jungle recently?'

'How do you mean?' Hisham asked.

'Anything out of the ordinary,' Anwar said. 'Any sudden stillness, unusual screeches, or calls, that sort of thing.'

Hisham's brow furrowed. 'Why do you ask?'

Anwar continued, 'There was such an event recently and I'm trying to discover its cause.'

He turned to Aashif. 'I know you had an almighty shock discovering that poor young girl. Can you remember hearing any strange noises in the jungle near the shack where you placed the girl?'

Aashif recalled what had happened when he and Hisham were picking durians but decided to leave it to Hisham to mention that. 'No,' he said, 'only the sound of her crying.'

'And no sudden quietness?'

'No,' Aashif replied.

Anwar bristled as he recalled the chief's expression as he had relayed his villager's experience.

'What's this all about, Anwar?'

'The chief from a village close to the shack came to see me. It transpired that one of his villagers went to the same area to fish. The man claims that after he'd taken his equipment to the shack and stepped outside, he was confronted by a pontianak that sat on the branch of a tree and laughed at him.' Anwar made no attempt to conceal his incredulity.

Anwar noticed Aashif turning to look at Hisham. 'What is it?'

'We were gathering durians near the path leading to the graves of the warriors,' Hisham said, 'when we heard a blood-curdling screech followed by an intense hush. I'm sure you've heard the claims that the guards of Hades are up there. Apart from those myths, there was no other explanation.'

Anwar stared at Hisham. 'Why haven't you mentioned this before?'

'You've got too many important concerns to spend time investigating such unaccountable events.'

Anwar nodded. 'The chief believes that the tree spirits were angered by what happened in that shack.' He sighed before continuing, 'The villager is half mad and the rest of the villagers are terrified. They only have a handful of warriors to protect them, so I'm going to send a contingent of men to search the area and make sure they are safe.'

* * *

When Aashif left the kitchen, a mix of emotions were stirring inside him. His mind was made up; he was leaving, come what may. Still, he was melancholy as he took in the land that had been his home for the last fourteen years.

To his delight, he noticed Fatima in the distance. She was dressed in an emerald-green baju, and he was reminded of his mother—green had been her favourite colour. He was even able to recall her gentle face, and tears welled up in his eyes.

He put his hands to his mouth and gave a hopeful shout and was ecstatic when Fatima waved back at him. The closer he got to her, the more he realized that she was everything he hoped for in a woman. She greeted him with a small bow, and they stood gazing into each other's eyes, transfixed.

'How are you?' he asked. Before she could reply, he spoke again. 'You look nice.'

Fatima laughed happily. Aashif struggled with what to say next and was trembling with nerves. 'Fatima, would you walk with me? There's something I want to tell you.'

Chapter 26

As they strolled across the field, Aashif racked his brain for something to say. Nothing came to him, and he had to content himself with the pleasure of Fatima's company.

When they were out of the view of others, they came to an abrupt halt. They were under the shade as Aashif stared into her eyes. 'I'm leaving, Fatima. Tomorrow. See that mound of clay behind that tree? Under there, in a small box, are my things—a change of clothing and stuff.'

Fatima looked at him silently as he took a deep breath. 'It's hard for me to know where to begin, but I will come back.' He paused, daring himself to say more, 'I'll come back for you.'

For a moment, he wished that he had kept his mouth shut. But then, without warning, Fatima leant against him and kissed him on the cheek. He stared at her in disbelief, and for several moments neither of them spoke.

'I shall miss you.'

When she didn't respond, he looked at her closely, worried that he had said too much. 'I only have you and Hisham to tell—I can't leave without telling him. He's been like a father to me,' he babbled nervously.

Fatima said nothing.

'I can't be a slave any more. I have to be a free man. I've always dreamt that I will one day have a wife and children, but I could never let them live in a slave's kampung. First, I will do my Haj, and then, I will go in search of my father.'

Frightened of Fatima's silence, he couldn't stop talking, 'My journey will be long. I plan to go over the mountains to the coast and then across to

131

Africa. Once there, I will make my way to the Holy Land. I know it will be dangerous, but Hisham has prepared me well. For years he has taught me how to protect myself—I have no fears about what I may meet.'

As he stopped speaking, it dawned on him that while he was struggling to string sentences together, he was not stammering. He stared at Fatima as the image of his mother's face came back to him. He had always failed to recall her face, but now he could visualize her, seated by the water's edge with the other mothers while he and his friends laughed and screamed as they tumbled about in the water. Every minute detail had been inspired by the sight of Fatima in her green dress. Though he must have seen other women dressed in emerald green, none of them were people he loved. He wanted to throw his arms around her, show her to the world, and tell her how much he loved her.

* * *

Fatima had been wandering around the compound for nearly two hours, fighting back tears of frustration, when Aashif called out to her. She had been with Toh in the throne room when Dato Hamidi strolled in. Toh's reaction had shocked her—the princess had turned her back on her husband and quietly told Fatima to leave immediately. Fatima had wanted to ask where she should go, but she had to suffer his taunting glare as she passed him and hurried from the building.

Outside, she stood perplexed. Faced with the choice of going for a walk or visiting Suraya in the kitchen, she chose the former and took every route around the compound that avoided the other slaves.

Tears of rage had replaced tears of frustration and she filled her thoughts with Aashif. Apart from Suraya, he was the only person she could confide in. When she heard her name being called and saw that it was him, she was overcome with relief. As they neared one another, she was battling to control her rage and she was glad that he did not engage her in conversation until they reached the trees. She needed a period of quiet to gather herself and cast aside the negative thoughts that threatened to crush her. By the time they stopped, she was ready to tell him all about her morning, but then Aashif knocked the wind out of her. *Leaving*. The word kept spinning around in her head. She threw her head back and tried to bring her mind into focus.

The thought of being abandoned by Aashif drew fresh tears to her eyes, but she managed to suppress them. She was taking deep breaths when he told her that he intended to come back for her. Despite herself, she fell against him and kissed his cheek. She didn't care whether she was acting inappropriately—the joy of feeling wanted was overpowering. She loved him but she didn't have the nerve to tell him in case her feelings were not reciprocated.

She had tried to take in what he was saying, but she was having difficulty concentrating. She listened to him talking about his drive to be a free man, but all she could think about was his failure to react to her gesture. She kept asking herself if she had gone too far.

It was when he spoke of having a family that she knew she had to fight for her future. She was not about to surrender to a life without him, and she decided there and then to embrace her hopes and dreams. She gazed at him earnestly, 'Take me with you.'

* * *

Could it be that someone would love her more than he could? Aashif took hold of Fatima's shoulders and they fell into each other's arms, holding one another tightly until Aashif spoke, 'It would be far too dangerous for you.'

'No more dangerous than for you. Besides, I don't want to spend one night more than I have to in that dormitory.'

'Let's walk,' he said.

After only a few steps they stopped, and he listened intently to what she had to say.

'All my life I have valued my existence. And now I've been cast aside because of the actions of another—a so-called "free man". I keep thinking of that poor girl you found and how she must have suffered—most likely because of the actions of another free man.'

'The jungle can be a treacherous place,' he said, before telling her about the rumour of the pontianak and the incident he and Hisham had experienced.

'Do you believe the story about the pontianak?'

'No.'

'Then how do you explain the villager's claim that he was chased by it?'

'We were never able to find the girl's baju. Anwar believes that the person who killed her threw it away, but I suspect it got stuck in a tree branch and was spun in the air by a whirlwind. A similar thing happened when Hisham and I were out picking durians.'

Fatima was quiet for a moment. 'Until that poor girl died, I was blind to everything around me. The only thing that bothered me was the thought that I could not have my hair as long as Toh's.'

'You will miss the princess.'

'I will, but all I want is to be free like her. And if that means taking chances, I'm ready.' She was in full flow and fearlessly unabashed. 'Aashif, I want to come with you.'

He gazed at her speechless as she tutted, 'Aashif, kiss me.'

He bent low and clumsily brought his lips to hers. As their bodies pressed together, he realized that he would protect her to the end.

When they broke free, he spoke. 'They'll come looking for us.'

'I know.'

'Where we're going, it will be cold at night—you'll need a change of clothing.'

'Anything else?'

'Bring some spare pairs of footwear, if you can. The route we will be taking will be rough.' He paused. 'It will be brutal, Fatima, but I will help you in every way I can.'

'I know you will, but I don't wish to be a burden. And by the way, you've stopped stammering.'

Aashif knew that it was her calming influence that allowed him to relax but was embarrassed to say as much. Instead, he became grave, 'A change of plan. We'll leave the day after tomorrow. You need time to gather your things. Give them to me and I'll bury them with mine.'

Fatima nodded solemnly, 'Can I say goodbye to Suraya?'

Aashif explained that he had planned to tell Hisham, but no one else. 'The fewer people that know, the better.'

'Suraya has been like a mother to me, Aashif—to you too,' she said sadly.

He looked at her sheepishly. 'In that case, don't tell her when—simply say that it will be in a few days' time. And try not to let anyone see you carrying your belongings. The less anyone knows, the better our chance of escape.'

Chapter 27

Aashif and Hisham were working on the outskirts of the gardens, busily clearing away the lalang that could swallow up hedgerows with ease if left unattended. It was early morning, and the sun was on its rise.

Aashif had spent the day before thinking about what he would say to Hisham. He had long been dreading this moment, and when it came, Hisham was fierce. 'How dare you?' he bellowed.

Startled, Aashif stumbled backwards as Hisham continued to shout, 'I always knew this day would come, but to invite Fatima to go with you is beyond the pale.'

Aashif had never known his mentor to be in this sort of mood.

'It was my intention to back you all the way, but no longer. Unless you promise to abandon this plan, I will report you and put an end to this madness.'

Aashif gazed at him in astonishment. 'Sir, I did not invite her. She asked to come.'

'And you didn't say no?'

Aashif's tongue quivered, but he eventually managed to stammer a reply. 'I told her it was too dangerous.'

'Too dangerous?' Hisham shouted. 'She's a Perak girl—she'll die out there, you stupid fool.'

Tears spilled down Aashif's face. 'She's adamant, sir. I told her about the dangers.'

'Told her?' he snapped. 'You'll tell her that you're not taking her, that's what you'll do.'

'Sir, I know that she's a Perak girl, but we are in love.'

Hisham stared at Aashif in disbelief. 'What do you know of love?'

'I know that we love through our fears, our flaws, and our mistakes. Those were lessons taught to me by you, sir.'

'Well, what do you think about exposing the woman you claim to love to risks and dangers?'

'Sir, if she remains here, she will be left to the mercy of Dato Hamidi. She's terrified of him, after he appeared naked at her bedside. Princess Toh knows of her constant peril, which is why she ordered Fatima from the palace. She now spends her nights in the female quarters, where many of the women openly entertain men. She is frightened here.'

Hisham continued to stare at Aashif.

'I want to protect Fatima. If I leave without her, I will be leaving her to far greater danger. Some of the things the other men say about what they would like to do to her would disgust you. Like me, she is a slave, and like me, she does not want to be a slave any longer.'

After listening to Aashif speak, Hisham looked at him closely. 'There is a bounty to be had for escaping slaves, Aashif. I have no doubt that if you were caught and banished, you would survive. But what chance would that young girl have?'

'Perhaps more than that young slave I found,' Aashif answered. 'And anyway, I don't believe Princess Toh would permit that. Sir, I know the journey will be tough, but I don't want to leave her to the mercy of the Dato. All I can do is make certain that she comes to no harm.'

'And if something happens to you?'

'But what if something happens to the princess? I can't protect her if she is alone in the palace with that man. And I can't protect her in the women's dormitory unless I sleep next to her every night.'

* * *

It was the middle of the morning, and Hisham, Aashif, and Fatima had gone to the kitchen to see Suraya. All four were seated around a small table, and the place was empty apart from a few stragglers.

'I am most unhappy with your plans,' Hisham began.

'Hisham, let me say a few words,' Suraya said. She looked around to check that they could not be overheard before staring at the two slaves. 'Hisham and

I have no intention of standing in your way, but we shall miss you terribly. You have been like children to us.' As she paused, Aashif glanced across the table at Hisham and was shocked to see that the old man's face was marked with dark, heavy folds.

'I'm only going to ask you once: Please don't go.'

All four were silent and Aashif and Fatima looked at one another.

Fatima addressed Suraya but also drew Hisham in, 'Auntie, Uncle, we're going to miss you both dreadfully. If we thought you could come too, we'd plead with you both to join us, but we have to do this. We each have our own motivations, but they amount to the same thing: We are desperate to be free and to be together.' She turned to Hisham. 'Uncle, I know that the journey we are about to embark upon will be tough, but it will be made easier if we have your blessing.'

'I will not lie to you,' Hisham replied. 'We are displeased by your plan, but we are willing to go along with it for your sakes. You have no idea what you will find out there. Young lady, have you thought how you will cope with the wild animals, many of them hungry? Or with the poisonous plants and hidden snakes? And besides all that, demons and spirits will be waiting for two foolish individuals like you.'

Suraya stretched behind her neck, grabbed her chain, drew the amulet free, and stared at Aashif. 'This was given to me by a dear friend. It is said to reflect the footprints of King Solomon.'

She handed it to Aashif, who weighed it in his hand, and then she removed a small charm from around her wrist. 'Aashif, this amulet is too heavy for Fatima to wear around her neck, so I want you to look after it for her. Stay close to Fatima at all times, and the amulet will protect her.'

She turned to Fatima. 'This small piece of jewellery is a talisman that was given to me by the same person.'

'Is this the person you spoke of before, Auntie?'

'Yes. It also has magic powers that will guard you on your journey. Wear it all the time and it will bring you good luck.'

Struggling with her emotions, Fatima threw her arms around the kitchen maid. 'Thank you, Auntie. I shall guard it with my life.'

Fatima stood up, hurried around to Hisham and embraced him too. 'Uncle, I shall make sure he has a long and happy life—I promise.'

While Fatima's arms were around Hisham, the old man and Aashif looked at each other and they both nodded without uttering a word.

When two workers wandered into the kitchen, Suraya leapt to her feet and hurried to attend to them. Hisahm said, 'You have my blessings, both of you. Aashif, put everything I taught you to good use, and maybe one day you will return.'

* * *

Aashif went with Hisham to fulfil their daily chores while Fatima remained with Suraya. The meeting ended with the news that Aashif and Fatima would set off the following day, though neither slave would reveal which direction they planned to go.

Fatima agreed to stay behind to help Suraya prepare lunch, on the understanding that she would leave immediately if she was called to the palace, though Dato Hamidi's presence seemed to make that unlikely.

'Hisham is going to miss Aashif greatly,' Suraya said. 'The reason why he never married and had children of his own is his dedication to the royal family; he knows that now. He's a clever man, and he's taught Aashif survival skills. If you follow Aashif's advice, you'll be safe. You see, Hisham always knew this day would come.'

'I will, Auntie. I promise.'

Suraya embraced Fatima again. 'You'll need to take some bread with you, so let's get baking.'

'But it won't be ready in time, Auntie.'

'The bread we bake will replace the loaves I'll give you. It will only be enough to sustain you for a few days, but Hisham has taught Aashif how to forage for food, so I have no worries there.'

Suraya went to collect flour from a cupboard and when she returned, she spoke softly, 'Fatima, dear, have you ever been with a man?'

Fatima stared at her.

'At nighttime you will need to be close together, to stay warm as well as safe. Aashif might find himself overcome by desires he had not anticipated.'

Fatima smiled. 'Auntie, I've been sleeping in Toh's room nearly all my life. I may not have seen things, but I've heard noises. I do not know what will happen, but I love Aashif very much.'

Suraya took hold of Fatima's hand and squeezed it gently.

* * *

'Anwar is no fool,' Hisham said to Suraya. They were alone in the kitchen as the day drew to a close. 'He will suspect our involvement in their disappearance, and we must not admit anything. If we do, he will be obliged to report us— and there is no telling how we would be punished.'

'I hope we've done the right thing, Hisham. You can see from their eyes that they find wonder in one another.'

'Fatima is a fine young woman, and it is comforting to know that she will have Aashif at her side. I have little doubt they'll be safe in the jungle; it is their journey beyond that which worries me. I hope we are doing the right thing staying silent.'

'We can't break our promise to them,' Suraya replied. 'And anyway, they are good for each other.'

Part 3

Chapter 28

As dawn broke, Fatima met Aashif next to the tree where their possessions were buried. She was wearing her emerald-green baju, while Aashif was dressed in black. Their outfits would help them to hide among the trees.

Fatima greeted Aashif with a smile, and they kissed briefly. Aashif bent low and picked up one of the two bags he had made for the journey. He brushed loose soil from them, and Fatima asked if she could help.

'I'm nearly finished,' he said. He rummaged through his bag and produced a small tin container, before removing the lid, pouring some of its contents on to his hands, and rubbing it into his exposed flesh. 'Citronella leaves and coconut oil. It will protect us from mosquitos.' He passed the can to her and watched as she worked the mixture into her skin, remaining silent when she exposed her arm, which was withered like the bark of an old tree.

'We can make more of this mix as we go along,' he said, sealing the container and returning it to his bag.

'Can you help me fold these?' He unravelled two blankets wrapped in oilcloth. Together, they doubled them until Aashif was able to tuck them into the bags.

'Will there be enough room for the bread?'

Aashif took the loaves from her and placed them carefully in the bags. He lifted the heavier of the two and slung it across his shoulders before helping Fatima with hers.

'We'll work our way to the rice fields and then double back in case anyone spots us.' He picked up two sturdy sticks that he had trimmed into poles. 'While we walk, we can pound these into the ground to warn snakes of our presence.

Pausing, he gazed at her affectionately. 'Ready?'

She nodded and smiled.

'Let's go.'

The sun was peeping over the treetops when they set off. 'I'll lead if that's all right with you?'

'It is,' she laughed.

They stuck to the outer reaches of the palace grounds, being careful to stay hidden among the trees. They reached the rice fields and then headed for the path that led to higher ground. When they got there, Aashif stopped. 'Do you know the story of the warriors' cemetery?'

'Yes—the Raja often spoke about it,' Fatima answered.

'And of the jinn?'

'Yes,' she said.

'Nobody will suspect that we went that way; and if they did, they would be too scared to follow us.'

Fatima seemed troubled by what Aashif was about to say.

'That's why I think we should go that way. They'll never suspect that we went over the mountains.'

'Will it be safe?' Her expression was tense.

He looked at her earnestly, 'You remember when I was speaking to Suraya about spirits?'

'What of it?'

'I wanted to believe that there were such things, something that could reveal who killed that poor girl, but I don't believe any of the stories I've heard.'

She stared at him sceptically, recalling his account of the villager who had been chased through the jungle.

'So, you're not scared of entering the cemetery?'

'No,' he said firmly.

'In that case, neither am I.'

'Then let's go. I'll lead, but at no time must you allow me out of your sight. Do you understand?'

'Yes.'

A calmness seemed to come over Aashif at the knowledge that they were finally on their way. But as soon as they entered the jungle, its noise engulfed them. Fatima quickly fell into a routine of thumping her pole into the ground every time Aashif did. When they got well into the jungle, she shuddered at the sight of a thick cobweb across some outstretched branches. The largest spider she had ever seen was in the middle of the web, and she only just managed to stop herself from calling out to Aashif.

* * *

Fatima was determined not to reveal to Aashif how weary she was—she was intent on getting through the day. When she noticed the spider, which spread far wider than her hand, she raised her pole, ready to defend herself. When Aashif turned round, she pummelled it into the ground.

'Everything all right?'

'Keep going,' she answered sharply, struggling to keep the panic from her voice. Although he was physically stronger than her, she was resolved to be his match mentally. Come what may, she would not be a burden. As they climbed, she kept a close watch on their progress, following his trail in the knowledge that it was safe. She was already weary from the weight of the bag across her shoulders and was contemplating removing it, when she watched him slip and stumble to the ground.

'Are you hurt?' she called out, rushing to his side.

'I'm fine. I just lost my footing—don't worry,' he said, smiling self-consciously.

She kissed his cheek. 'Can we have some water?'

He brushed himself down, took hold of Fatima by her shoulders, kissed her forehead, and turned her around before burrowing into her bag and digging out a bottle of water.

'There'll be plenty of water ahead, so drink as much as you need.'

Bathing in the warmth of his kiss, she drank happily, and they pressed on, listening to the drone of insects and warbling birds, broken intermittently by the calls of monkeys.

Fatima watched as flocks of birds soared from the treetops.

'I wonder what disturbed them?' she called out to Aashif.

He stopped and glanced back towards her. 'Monkeys, probably. Let me know when you want to eat.'

'I will,' she replied, but she had no intention of stopping.

When they reached a small clearing, the height of the sun in the sky told them that it was mid-morning. 'This is as good a place to stop for a rest as any,' Aashif said.

They unknotted their bags, dropped them to the ground, and removed their bread. 'I'm starving,' Aashif said.

'Me too,' Fatima replied. To her delight, Aashif passed her small slices of chicken.

'Where did you get this?'

'Suraya. She insisted I take it.'

They broke off chunks of bread from their loaves and ate in silence.

'How are you feeling?'

'Good,' she said, fighting back tiredness. 'How long before we reach the cemetery?'

'Sometime tomorrow, I'd guess.' He gazed at her a moment, 'Do you want to rest here for a bit longer?'

'Let's keep moving.' In truth, she wanted to be past the graves of the warriors as soon as possible. She accepted that her bag was too cumbersome to carry in her arms and let Aashif tie it across her shoulders again. Once he had strung his own bag in place, they moved off.

Tiredness was starting to play havoc with Fatima's mind. It had gone midday when she was attacked by stomach cramps, but she tried to ignore it. While she concentrated on Aashif's progress, her mind returned to Toh and the anger the princess would feel once she found out about their escape.

She took hold of her sleeve, dabbed beads of sweat from her brow, and remembered how Aashif had stared at her disfigured arm. Accustomed to hiding it, she squeezed herself tight and fondly recalled the memory of him ignoring its ugliness.

They both continued to pound the ground, with Aashif turning to check on her at regular intervals, always wearing a cheerful expression. She was carefully placing her feet in his footmarks when another attack of cramps struck her, this time more severe. She gasped softly. They were surrounded by trees, and she couldn't fathom where she might safely attend to her needs.

'Aashif,' she called. 'I need to relieve myself.'

He glanced round, 'There's a clearing up here.'

Aashif increased his speed and practically ran up the edge of the mountain, frequently glancing back to make sure she was still behind him. Once they reached the clearing, they glanced around, and Aashif looked at her in her baju, aware that she was going to have to undress. He used his axe to loosen the soil before digging a hole for her with his hands.

'I've still got plenty of water left.' He turned his back to her. 'Take the container from my bag.'

Once she had done as Aashif asked, he stepped away from her, plucked several leaves from the trees and passed them to her, avoiding eye contact. 'I'll step over by that tree and wait for you.'

Fatima winced, embarrassment crawling all over her. As soon as Aashif had walked away, she stripped and attended to her necessities.

'Ready,' she called out when she was done, and Aashif set off again slowly. He called back to her. 'It's brighter up ahead. The next clearing we come to, we'll take a rest.'

By following his footsteps, Fatima quickly caught up with him but stopped abruptly at a hissing sound. A shiver ran through her body at the thought that it could be a venomous snake. She pounded the ground furiously and pushed on.

When she was close behind Aashif, she spoke, 'Did you hear that?'

Aashif glanced back over his shoulder. 'What?'

'That hissing noise.'

'No,' he said, and they stood still for several moments.

'I think it's all clear,' he said, when there was a sudden agitation of foliage. 'The wind,' he said, and they moved on.

Fatima had an overwhelming sense that the jungle was watching their every move. Aashif was on the verge of disappearing from view, when the air seemed to change.

'Psst.'

Noticing that Aashif had not reacted to the sound, she shook her head and a tiny breeze brushed past her. Instinctively, she touched her face and spun round, but there was nothing there.

She gazed skywards, noticing that the small spaces around her were growing brighter. She felt relieved and her tension melted away, but then she heard the noise again.

'Psst, psst.'

She shuddered and then stood stock-still, gritting her teeth. She wheeled around, expecting someone to be standing behind her—but nothing. She charged after Aashif, staying as close to him as she could without getting in his way.

When they reached the clearing, it felt like they were strolling into a new day. It was bright and fresh, the sky, a glorious blue. Fatima shaded her eyes from the sun with her hand. The clearing was a circle of land devoid of trees, with smaller, matching circles surrounding it. The place was scattered with clumps of wild orchids, but it was completely silent; the humming, cawing, and screeching of birds and animals had gone.

Fatima searched for somewhere to rest without disturbing the flowers and wandered into one of the small circles.

'Psst.'

To her astonishment, a small child stood at the circle's edge, partially in shadow and dressed in ragged clothes, with long, unkempt hair. She stared at the child, transfixed, and it raised its hands and stretched them out to her, inviting her forward.

Chapter 29

Toh was finding Dato Hamidi's snoring increasingly jarring. Tormented by his conduct towards Fatima, the sacrifice she was making for the sake of her marriage felt so overpowering that at times she barely had the strength to carry on. She sat on the edge of the bed, tempted to go to the women's dormitory to check on Fatima, but it was still too early. Instead, she decided to wander around the palace.

The corridor guard sprang to life when Toh approached. 'Your Highness,' he said. 'May I assist you?'

'My apologies, Abdul,' she said. 'I had not intended to wake you.'

Abdul bowed respectfully, and Toh strolled along the corridor, before going up the flight of stairs to the throne room. She wandered over to the stage, climbed the steps and stood behind the throne. Gloom settled over her as she pictured her husband sleeping contentedly, claiming more rest than his lazy ways demanded. Reluctantly, she set off for her chamber, hoping that he would still be asleep when she climbed back into bed.

When she reached the store cupboard, she stepped inside. Full of remorse for evicting Fatima from the palace, she sat on the small bed and wondered whether Fatima was still asleep. Indignation crept up on her at the thought that Dato Hamidi was sleeping so comfortably while Fatima had spent several nights sleeping in these cramped conditions. And now, she was sleeping among strangers. She had much to make amends for, Toh thought, as she made her way back to her chamber, nodding at Abdul as she passed.

She opened her bedroom door and was greeted by the sound of the Dato snoring, which stoked her rage. She climbed back into bed and at some point, must have fallen asleep; when she woke up, the room was empty, and daylight was spilling in through the curtains.

Toh jumped out of bed, rushed across to the door and called out to Abdul, 'Where's Fatima?'

'I don't know, Your Highness,' the guard responded.

'The breakfast hasn't been delivered?'

'No, Your Highness.'

Toh closed the door. It was so unlike Fatima, she thought. She attended to her appearance, before calling Abdul to her again, 'Can you go to the kitchen, ask Suraya to make the breakfast and then summon Fatima to see me?'

Toh had asked Fatima to resume delivering the breakfast from this morning. Unease entered her mind. She had never known the girl to fail her before; it struck her that Fatima might be unwell.

When Toh heard the guard returning, she hurried from her chamber and followed him to the throne room. She sat at the table and allowed Abdul to serve the food. 'Is Fatima on her way?' she asked.

'I gave Suraya your instructions, but she said that she hadn't seen her all morning.'

'I was clear in my instructions to her yesterday. Abdul, can you go to the female dormitory and check that she is not ill? And if she's not there, ask the other women where she might be.'

Abdul bowed and left.

'On your return, go to Suraya again, in case she has appeared,' she called after him.

A thought struck Toh that her husband might be involved with Fatima's disappearance, but she rejected the idea immediately—surely, he wouldn't dare confront her outside, where everyone could see.

Abdul returned as Toh was washing her hands. 'Is she all right?'

'I don't know, Your Highness. There were five women in the dormitory, and none of them have seen her. The rest of the slaves are working. I went back to the kitchen, but Suraya hasn't seen her either.'

'How odd. That's most unlike Fatima,' Toh said, puzzled.

At this moment, Dato Hamidi wandered in and strolled up to the table. Toh swept a hand over the food, indicating that what was left was for him, before hurrying from the room. She stopped at the top of the stairs and addressed Abdul, 'I'll go and talk to Suraya. Once my husband has eaten, please take the containers back to the kitchen.'

'Yes, Your Highness. But allow me to go ahead of you and arrange for guards to accompany you.'

By the time she had descended the stairs, two guards were waiting for her. As they led her across to the kitchen, Toh found herself constantly looking around to see if she could spot Fatima. When they entered, several stragglers who were still eating stood to attention. Toh walked across the room to Suraya, who was busy by the stove.

'Your Highness,' Suraya said, giving a small bow.

'Abdul tells me you haven't seen Fatima today,' she said.

'No, I don't think she's been in.'

'You would have noticed if she had been here, surely?'

'Well, there are over two hundred slaves in here at any given time, during the course of the morning.'

'I asked her to collect this morning's breakfast, but there's been no sign of her. I'll go check the dormitory and come back.'

Filled with anxiety, Toh marched to the women's quarters. The few slaves in the room responded to the princess's appearance in the same way as those in the kitchen, by leaping to their feet.

When Toh asked if anyone had seen Fatima, the slaves shook their heads or mumbled no.

'Show me Fatima's bed,' Toh ordered the nearest girl, before following the slave to the end of a long row of beds. The slave pointed at Fatima's bed, which was unmade. That was unlike Fatima, Toh thought; she normally made her bed first thing every morning.

'Where do you keep your possessions?'

'In the side cupboards. That's Fatima's cupboard,' the slave said, pointing to a small cabinet at the end of the bed. 'The rest of our stuff, we hang on the poles overhead.'

Toh bent down and opened the door, before glancing at several poles with garments draped over them. Fatima's cupboard was empty, and her pole was bare.

Toh stared at the slave. 'When did you last see Fatima?'

'At around midday yesterday,' the slave said. 'She was in the company of Suraya, Hisham, and Aashif.'

'In their company? What do you mean?'

'They were seated together around one of the tables in the kitchen.'

Toh hurried from the building and rushed back to the kitchen, where Suraya was wiping down the main table.

'Show me where you, Fatima, Hisham, and Aashif sat yesterday,' Toh demanded.

* * *

Dato Hamidi sat, eating his breakfast and smirking at what he was about to do. He had no intention of allowing people to approach him unawares, so over the past two days he had arranged for sheets of looking glass to be delivered to the palace. They had been stacked beneath the bed in the storeroom.

As soon as Toh had left the palace, he went outside and waved to Shaz, one of the senior slaves, who approached him with three other slaves.

'Until my hearing returns, understand this: When I speak, you will nod that you understand me and shake your head if you do not. Understood?'

All four men nodded.

'Good. Your task is to install the sheets of looking glass in the palace at my direction. Follow me.' He led them into the palace and took them to the storeroom, before continuing to give them orders. 'I want to be able to detect movement throughout the palace. 'Take two sheets from under there and come with me.'

Dato Hamidi sat at the table in the throne room, his back to the wall. He ordered the slaves to place the glass at such an angle that he had a full view of the corridor that led to the bedroom. He told one slave to stand a few steps down the stairs until only his head was visible. Then he moved around, calculating the best angle and arranging the position of the glass accordingly.

'Shaz, come and sit here.'

The head slave did as he was told, and he and Dato Hamidi swapped positions until Dato Hamidi was satisfied that they were both viewing the same scene. 'That's where I want that glass placed, and at that angle.'

Shaz chalked out the position of the glass on the floor, and then Dato Hamidi took the slaves to the bedroom. He commanded them to wait several steps from the door before entering the room and sitting on his side of the bed. He called on Shaz to come to the doorway—he would not allow any slave to enter his chamber, let alone view the interior.

Shaz moved the second pane of glass at Dato Hamidi's direction, until the Dato was satisfied that it was positioned as he wanted it. He would soon have a full view of the corridor, and of anyone who came up the stairs.

Dato Hamidi helped Shaz position the looking glass while the head slave chalked out its location. They spent an hour repeating the exercise throughout the palace, until Dato Hamidi was satisfied that he had all the approaches covered.

'Splendid. Now fetch enough wood to build whatever you need in order to secure each looking glass in place—and I want this done before the day is out.'

He returned to the throne room and stared into space, his brooding eyes imagining how Toh would react to the sight of the looking glasses jutting out all over the palace.

* * *

'Come,' Suraya said, her voice placid. She led Princess Toh to the table where the four had sat the previous day. 'I sat here, Hisham here, and Fatima there. Aashif joined us later. Fatima had come to see us because she was upset. It wasn't hard to tell that she was distressed; it took a while, but Hisham and I managed to coax out of her what was bothering her. She was unhappy at the harsh way in which your brother interrogated Aashif.'

Suraya watched as the expression on Toh's face grow more serious but took no pleasure in deceiving her.

'But unfortunately, that isn't the worst of it,' Suraya paused, choosing her words carefully. 'What's upsetting her most is sleeping in the women's quarters.'

'Oh, Suraya,' Toh exclaimed. 'She told me she was getting along well with the other women. I've been missing her dreadfully.'

'She didn't want to disappoint you, but she feels wretched. It isn't that the other women are cruel to her, it is simply that she is missing you. She hates the fact that so many of the women freely entertain men, but there's more—she's terrified of Dato Hamidi. Hisham and I advised her to talk to you, to be open and honest, and that's when Aashif joined us. Her face lit up when she saw him.'

Toh paled and Suraya decided to reveal all without breaking her promise.

'Don't feel hurt, dear, but Fatima told us what Dato Hamidi did to her.' Suraya was determined that the truth should be told—she was already missing the girl and was sick with worry for her and Aashif. 'She was agitated because she'd done nothing wrong.'

'Suraya, after two dreadful marriages, I wanted to try and save this one— not because I love Dato Hamidi, but to retain the respect of my people. I fear that after the brutal slaying of that young slave, the slaves might rebel. It is a sacrifice I have to make.'

Suraya could tell that Toh felt great sadness; nonetheless, she was determined to see justice done for Fatima and for the Dato to be punished for his misconduct.

'Suraya, Fatima's things are missing.'

Suraya managed a false look of concern. 'Is she planning to move back into the palace, do you think?'

Toh shook her head and stood up slowly, 'I'll have a wander and see if I can spot her. And maybe I'll have a word with Aashif, too.'

Chapter 30

Mesmerized, Fatima struggled over what she might say without scaring the child off.

Its long hair was wild and straggly—it had clearly never been combed. Its clothes were in shreds, as if it had been in a fight with some vicious animal, and she doubted if it had washed in years.

It was when she was right up close that she noticed its fingernails were long and twisted. Without warning, it raised its head, and a chill ran through her, despite the humidity of the day. Its face was ashen, its eyes hideously bloodshot.

Fatima bent down and they were both silent as they stared at each other.

All of a sudden, a wind picked up and whistled through the trees. Then, a smile played around the corners of the child's mouth and turned into a snarl. An expression of unmistakable evil came over it, and it released an odd laugh, so shrill and piercing that it seemed to silence the wind. Fatima froze.

'Fatima,' Aashif bellowed. His shout was loud enough to scare the birds, which flew from the trees, disturbing the foliage so much that it sounded like the leaves were applauding Aashif's effort to rescue her. He charged past Fatima, knocking her to the ground, while removing his top to get at the amulet Suraya had given him.

When he was just inches away from the creature, Aashif poked the amulet into its face. It howled out in pain and sprung back, screaming like an animal snared in a trap. Driven by the terror in its eyes, Aashif went after it, still holding the amulet towards its face. Screeching, the figure jumped into the air and landed on an exposed tree branch. Aashif continued to point the amulet in its direction, holding his axe in his other hand and waving it threateningly.

The creature began to swing from branch to branch in a desperate attempt to escape, and Aashif chased after it, climbing up the tree until it had disappeared from view. When he was satisfied that it had gone for good, he turned to Fatima, stooping down and attending to her. 'Are you all right?'

Fatima sat up, stunned, and blinking fiercely. 'What happened?'

'I'm sorry—I knocked you over.'

'You did?' She looked around. 'Where's the child?' She shivered and grabbed hold of Aashif's arm, 'It was a child, wasn't it?'

As Aashif hesitated, Fatima tightened her grip. He brought his head closer to hers, turned her to face him, and kissed her briefly. 'Yes, it was a child. A wild one, judging by its behaviour. It was probably from a remote village and allowed to roam free.'

'Its hair and nails—did you see them?'

He attempted to smile.

'What's happened to your shirt?' she demanded, before noticing Suraya's amulet swinging from his neck. 'You showed the amulet to the child?'

'That, and my axe,' he said. He could not bear to tell her that he thought the creature was a pontianak—it would only add to her anxiety. He knew from Hisham's tales and the incident involving the terrified villager, that they could move around like that.

'Let me help you up.'

Aided by his support, Fatima got to her feet and Aashif embraced her warmly. 'It won't come back. Especially after it saw the sharpness of my blade. Let's move on —we'll take shelter further up.'

They gathered up their bags. 'Let's stick closer together,' Fatima said.

* * *

The pair pressed forward, staying side by side. They agreed that when they had to proceed in single file, Aashif would lead with Fatima following close behind. Aashif checked on Fatima so frequently that he practically made the climb backwards. His thoughts were filled by the memory of her warm soft body when they'd embraced. The feeling of her small breasts pressed against his body aroused in him a sensation he had never experienced before. He was confused and anxious about the thoughts spinning around in his head. Memories of their first encounters crossed his mind and he understood how lucky he was to have her by his side—it reinforced his resolve to ensure nothing happened to her.

At the sound of a small yelp from Fatima, he swung round to find that she had lost her footing. Before she knew it, he was untying her bag.

'It's getting steeper. I'll carry this,' he said.

'No,' she protested, 'I can manage.'

'I'm sure you can, but if I carry this ahead of me, it will stop me from toppling backwards,' he said, lying in order to help her. 'You hold on to my baju and keep pounding the ground. We'll reach open space much sooner—hopefully before dark sets in.'

For the next hour, they continued to climb in silence. Then, without warning, they entered a twilight world, and he knew that dusk was fast approaching. They reached a small area of level ground with a line of trees on one side, the air fresh.

'We'll be able to rest here,' he said, and she gave a relieved laugh. He took hold of her, and they kissed fleetingly. 'You rest while I build us some cover,' he said.

'While you're doing that, I'll empty the bags and prepare us a feast,' she said, laughing at their situation, though fear still was evident in her features.

Fatima watched as Aashif hacked away at the surrounding trees, chopping branches off at such speed that she was astonished by his strength.

'Can you remove the string we use to tie the bags?' he asked.

She unwound the string as he sharpened one end of each of their poles and drove them into the ground, several feet apart. Next, he balanced a long branch between the poles and secured it in place with the string. Then, he rested other branches against it so that they spread away from the frame and formed a slanted roof.

'I'm going back into the jungle. Call if you can't see me—I don't want us to lose sight of each other,' he said.

Several minutes later, he reappeared, carrying an armful of large leaves. They brushed them clear of insects and Aashif spread them over the roof, before placing more branches on top.

'It's not the most comfortable of shelters,' he said. 'Let's hope we get some sleep.'

* * *

While Aashif was putting the finishing touches to the shelter, Fatima surveyed their surroundings. Only when she peered through the thin line of trees did she realize that they were on a ledge, overlooking a vast layer of thick green that stretched as far as the eye could see. She caught Aashif placing the unfurled blankets side by side under the shelter, and her heart warmed as she watched him.

'That should do it,' he said, stepping back to admire his work.

'A handsome home for two,' she said, attempting to be light-hearted.

He was brushing the entrance to their sanctuary when Fatima called him to her and pointed down at a tiny scene below. 'Isn't that the palace?'

'It is,' he said, pleased at the progress they had made.

They stood for a long time, gazing at what once was their home, different thoughts filling their minds.

Aashif stepped back, grabbed his bag, and rooted inside for the container of citronella and coconut oil. 'You first,' he called to her.

Fatima scrunched up her face, 'But it's so messy.'

Aashif eyed the small amount of the oily mixture she had poured on to her hand and stepped forward. 'Allow me,' he said, pouring a generous amount on to one hand and rubbing it into his palms. He took hold of her hand, only realizing too late that he was holding her damaged arm. He looked at her impassionedly. 'Do you mind?'

She shook her head, and he began to gently work the oil into her hand, paying attention to each finger. 'Can you pull your sleeve up?'

She did as she was asked without speaking, and he gave the same attention to her arm. 'Now the other hand.'

When he'd finished, he asked her to turn round and slowly massaged the oily mix into her nape, before stopping and rubbing the remnants on himself.

'I'll do that for you,' she said.

He grimaced shyly, 'I'm nearly done.'

She grinned at him, 'Time for dinner then.'

They sat together and took the remaining bread from their bags while Aashif presented the last of the chicken. 'There's enough bread for tomorrow. I'll do some foraging then, and maybe some hunting.'

'We'll pass the graveyard?'

'Yes, in the morning, I hope. And then we should begin to make progress across the top of the mountains.'

'How do you know all these things?'

'From Hisham.'

They fell silent, devouring the bread and chicken as if it was the first meal they'd eaten in days. 'This is much tastier than earlier,' Aashif said.

'That's because you have more of an appetite.'

Fatima lay back on her elbow. 'Will you miss Hisham?' she asked.

'Yes—I'll miss him a lot. As I told you, he's been like a father to me all these years. How about you and Princess Toh?'

Aashif noticed that Fatima had become melancholy.

'We've never been apart before,' she said quietly.

Aashif remained silent and gazed up at the sky, 'It'll be dark soon. I'll just pop into the trees for a moment.'

When he returned, he found Fatima lying under the shelter on one blanket and with the other covering her. He swallowed and quickly turned away, fearful of making eye contact. With his pulse racing at the thought of them lying together, he stood in the centre of the clearing, desperate for something to distract him. He was casting his eyes around when he observed the number of crumbs on the ground.

He stooped to pick them up and Fatima called out to him, 'Aren't you coming to bed?'

'I'm just clearing these crumbs away—we don't want to attract insects,' he answered hoarsely.

He wandered to the edge of the clearing with the crumbs, before strolling back towards the shelter. As Fatima watched him, he was overcome by uncertainty. He had never laid with a woman before; all he knew was the smutty language of his peers.

He stooped to enter the shelter and she grinned, 'I hope we find somewhere to bathe tomorrow.'

'Yes.'

'I thought that if we lay together, we could keep ourselves warm,' she said. And as she nestled up against him, he thought that his heart would burst.

Chapter 31

Toh walked out from the kitchen into the heat of the raging sun. Accompanied by her two guards, she wandered around the gardens in search of Fatima, Aashif, or Hisham. She eventually spotted Hisham near the allotments and hurried to talk to him, half expecting that Aashif would be with him.

When she reached Hisham, she got straight to the point. 'I can't find Fatima anywhere. I understand you were with her yesterday. Have you seen her this morning?'

'No, I haven't. I last saw her yesterday when she and Aashif left the kitchen.'

'Suraya told me what you were talking to her about.'

Hisham tilted his head to avoid the glare of the sun. 'She's most unhappy, I'm afraid.'

Toh was disinclined to go over the events. 'Is Aashif around?' she asked.

'He should be over by the rice fields,' he said, troubled by the princess's sadness.

Toh continued to look at Hisham until his stare began to unsettle her. 'You've done a wonderful job with the gardens,' she said, walking away. She felt uncomfortable knowing that Hisham was aware of her difficulties and was glad to be away from him. She continued to search the grounds for Fatima, until she reached the paddy fields. When she worked out that Aashif was not among the slaves tending to the rice, she headed back towards the palace.

Anger building up inside her, she marched to the men's barracks and stood by the door, allowing her guards to enter. She listened as one of them called whoever was inside to attention before informing her that she could enter. Apart from one slave who had a towel wrapped around him, the other seven slaves present were fully dressed. All of them stood to attention.

'Have any of you seen Aashif?' she asked.

They all replied that they hadn't.

'Take me to his bed,' she demanded of the nearest slave, and she and her guards followed him to the far end of the aisle.

'Who sleeps on either side of him?'

'Faiz and Reza, Your Highness.'

'Are they here?'

'No, Your Highness.'

'Kindly fetch them. My guards and I will wait.'

The slave scurried away.

Puzzled that Aashif's bed was one of only a small number that was made, Toh instructed one of her guards to examine his possessions. Having opened Aashif's cupboard, he turned to the princess. 'It's empty, Madam.'

'Search under his bed.'

The guard inspected the bed frame and discovered an opening built into the structure. 'It's some sort of secret compartment,' he suggested.

At that moment, the slave rushed back into the dormitory, followed by Faiz and Reza. All three stood to attention as Toh addressed the two slaves. 'You two sleep either side of Aashif—correct?'

'Yes, Your Highness,' they replied.

'Who sleeps where?'

Faiz explained the sleeping arrangements to her, casually slackening his posture.

Toh looked at him coldly and he stiffened. 'Have you seen Aashif today?'

'No, Your Highness.'

Toh turned to Reza, who gave the same answer.

'When did you last see him?' she asked, rage filling her eyes.

'Yesterday, I suppose. I don't remember.'

'And you?' Toh asked Faiz, the pitch of her voice rising.

Faiz blinked and looked down. 'Yesterday morning, I believe, Your Highness.'

'His bed looks as though it hasn't been slept in,' Toh said.

Neither Faiz nor Reza responded.

'And underneath his bed, there appears to be a hidden compartment. Do either of you know anything about that?'

The two slaves seemed startled. Reza said no while Faiz shook his head.

'You don't appear to know very much about your immediate neighbour,' she said.

'He's a private person,' Faiz said.

'Is that by choice or necessity?' Princess Toh snarled. 'And I suppose neither of you knows where he is now?'

'No, Your Highness,' they answered together.

Toh glowered at them, before turning and hurrying from the building. She could only think that Aashif must have had something valuable, to go to the trouble of hiding it—and now, whatever it was, it had gone missing.

As she walked back to the palace, she became alert to banging noises coming from the building. What was her husband doing now, she wondered. The closer she got, the more rage she felt bubbling up inside her.

When she reached the palace, the guard who normally protected the stairs was standing outside. As she ascended the staircase, her anger exploded. 'What on earth is happening?' she asked Abdul, who shook his head and shrugged his shoulders. 'The Dato has brought the builders in.'

'What on earth for?' she asked.

'He's installing looking glasses throughout the palace. According to the builders, he says that if he can't hear anyone approaching him, he will at least be able to see them.'

Her irritation at Fatima and Aashif's absence, combined with all the noise, caused fury to enter her face.

'Where is he now?'

Abdul nodded towards the bedroom. Toh marched along the corridor and barged into the room, only to discover Dato Hamidi sitting on the edge of the bed, staring at her. She pointed behind her at the door, before gesturing to him that he should stop the work. At this, the Dato looked embittered and snorted, before making a thin laugh that he knew grated on his wife, 'I still have my sight, and I'm using it to its best endeavours.'

She scrutinized him, frustration mounting inside her, still bedevilled by the image of him semi-naked before Fatima.

'I shall explain to your brother that I have no way of helping to defend this palace if it is attacked,' he continued.

Toh glared at him, enraged. A chill ran down her spine at the sudden realization that Fatima and Aashif may have disappeared together, and she shuddered. Desperate, she decided that she must speak to the Bomoh—he was the one person who could counsel her.

* * *

Toh descended the stairs, to find her guards waiting for her. They sprang to life as she approached.

'Any news?'

'No, Your Highness, there's been no sighting of either of them.'

'Where's Anwar?'

'Training, Your Highness.'

'Take me to him.'

Beyond the living quarters was an open clearing in the forest, where the warriors trained in hand-to-hand combat and other fighting skills. Toh gaped at the half-naked warriors attempting to wrestle each other to the ground, taking in Anwar's booming voice intermittently shouting encouragement at the men. Her presence soon became apparent, and the warriors stopped fighting and stood to attention.

Anwar hurried to her, 'Princess, I've never seen you out here before.'

'Fatima and Aashif are missing,' she said without preamble.

'Missing? What do you mean?'

Toh recounted what had happened since she called Fatima to the palace that morning, telling him about the state of their sleeping quarters, the absence of any possessions and Aashif's empty hidden compartment.

'Anwar, it's clear that you are busy, but I need to pay an urgent visit to the Bomoh. There are troubling matters that I must discuss with him.'

'I'm afraid I'm planning to resume my search for the slave's murderer tomorrow morning. Arrangements are already in place.'

'Then I must ask you to accompany me now. All being well, we should be back before dark.'

* * *

The moment the Bomoh realized that Princess Toh and her guard were approaching, he fell back into the maudlin mood that captured him every time he met her. The dark, heavy folds in his face, already weathered by old age, tensed and he returned to his cave. How many opportunities did the woman need to find happiness, he wondered. If he could endure loss for so many years, why was she so unwilling to accept an imperfect world?

Unknown to anyone, his cave had two openings. Years ago, when he was an agile young man, he had divided it into two sections, each of which was thirty yards or so in length, separated by a solid door. His living quarters, palatial by the standards of any village chief, had never received a single visitor.

He calculated how long it would take Princess Toh and her guard to reach him and retired to his living quarters, in search of some tranquillity. Minutes before she entered, he returned to the other section, prepared the fire so that it cast a dim light, and settled himself into his seat.

'Hello, Bomoh. It's me, Princess Toh.'

The Bomoh was vexed by the tension in Toh's voice. He waited for her eyes to adjust to the light; once she had made out his shape, she gingerly moved towards him. He patted the seat next to him and she sat beside him uneasily.

The Bomoh stretched out and poked the fire, causing more light to spread through the cave.

Toh began by recounting Dato Hamidi's recent behaviour before talking about her search for Fatima and Aashif. The Bomoh turned to her, and she found herself staring into his dark, piercing eyes.

'I was unaware that Fatima had befriended Aashif, and now they have both gone missing. I do not know this Aashif well, and I have no reason to believe that he is trustworthy. The fact that he has gone missing at the same time as Fatima indicates that they have run away together.'

Her voice was tight when she continued, 'Bomoh, I want you to perform *main peteri*.' She glanced around the cave, wondering if it was a suitable place to carry out the ritual. She was aware that this act of prayer usually took place at night, in a room decorated with flowers to attract the spirits. Toh knew that she would not need to attend; she could keep her promise to Anwar to be back at the palace before dark.

'I want you to ask the spirits to stop this slave from winning Fatima's heart.' Toh gazed at the Bomoh as he sat upright, contemplating her instruction. 'My one hope is that after the Dato's abuse, Fatima will be too scared to allow this Aashif to touch her. I want her back, Bomoh. Please bring her back for me.'

He continued to stare at her fiercely as he reflected on her words. He then rose slowly, his movements cumbersome, as if there was a great weight on his shoulders.

'She's my little sister, Bomoh. I love her dearly. Please do this for me.'
The Bomoh slowly nodded, before speaking in a rough but precise voice:
'A search party, orderly and complete
Will return to you she who is so sweet.'

Chapter 32

Fatima woke to find herself wrapped around Aashif, who was fast asleep and snoring softly. She lay there for a while, anxious not to disturb him; she was fearful that if she did, his soul would go out of him. Long ago, Princess Toh had told her that it was a man's *roh* that set him apart from the rest of creation. It was believed, she said, that if a man was woken up abruptly, the roh may disappear—and that a man without a roh could transform into a weretiger at night.

Fatima carefully peeled herself away from him, edged out from the shelter, and wandered to the edge of the clearing. She turned her attention from the vast spread of trees to the palace below, watching as ant-like figures went about their business. She wondered if Toh might be among them and hoped that the princess was not too distressed by her absence.

She swung round, startled by the sound of leaves rustling, convinced that she was being watched. She hurried back to the shelter and lay down next to Aashif, who blinked his eyes open.

'Morning,' he said.

She gave him a wide smile.

'How did you sleep?'

'Very well; I woke up a short while ago,' Fatima said. 'But Aashif, I think we are being watched.'

Aashif stiffened and Fatima looked towards the trees. An anxious expression formed on Aashif's face. He picked up his axe and stood, Fatima following him.

'Stay close behind me, but not too close—I may need room to strike out.'

They gingerly stepped away from the shelter and Aashif tried to peer through the foliage.

'There,' Fatima gasped, and Aashif noticed a movement in the leaves. He swung round briefly, placed a finger on his lips, and stood still, readying himself for an attack, but stared in disbelief when a bluish-grey thrush flew out from the foliage.

The strain lifted from them both, and they burst out laughing.

'What a fool!' Aashif said.

'You or me?'

'Both of us.'

They settled down again. 'I hope we find water soon. Somewhere where we can bathe,' Fatima said.

'Yes, that would be nice.'

'So, today is the day we meet the dead,' she said, trying her best to sound casual.

'You're worried?'

She shrugged. 'I suppose so.'

He stretched out his arms to her. 'Don't be. If the dead were able to come back to life, our world would be full of them.'

She fell into his arms and took solace from the strength of his body.

He released her. 'We'll have some of the bread, tidy up here, and move on. Unfortunately, even if we had something to cook, it wouldn't be wise to light a fire—someone might spot the smoke.'

They returned to the shelter and rummaged through their bags for the bread and the citronella mixture. After they had covered their exposed skin, they sat on their bags and began eating the bread. Aashif shook his head at their meagre rations. He caught Fatima looking at him and they both laughed.

'I'll cut down a few coconuts later; we can drink the milk and eat the flesh. I'll also find us some bananas.'

'It sounds like you're planning a feast.'

'We'll eat and drink as we go along, rather than overloading ourselves with provisions.'

'Do you think they've sent out a search party yet?'

'I doubt it, but I expect they will soon enough. They won't find us if we're careful—we've had too much of a head start. We'll have to clear up as we go along, though. We should dismantle the shelter.'

'We'd better get started then,' Fatima replied.

Aashif picked up the crumbs from the floor around them. 'A clever tracker would notice ants swarming all over the place, so let's make sure we brush away the crumbs.'

Next, Aashif dismantled the shelter and carried it into the jungle where he broke up the frame. He retained the two poles and disposed of the rest.

Together, they folded the blankets, shoved them into their bags, and tied the bags across their backs before Aashif brushed the floor with his feet, so that it appeared undisturbed.

'Ready?' he asked.

Fatima nodded brusquely, aware that the graveyard was fast approaching.

* * *

They set off with Aashif leading, and soon the trees were pressing in around them. He tried as best he could to shake off his concerns at what they might face, without revealing his anxieties. Because of the denseness of the jungle, progress was slow. Every now and then, Aashif would pause to check on Fatima. At one point, she lost sight of him and rushed to catch up, shouting out when she caught her baju on an overhanging branch. Aashif swung round sharply, to find her struggling to free herself.

Fearful that she was ensnared by some hidden animal, she yanked herself free, ripping the garment in the process. She put her hand to her chest to try and stop the tear, revealing her breast.

'Don't move,' Aashif said, hurrying to her and prising her baju free. He held on to the material, staring at her nakedness and unsure what to do. 'As soon as we are out of the forest, I'll try to mend it.'

Fatima held the torn cloth over herself, and Aashif turned away. 'Take the citronella mixture from my bag and rub some on to yourself so you don't get bitten.'

Fatima quickly did as he suggested before replacing the container.

Aashif deliberately stared into her eyes. 'I'll call you each time I turn to check on you,' he said awkwardly.

Fatima blushed and they set off again. The sight of her naked breast lay heavy on Aashif's mind, and he fought to focus on the need to stay vigilant.

'I'm turning around,' he said, but at that moment a gibbon screeched. His heat intensified when he found that Fatima had failed to cover her breast. 'Sorry,' he said.

'The gibbon—I didn't hear you.'

Aashif tried to smile and quickly turned away. The next time he called to tell her that he was turning around, Fatima heard him and covered herself. Aashif's heart was pounding at the thought of her pert breast and protruding nipple. He finally came to a halt as the trees began to thin, and he glanced up at the milky sky. 'Please don't let it rain,' he pleaded out loud. 'Let us get across the mountaintop first.'

Fatima joined him and they gazed through the trees at the barren, rocky landscape ahead.

Aashif untied his bag. 'Let's get you fixed up,' he said, unravelling his blanket and passing it to Fatima, who wrapped it around herself and removed her baju. He then took several strands of his twine and rolled them into a thread, before using it to tie the torn fabric back together.

'That should hold,' he said, passing the repaired baju back to her.

'Thanks,' she said, before stretching up to kiss his cheek. When she stumbled on the uneven ground, he clasped his hands on her shoulders to stop her from falling.

She asked him to turn around as she dressed.

'Done,' she said, once she had wriggled the baju into place.

They made their way through the trees and on to the rocks. Fatima sighed, relieved that there was no sign of a graveyard. 'It's like being on top of the world,' she said.

Aashif was troubled by the silence, but he said nothing to Fatima. Wary of tripping on the uneven surface, he warned her to watch her footing. A little way ahead, Aashif noticed that the ground dropped sharply. When they reached the ridge, he looked at Fatima and saw that her face was ashen. Ahead of them was a stretch of land covered by row after row of graves.

Fatima looked around desperately, and Aashif guessed that she was searching for a route that avoided the graveyard. However, it seemed to stretch endlessly on either side, and he knew that their only way to reach the other side was by continuing straight ahead.

'Are you ready?' he asked.

Fatima stared at him, biting her lower lip. 'Is there no other way?'

'We'll be fine—I promise. Hold my hand.'

The short drop was steep in places, and they practically ran down the bank. When they reached the graveyard, Aashif was troubled by the neatness of the place. Many of the graves were covered in weeds and shrubs, but some of them were clearly tended.

'We shouldn't step on the humps,' Fatima said. 'I'll follow behind.'

They set off briskly and were nearly halfway across the graveyard when Aashif came to an abrupt halt. 'That smell,' he said.

A sweet fragrance was bothering him greatly—after all, there were no flowers in sight. Immediately ahead of him was a small mound of recently turned clay; he recalled Hisham's warning of how the grave of a young girl would smell.

Chapter 33

Dawn had yet to break when Princess Toh climbed from her bed and rushed along the corridor to speak to her guard.

'Abdul, would you fetch Anwar? I'll be in the throne room waiting for him.'

'Yes, Your Highness,' Abdul replied, bleary-eyed, and dashed down the stairs.

One or two slaves were already awake when Abdul reached the guards' quarters. Anwar was already dressed, and he followed Abdul back to the palace.

By the time Anwar entered, Toh was seated at the table, writing a letter.

Though her heart lifted at the sight of him, her voice was grave. 'I'm glad I caught you in time,' she said. 'I need you to change your plans.'

'Madam,' Anwar stood to attention.

'I want you to raise a search party and bring Fatima and Aashif back.'

'When?'

'Now.'

'In an hour's time, I'm due to continue the search for the young slave girl's killer.'

'Can someone go in your stead—or can it be delayed? The girl is dead, after all, and finding her killer won't bring her back. I'm worried for Fatima's welfare.'

The pleading tone in Toh's voice touched Anwar and he stared at her, his mind racing.

'I'll never be able to forgive myself should anything happen to her,' she continued.

Anwar's thoughts were conflicted between the Raja's instructions to find the killer and the princess's genuine concern.

'There is someone I can instruct to continue the search for the murderer,' he said, thinking of Shafie, who he had introduced to the chief whose slave had gone missing.

'How soon could you depart?'

'By lunchtime, I would think. I'll need to give out fresh instructions and organize a small party to accompany me.'

'Come and see me before you leave.'

* * *

When Dato Hamidi had gotten married two years earlier, he had been driven by a need to know everything that was going on in the palace. To achieve his goal, he had befriended Shaz. The slave's shifty eyes had suggested to the Dato that the man would be perfect as his spy, and he had not been wrong. They soon reached an arrangement where all the gossip from the palace would be passed to him in return for a coin or two.

That morning, the Dato awoke to find his bedroom empty. Eager to remain up to date on the happenings at the palace, he washed, dressed, and set off to meet Shaz, who was supervising the final touches to the decoration work. Dato Hamidi stood apart from the workers and Shaz strolled up to him, carrying a small slate.

'Do you have anything for me?'

Shaz showed him the slate, as if they were discussing the ongoing renovations. Written on it was a message: 'Fatima and Aashif have run away together.' Dato Hamidi read the words, astonished. 'When? Who told you?'

Shaz wiped the slate clean and wrote another message on it, while pointing at the palace as if he was sketching a plan, 'Learned over breakfast. Everybody knows. Search party forming.'

Dato Hamidi laughed out loud as he imagined voices throughout the palace, whispering all manner of malicious thoughts about Toh. 'Good man,' he said. 'Be sure to send a messenger if you have any further information.'

And with that, Dato Hamidi skipped away.

* * *

It was mid-morning when Toh strolled to the kitchen.

'The same guards are waiting for you, Your Highness,' Abdul told her.

They walked into the kitchen and the guards stood inside the entrance. Furniture scraped across the floor as several female slaves who were eating breakfast, rose. Toh greeted them and watched as they hurried from the room.

'I had no desire to interrupt them,' the princess said to Suraya.

'If you hadn't arrived, they'd probably still have been here at lunchtime. I was about to take a break. Will you join me?' Suraya offered, gesturing to Toh to take a seat at the large table.

'I'm so worried about Fatima,' Toh said.

Suraya poured two mugs of water and sat next to the princess, struggling to manoeuvre her mind around her own treachery. 'I'm sure she's safe.'

Noticing that Toh's attention had wandered, Suraya waited for her to speak again. Finally, the princess said, 'I suppose you heard all that banging yesterday?'

'You mean the Dato installing looking glasses?'

'How did you know that's what it was?'

Suraya pulled a face, 'News travels fast.'

Toh took a sip of water. 'What's this slave Aashif like, Auntie?'

'He's a good man.'

Toh cried softly, 'I keep picturing the confusion on Aashif's face when my brother interrogated him. The Raja was too fierce.' She paused. 'Fatima's only been gone a short time, and I already miss her dreadfully. Auntie, you say that Aashif is a good man, but if that were so, he would not have placed Fatima in danger.'

'If it is of any comfort to you, Hisham says that he trained Aashif as well as any warrior here. Furthermore, he knows the jungle better than anyone.'

Toh muttered, staring hard at Suraya as the older lady continued.

'Hisham is pained because Aashif has gone. He's very proud of him and thinks of him as a son. Apart from teaching him the ways of the jungle, he taught him to read and write. But what gives him the most pride is Aashif's reason for leaving.'

Suraya watched as Toh struggled to cast aside the pain she felt at Fatima's disappearance.

'Hisham taught Aashif the ways of all believers, to the extent that he became driven by a desire to fulfil his Haj.'

Toh stared at Suraya, dumbstruck. 'He's trying to reach Mecca?'

Suraya nodded, 'According to Hisham, that has been his desire ever since he became a believer.'

'So why didn't he say anything?'

Suraya shook her head, 'I can only assume that he feared he wouldn't be allowed to go. After all, if he was granted permission to make a trip to Mecca, every other slave would claim the same right.'

Toh spoke quietly, 'Do you think they are in love?'

'From what I saw of them in recent times, yes,' Suraya said.

'She's my baby sister and my best friend,' Toh said. 'We told each other everything, but she said nothing to me about being in love.'

'Perhaps she didn't know how. Love can often carry with it great confusion.'

'But he's not Malayan,' Toh said. After a prolonged silence, the princess got to her feet. 'I must get back and meet Anwar. I've asked him to take a search party and bring them home.'

Suraya stared at Toh.

'I have little choice. If I don't, my brother will reprimand me. To let them escape would unsettle the other slaves. Before I know it, they'll all be trying to escape.'

* * *

Toh was sitting in the throne room, writing a letter, when Dato Hamidi strolled in, an unsettling glint in his eyes.

'So that lying brat Fatima's run away?' he smirked.

Toh glared at him in contempt.

'You didn't want to listen, did you?' he snarled, enjoying a new sense of power over her. Fuelled by the distress on her face, the Dato continued, 'It's the talk of the guards, the slaves—everybody.'

The behaviour of Toh's previous two husbands came back to haunt her, and she found herself wishing that she had let the Bomoh do his damnedest. But seeing the tiredness on her face, Dato Hamidi carried on, 'Time and again, I warned you not to trust these slaves, but you wouldn't listen. And what's happened? Not one, but two of them have gone missing. I'm sure your brother will be proud of the way you're running this place.'

At this, Toh's features hardened, and she gestured to her husband; opening her mouth wide and then covering her ears to remind him how he had lost his hearing. She pointed at her mouth and placed a finger to her lips, suggesting that if he shouted again, he might also lose his voice.

'Please don't show that filthy mouth of yours—it disgusts me.'

Toh struggled to retain her composure. At the sight of her discomfort, Dato Hamidi was roused to continue his insults, 'It's pathetic, really, the way you wander around this estate, thinking that you have the workers' respect. To gain any respect from them, you'll need to prove that you can keep a man happy. But you can't, can you? Not after three marriages. What they want is a man to rule them—not a woman they perceive to be a witch. It's obvious that your lying little brat's lover, that slave they call Aashif, has also been lying. He's the murderer of that poor slave.'

Toh placed her finger to her lips again and laughed in her husband's face.

'I heard rumours that your brother interrogated him,' he continued. 'Well, clearly not fiercely enough. But I can tell you this, I'll lash the truth out of him.'

Toh reclaimed her composure, deciding not to stoop to his level of abuse as the Dato continued to rant.

'It's clear to me that he raped that poor girl and made a fool of you all in the process. No wonder he's run away. I dread to think about the suffering that young slave must have endured,' he persisted. 'I wonder how much time he spent abusing her.'

Toh puckered her lips in her resolve.

'Mark my words: once a rapist, always a rapist. He's probably already raped that little brat of yours. And if he hasn't done so yet, he will soon enough.'

Toh's eyes widened, appalled at the thought of Fatima being assaulted.

'Actually, having been led on by her myself, I wouldn't be at all surprised if he hasn't already taken her. She's the real witch, seducing men while they sleep.'

At that moment, Abdul and Anwar entered. Dato Hamidi stiffened, and he swung round, bowed humbly at Toh, and rushed from the room.

* * *

Anwar and Abdul had scorn in their eyes as they watched Dato Hamidi slink from the room, with his shoulders drooped. His puerile behaviour disgusted Anwar, who glared at him as he passed.

Pulling a face that made her shame clear, Toh asked Abdul to leave and beckoned Anwar to sit opposite her, 'Allow me to finish this.'

Anwar watched as she put some final words on the page, before folding another sheet into a square and wrapping it around the letter. When she took hold of the melting spoon, Anwar sprung to his feet. 'Allow me, You Highness.'

Toh handed the spoon to him, and Anwar broke a small portion of wax into its bowl, before holding it over the burning candle until the wax started melting and pouring a small amount over the document. Toh removed the royal seal from around her neck and passed it to Anwar, who pressed it into the wax and returned the letter to the princess. He watched as she wrote 'Fatima' on the front.

'Anwar, please keep this safe and give it to Fatima. I've explained in it that she should pass it to you once she's read it.'

Toh rose to her feet. 'Before you depart, can you tell Abdul how to reach the Bomoh's cave? I know we've only recently got back, but I must return urgently.'

Anwar nodded.

'Go safely,' she said.

Anwar bowed and left to speak to Abdul before joining his small search party.

Chapter 34

The fragrance emanating from the freshly tended grave troubled Aashif.

'When I was a little boy,' he said, 'I remember Hisham telling me about a young girl who became so distressed at the death of her first lover that she couldn't eat or drink, and she eventually withered away. Years later, when there was cause to move her body, there was a sweet small coming from her grave. To everyone's surprise, they found that she had a most beautiful body. Hisham told me the story when I was refusing to eat—I was sulking because I wanted to be a warrior. That was when he began to train me.'

Fatima shivered. 'And you think this grave might contain such a girl?'

'I don't know. This is a warrior's graveyard. Why would a girl be buried here?'

'Perhaps she was the daughter of a warrior?'

They were shaken from their reverie by a bird flying overhead, flapping its wings loudly before disappearing from view.

Fatima blanched. 'Is that some sort of warning?' she asked, clearly tense.

'It's just a bird,' Aashif said. 'Let's keep moving.'

It was a hot, still day and they made their way across the graveyard without incident. They carefully passed through a thick copse and came to a small pool of water covered in dark-green weeds. The ground surrounding it was muddy.

'Do you think it's clean? I'd love a wash.'

Aashif looked at it warily, 'We don't know how deep it is.'

'Maybe I could scoop up some water to wash with?'

'It looks dangerously slippery around the edge.'

Aashif noticed Fatima's disappointment. 'Let's use a container to scoop up some water.'

It was while he was manoeuvring his bag free that he sensed movement under his feet. The next moment, the air was filled by a thunderous sound somewhere between a screech and a roar.

Aashif surveyed their surroundings and noticed that they were near the edge of the jungle. He snatched Fatima's hand and as they ran for cover, a strange whistling sound filled the air. A sharp draft of wind rushed past Aashif's face; a split second later, a long pole embedded itself in the trunk of a large rain tree with a thud.

'A spear!' he exclaimed. He tightened his grip on Fatima's hand and dragged her through the shrubbery and behind the rain tree, causing her to gasp for breath. He pushed her against the trunk on the opposite side and held her tight. Moments later, the air was filled by another whistle and a second spear followed. Then what sounded like a great storm broke. Spears bounced off the trees all around them, with one striking the side of the rain tree, just above Aashif's head.

It was then that he spotted a huge, felled tree, which looked like it had at some point been struck by lightning. To the side of it was an enormous fig tree. He bent low and whispered into Fatima's ear. 'Look ahead of me and you'll see a fallen tree, with a fig tree next to it. When I shout 'Now', follow me. We'll be safer over there.'

He began counting the seconds between each attack. 'Now,' he bellowed and sprinted into the open, leapt over the tree trunk and waited for Fatima to join him.

'There,' she called out, pointing towards a hole beneath the tree.

The whistling sound rushed towards them again. 'Get inside,' Aashif shouted.

Fatima threw herself headlong into the opening, dragging her bag after her. Aashif followed and quickly jammed both their bags against the entrance. A shower of spears rained down on the jungle surrounding them, slashing everything in their wake. One of them bounced off the tree and glanced off Aashif's bag. They lay there until the attack ended, terrified. Aashif began counting, his blood pumping; sure enough, the next wave came on the same count.

Fatima nudged her head into the crook of Aashif's arm and gripped his hand when a wayward spear bounced off the fig tree and lodged itself into the soil behind their two bags. As Aashif started counting again, Fatima stiffened and tightened her grip on him. 'There's a snake in here,' she whispered, as something crawled over her body. Aashif knew he had to calm her down before she began to panic.

'Shh,' he whispered, 'don't move, whatever you do. And keep your eyes closed.' He was worried that the snake might spit venom into her face. He kissed her forehead and kept his lips pressed against her.

Fatima held her breath, desperate to shake off the reptile and bury herself under Aashif's body. A brief period passed before the next attack, and the reptile didn't move from her back. Like the previous attacks, the assault ended abruptly, but the snake remained still. Fatima was desperate for Aashif to remove it from her, but she was too frightened to make any noise.

Aashif felt something drip on to his arm. He was shocked to realize that it was a tear from Fatima, but when the snake slithered across his arm, he became distracted. Opening one eye, he was relieved to see that the creature was a red-tailed pipe snake—not a venomous species. He sighed and took hold of Fatima in a firm embrace.

'It's all right,' he said, trying to alleviate her fears. 'It's not poisonous.'

Fatima broke down in tears. 'I'm sorry,' she wept, 'I was terrified.'

He tried to kiss her on her lips, but she pushed him away. 'Not now.' She edged forward, placing her cheek against his, 'Let's get away from here.'

He wiped her tears and kissed the tip of her nose. 'I think it's over,' he said, pushing himself forward to take in the scene outside. He was stunned to see hundreds of spears jutting upwards, like an overgrown field of sugarcane. He shoved the bags aside and he and Fatima worked their way free.

'The souls have stopped marauding?'

'I don't believe that stuff about dead warriors coming back to life.'

'So, who was it then?'

'I don't know.'

They rose slowly, ready to dive back into their hiding place if it became necessary.

'Why do I get the feeling we're being watched?'

'Because we are—by the animals, too frightened to show themselves.'

They kept glancing around when Aashif spotted a thick mass of bamboo grass and understood what the spears were made from.

'Be careful of the bamboo,' he warned her, stepping up to a clump of the plant. 'The tiny hair on them can be sharp,' he said, pointing at the stems. 'They can irritate the skin, especially where it is soft.'

'I'll be careful.'

The jungle broke up into small thickets of trees that became denser as they hiked. At some point in the middle of the afternoon, they sensed that they were walking downhill.

'I'm parched,' Fatima called. 'Do we have any water left?'

'I've got some,' he said. Without Fatima noticing, he had been taking small sips of his own supply. He unstrung his bag and passed his canister to her. 'Now that we're going downhill, we should come upon water.'

It was while Fatima was quenching her thirst that he spotted a group of citronella plants and stuffed a few leaves into his bag. 'Once we hit a stream, I'll do a bit of foraging,' he said.

* * *

After Anwar had seen off Shafie and the small group of warriors he had selected, he strolled across the courtyard to join Osmin, Haron, and Farouk, one of his most trusted warriors.

Having learned from Hisham of Aashif's ambition to visit Mecca, Anwar concluded that he must be travelling west. Had it been anybody else, he reasoned, they might well be wandering lost in the jungle. But Aashif was different; he had been trained by Hisham.

He gazed up at the mountains in the distance as he contemplated the route Aashif might have taken. He assumed that he would have gone over the mountains via the graves of the warriors, but his own men were terrified by stories of the jinn and would have mutinied if they were asked to take that route. Shortly before his death, the Raja's father had told Anwar the secret behind the legend of the graveyard, but he was not prepared to breach that confidence in order to shorten their search. Instead, he would travel south, taking the familiar path up the mountain towards the Bomoh's cave.

Chapter 35

Princess Toh had no desire to trek for hours in the company of warriors who meant little to her in her current condition, so she chose not to accompany Anwar and his men. But it was that same condition that stimulated her visit to the Bomoh, and she feared that time could be against her.

It was the middle of the morning by the time she began the trip with Abdul.

'I escorted your brother to the Bomoh a couple of times, but my memory may not be too clear, princess.'

'Then I shall guide you as best I can.'

Abdul was a strong man, a good-natured and respectful warrior whose ferocious reputation gave Toh peace of mind. He was glad that no rain had fallen in the past twenty-four hours; he would be able to follow the tracks made by Anwar and Princess Toh's horses the previous day, as well as those created by Anwar's troop that morning.

In the dense foliage, Abdul occasionally lost sight of the prints, and Toh found herself struggling to keep her frustration in check—so desperate was she to get there and back as quickly as possible. She was relieved when they finally dismounted, and she knew that they would soon reach the cave.

It was as they began to progress on foot that a sweet scent got caught in Toh's throat. 'Abdul, what's that smell?'

'I'm not sure, Your Highness. Maybe it's from some sort of fruit that's hidden in the undergrowth.'

When they finally arrived at the cave, the smell was still lingering in Toh's nostrils. She passed her reins to Abdul and stared at him, 'A while ago, Anwar made the mistake of entering the cave after me. Under no circumstances whatsoever are you to follow me—I've learned that the Bomoh's powers do not work if someone is present who was not invited. Do you understand?'

'Yes, Your Highness. I shall wait here and tend the horses.'

Toh nodded. The last thing she wanted was for anyone to witness what was about to happen.

'I'm back,' she called out as she entered the cave. 'My husband has unsettled my mind, and I need your advice. If I do not act now, it will be too late.'

In the darkness, she identified the lumbering silhouette of the Bomoh crossing her path. Toh sighed. 'Can you kindly stoke your fire and bring some light in here, so I can at least see where I'm walking?'

She was unnerved by what she had to do, but if she wanted the Bomoh to cast a hex, she had no choice but to surrender to him. It was only when a flash of light appeared that she knew he was responding to her presence. 'I followed your advice and have sent a search party after them,' she added.

* * *

Even before the princess spoke, the Bomoh had noticed how tense she was. Nonetheless, he was irritated by her unexpected presence.

'I want you to cast a spell and bring them back,' the princess went on before pausing, as if unsure whether she was saying the right thing. 'I do not want you to do anything about my husband placing my slave's hand on his manhood.'

Unmoved, the Bomoh fixed his eyes on her. He was sorely tempted to order her away from his cave. How dare this young woman believe she had the right to limit his powers? It was only when he saw her wincing at his brutal stare that he decided to let her remain. He gave a menacing cough that startled Toh. Until then, the only sound that had ever emanated from him—apart from his couplets—was the occasional grunt.

'I believe the intentions of this African slave to be most dishonourable,' Princess Toh said.

The Bomoh was entertained as he looked at her sad eyes, and he expected her to show proper deference to his authority.

A new tension crept into the cave, brought on by Toh's nervousness. As the Bomoh watched her stare up at the bats, he wondered what she was thinking.

'I have learned that Aashif is well-trained in traversing the jungle terrain,' she said. 'The chances of the search party catching them before they escape these lands are not good.' She paused. 'If Aashif were to fall in love with me, he would return with Fatima—she would not be able to travel through the jungle alone.'

The Bomoh stared at the princess, wondering if she truly understood what she was saying.

'All my adult life, my menses have been regular. I know that tomorrow it will stop, so today is my last day of value before another month passes. This is the prime reason for my return.'

The Bomoh contemplated what she was asking of him, his heart pounding. It had been many years since he had enjoyed the pleasure of a naked woman, especially one so young and beautiful. For the first time in many years, he was aware of a sensation in his groin. He snatched the poker next to the fire and jabbed at the smouldering embers.

A couple of steps away from the embers was a small, scorched area where he would often light a fire to cook on. He rose and stood a small tripod over the blackened soil, before hooking a small pot underneath it and using tongs to place some burning embers beneath. Next, he poured a quantity of water into the pot and added a tiny amount of rice. He twisted round to face the princess, grabbed at his baju, and dropped his hands, indicating that she should undress. When she stood naked in front of him, he stared at her in silence. Her pert breasts and firm nipples, the heart-shaped shadow between her legs, the curve of her hips and the smooth flatness of her stomach held him transfixed.

When she indicated that she was ready, he carefully unhooked the pot, balanced it in the embers, and removed the tripod, before digging his hand into a bowl and sprinkling a handful of incense pellets over the fire. As fumes spread around the cave, he picked up a scoop and stood upright, staring blankly into Toh's eyes.

As steam began to rise from the pot of rice, he offered her his hand and led her towards the fire. He spread his legs apart, nodding at her to do the same, before guiding her over the fire. He tightened his grip on her hands and forced her to squat over the fire, waiting for the steam to dampen her private parts, as she intermittently wriggled at the intense heat.

The Bomoh gazed into Toh's eyes, held a hand in front of her face and spread two fingers apart before pointing between her legs, indicating that she should do likewise to her private parts—he wanted the steam to enter her body.

The instant he noticed the dampness between her legs turn a slight pink, he brought the scoop close to her and caught a single drop of her blood. He then stepped back from her, holding the scoop and handed her baju back to her. As Toh dressed, she watched as the Bomoh poured the blood into the rice and spoke:

'Aashif's heart beats as if willed
But soon this food will cause him to be fulfilled.'

The Bomoh glared at Toh and repeated the couplet. Toh recited his words, before the Bomoh rushed through a chant that she was unable to discern.

* * *

As soon as Toh left the cave, she was struck by the absence of the smell that had previously lingered in her nostrils. Contemplating the ordeal that she had just endured, she shook violently.

Abdul passed Toh the reins of her horse, noting the level of her concentration and saying nothing. The return journey was uneventful, and Toh used the quiet to reflect on what the Bomoh had said as he stirred her blood into the rice. Ever since her first visit to him, she had tried to memorize what he said and write down his words on her return to the palace. She had little difficulty recalling his verse; what troubled her was his chant, which he had reeled off at such a pace that she could not make out what he was saying. She concluded that she was not expected to do so, but there were words in there she believed to be important. One of them was semangat, which meant the spirit of the trees. Time and again, the Bomoh called upon such spirits. She recalled how he had called to Aashif: 'Come and sleep by Princess Toh and share her pillow.'

When they eventually reached the palace grounds, Toh glanced skywards and noticed a brahminy kite. Looking in wonder at the great spread of its chestnut-brown wings, she questioned if it might not be the Bomoh's famed homing bird.

Chapter 36

The wind was unrelenting as they made their way down. Noticing Fatima's concern, Aashif shouted to her over the gusts, 'It's because we're exposed to the elements.'

'It will be nice to be surrounded by trees,' she replied, her voice unsteady.

Aashif peered at the mass of green stretching out below. Each time he glanced back to check on Fatima, he surreptitiously looked behind her to make sure they were not being followed.

Aashif tried to imagine the actions of a search party. He was certain that Anwar would be leading it—he had observed the guard closely during their journey to the shack of the murdered slave and noticed how well-acquainted he was with the jungle.

'Is everything all right?' Fatima asked.

'Fine,' he lied, determined to cover his anxiety.

'You seem to be checking on me even more often than usual.'

'That's because I enjoy looking at you.'

'You're a fool,' she laughed.

They carried on until they came upon two enormous fig trees. Fatima watched as Aashif unstrung his bag before ordering her to step back. Then he flung his axe into the sky and watched a bunch of figs tumble to the ground, followed by the axe.

'That's some skill.'

'I'll bring down some bananas soon, and also some coconuts—we need them for the oil as much as the flesh.'

Fatima shook her head in awe of Aashif's knowledge.

'Let's rest awhile,' he suggested, helping her to release her bag. They sat side by side on the bags and ate the figs.

'Aashif, will we ever go back to Perak, do you think?'

Aashif paused. 'I hope I can return when I am a free man. I would like to see Hisham again.'

When Fatima beamed, he understood that it was the answer she wanted.

'I'd also love to find my father and to introduce him to Hisham.'

'Maybe Toh will one day find it in her heart to forgive me, to forgive us both. Then I, too, could return.'

Aashif said, 'Whatever my dreams, they would never be fulfilled without you at my side.'

Fatima leant towards him, and they kissed.

'An even better dream would be if we could befriend the Bomoh and have him make an elixir so that we could live together forever,' she said.

Fatima recalled the Raja claiming in a conversation with Princess Toh that the Bomoh had an inner eye, which allowed him to see ahead clearly. She wondered whether the Bomoh could be watching them now. 'Will they send more than one search party, do you think?'

'I doubt it,' Aashif hesitated, 'they'd only trip over each other looking for us.'

After a short silence, Fatima spoke again, 'What was your mother like?'

'All I can remember about her is that she was beautiful.'

Fatima struggled with the thought that she would never be able to understand the violence that Aashif had witnessed being done to his mother. There was a strength to his expression that reassured her, and he told her how he was reminded of his mother's face when he saw Fatima in her green baju.

'As a slave, I will never be at peace until I'm able to visit my homeland and pray before my mother's grave.'

Fatima could not bring herself to look into his face. She sat silently and waited for him to move when an image of Toh came to her. For a second, they were both in their own worlds, until Aashif slapped his thighs. 'Right, time to move on.'

They helped each other string their bags across their shoulders. 'Ready?' Aashif asked.

'Ready,' she replied.

Aashif resumed pounding the ground, while keeping his eyes peeled for any movement in the foliage. When they were some way into their descent, he noticed a new sound and stopped suddenly.

'What's wrong?'

'Shush.' He concentrated hard, before a smile formed on his face.

'It sounds like a waterfall.'

'We'll finally be able to wash!'

As they continued, Fatima became impatient to find the water. Aashif hoped that Fatima had failed to notice that he had gathered speed—he could tell that they were falling behind the necessary pace. He did not want to alarm Fatima, nor did he want to give Anwar any advantage.

In his haste, he stumbled over the roots of a tree and fell into two saplings, bringing them to the ground.

'Aashif!' Fatima screamed.

He pushed himself up and grimaced at his own stupidity. 'I'm all right,' he rushed, 'my own fault.'

'Maybe we should slow down.'

Saying nothing, Aashif brushed himself clean, relieved that his axe was lying on the ground in front of him.

They stood staring at each other. 'Listen,' Aashif said.

They both heard the sound of rushing water, and Fatima smiled. But then, as if to deliberately thwart their efforts to reach the water, the jungle became denser, slowing their progress.

'Can you come closer while I hack through these plants?' Aashif said. 'And make sure you keep an eye out for any flowers; they could be poisonous.' Closed in by thick trees that loomed over them, he was startled when he stepped into a sunlit clearing. In front of him was an oasis surrounded by trees; water flowed from a ledge above him and cascaded into a pool below.

* * *

The water glistened as Fatima stood and took in the dazzling scene. The prospect of standing naked in front of Aashif made her feel nervous, but she concluded that it was a small price to pay to be clean again. She sensed him looking at her.

'I'll turn away while you undress and wash,' he said tactfully.

'No—I'd prefer that you keep watch.'

They were silent, and Fatima wondered whether she might drape her blanket over herself. She recognized, however, that she could hardly do so after she'd washed —it would get soaked.

'I thought maybe . . . '

She undid the string of her bag and rummaged inside, withdrew her soap, and giggled. 'I'm less afraid of you seeing me naked than of you not keeping a watch on me.'

She felt a fresh flutter of tension in her stomach, but then noticed his awkwardness and a tiny sting pierced her heart. 'Kiss me,' she said, closing the gap between them. He kissed her on the lips, and it was her turn to feel awkward. She stepped away from him and removed her clothes, before rushing to the water's edge. She dipped her toes into the pool, shuddered, and jumped in, before gasping loudly, 'It's freezing.'

She rubbed the soap into her body as she gradually adjusted to the temperature. 'Come in!' she called.

* * *

Bewildered, Aashif had never imagined that the female form could be so beautiful. Flushed with confusion, he came to understand that his bouts of discomfort had actually been a deep longing.

A ray of sunlight struck the water, making its surface glimmer. Aashif watched Fatima sink into its depths; when she re-emerged, he imagined her being embraced by the clean air. The sight of her body moving this way and that captivated him. She called out to him a second time and his heart bounded as he slowly removed his clothes until he finally stood naked.

Overwhelmed by embarrassment, he covered his groin with his hands and leapt into the water. Unsure what to do next, he waded across to her and noted that she was staring at him, her eyes alive with excitement. She laughed and held out the bar of soap. 'Wash my back for me,' she said, turning around.

He took the soap from her and brought it to her flesh, his breath ragged with nerves.

'Harder, please.'

Afraid that he might become aroused, he ensured that his body did not touch hers and concentrated on breathing steadily.

'Thank you. Now I'll do yours.'

Unable to speak, he swivelled around and allowed her to rub soap on him. When her hand rested on his back, he could not stop himself from shuddering.

'Are you cold?'

'No,' he whispered, trying hard to control his breathing.

When she had finished, she handed the soap back to him. As he washed himself, she climbed out of the water and lay down on the thick moss that covered the bank. He rushed to rinse the soap from his body, left the water and sat down close to her. She twisted round and smiled at him, before stretching an arm across to him encouraging him to edge towards her. Their lips met, and he felt an ache in the pit of his stomach. Her hands stroked his back, and he did the same to hers. His touch grew more assured, and he drew her to him, so breathless that he was unable to speak. He pushed her on to her back and caressed her body. He tenderly massaged the moist area between her legs, looking into her eyes and attempting to demonstrate the depth of his love. He gradually parted her legs, and her eyes were slightly glazed as he rested himself on top of her, ensuring he kept his weight off her body. He slowly entered her, and she clasped him tight, releasing a little groan.

Chapter 37

Toh found herself reliving a recurring nightmare. While the rest of court slept, she was cowering against a tree trunk in the jungle, unable to see anything except the menace in her attacker's eyes.

He sniggered scornfully and leant over her before blowing air into one ear and then the other. She swung her arms at him wildly, but it was all in vain—it was like fighting off a shadow. She must have passed out; it felt like she was being lifted off her feet. When she blinked, she found herself alone with her attacker in a long dormitory.

Please, she begged, her voice too small to be heard even by the rats that scurried around on the floor. She was naked, but she could not recall losing her clothes. She was lying on the bed with her legs apart; when she felt his manhood pushing against her, she began to cry. Then, all of a sudden, she had a sense that she was Fatima, and she sat up with a jolt. Glancing about her room, she allowed her mind to settle.

Dazed, she eased herself from under the covers and climbed out of bed. She stepped into her slippers, put on her housecoat, and walked outside, where she nearly walked into one of the many looking glasses. She reached the staircase and Abdul bowed to her.

'I didn't hear the cockerel this morning.'

'It's nearly lunchtime, Your Highness.'

Toh blinked. 'I was tired when we got back.'

Abdul smiled.

'Where's Dato Hamidi?'

'He left the palace sometime ago, Your Highness.'

Relieved, she nodded her appreciation for Abdul before wandering along the corridor and up the stairs to the throne room. She went to the window and looked out at the tidy gardens below, but as her mind settled into the day ahead, her thoughts were distracted by a shriek echoing in the sky. It looked like the Bomoh's bird, its white and chestnut-coloured plumage beautiful against the blue sky. As the bird flew in large circles, her mind recalled the tale her father told her of how the Bomoh had spent years training his birds to undertake deeds on his behalf. 'His favourite bird is the brahminy kite,' he had said. 'Goodness knows why—they don't fly great distances, but he insists that he can train them best.'

She swung round at the sound of someone entering the room, to find her husband staring at her.

'You've decided to grace us with your presence?'

She looked at him with contempt, her nightmare rushing back at her. She realized that there was little point in talking to him and resumed her study of the kite, which disappeared over the top of the jungle.

'I see that your little brat and her boy have still not been captured.'

The memory of being naked before the Bomoh reminded her of how much she had sacrificed in her quest to have Fatima return, actions that she placed squarely on her husband's shoulders. She glowered at him and watched as he stood with his arms crossed. 'If the boy has Anwar to contend with, I've little doubt he will be put to the sword.'

Toh recalled Suraya's assurance that Fatima and Aashif were in love, and she crumpled at the thought of Fatima's distress over such an event. Only the existence of the two letters she had told Anwar to deliver to Fatima kept her emotions in check. Hard though she tried, she could not keep her fury hidden, and she glared at her husband.

'Ha!' the Dato scoffed. 'She'll probably offer herself to Anwar to save her ignorant slave's life. I certainly wouldn't put it past her, given how she behaved towards me.'

Toh looked him up and down derisively.

'You think it would only be Anwar? What about your first two husbands?' he jeered. 'You honestly believe that little brat didn't provoke them, too?'

Toh stormed to the doorway and shouted down to her servant, 'Abdul, fetch Shaz—and make sure he brings his slate and some chalk.'

Spite gnawed away at Toh, and she smirked at her husband, eager to see how he reacted when Shaz entered. Unbeknownst to Dato Hamidi, Toh had been keeping a careful watch on his activities—thanks to the help of Abdul and his fellow guards.

The Dato scowled at her, readying himself for another verbal onslaught. Despite his deafness, Toh shouted at him, letting him see her anger. At first, she did not acknowledge Abdul and Shaz, but then she stepped aside and gave them space to stand before her. As she did this, she took pleasure in seeing the confidence drain from Dato Hamidi's face.

She turned to Shaz. 'Your slate and chalk? Pass them to the guard.'

Shaz did as instructed, and then Toh raised her arm and pointed her finger at the doorway to dismiss him. She was resolved to demonstrate to her husband the full extent of her authority.

Dato Hamidi sniggered the scornful laugh that had featured in her nightmare and she stiffened.

'Abdul, I take it you can write?'

'Yes, Your Highness.'

'Then write down these words,' she continued, watching the flow of his hand as she dictated to him. Abdul's eyes bulged as he heard what he was to write. 'Now show it to my husband.'

The Dato looked at the slate, scarcely able to believe his eyes: 'I'm preparing a report for the Raja. Where were you on the day of the young female slave's murder? And do you have any witnesses to vouch for your movements?'

* * *

Anwar woke to the usual sounds of the jungle. He dusted himself down and was surprised to discover that unlike Osmin and Farouk, Haron was already awake.

'When did you wake, lad?'

'A while ago.'

Anwar stared at him.

'I'm not used to sleeping on the ground.'

Anwar gathered up his possessions and resolved to ensure the lad spent a couple of weeks outdoors when they returned to the palace, to acclimatize him to the elements.

A bank of thick dark clouds had appeared on the horizon, and Anwar feared that a storm would hamper their progress. Eager to set off early, he nudged Farouk awake with his foot and ordered Haron to wake Osmin.

Anwar ignored Osmin's tetchiness at being woken up and he ordered them to get ready—they would eat in the saddle.

As the morning wore on, Anwar became increasingly irritated by the banter between his men. The more Haron moaned about Aashif, the more Anwar concluded that the lad was not warrior material—he was too frivolous and lacking in discipline. He wished he could send him packing, but he feared Haron would get lost; he was simply going to have to tolerate him for the time being.

To give Farouk some respite from Haron and Osmin's chatter, he ordered him to take the lead. A couple of miles later, Farouk's horse whinnied and reared above the foliage. Farouk was a skilled horseman and managed to settle the animal before dismounting and drawing his sword. Anwar and the other two did the same.

'A snake?' Anwar asked.

'I don't think so.'

All four men peered at the ground, searching for something that would explain the animal's behaviour.

'There,' Osmin said, pointing at an animal's footprint, partially covered by a cluster of leaves. Farouk swept the leaves aside with his sword and studied the print. He searched the foliage for others, before jumping up with a start. There were several other prints, one of which was far smaller than the others. 'A weretiger,' he spluttered.

'Have any of you ever been this way before?' Farouk asked.

'Are you thinking what I'm thinking?' Anwar asked. 'Might there be a tiger town somewhere around here?'

Haron flung a hand to his mouth, ashen-faced.

'Control yourself,' Anwar barked at him.

All four men were familiar with the tales of tiger-folk that were said to live in human form in the heart of the jungle, only transforming into tigers when they left their enclosure.

'Sir, we must go back,' Osmin said desperately. 'The foliage around here is stricken with death.'

Anwar scowled. 'Keep your mouth shut and get a grip on yourself, man—and if I ever hear such superstitious nonsense again, you'll be sure to feel the heat of my sword.'

Anwar ordered his men to get back on their horses before leading them through an area that was wild with thick foliage. They all became mesmerized at the sight of large spiders spinning their webs in the undergrowth.

Anwar noticed that the shrubbery was gleaming, despite the heavy overhang of dark trees. He threw his hand up and brought his men to a halt, before turning round in his saddle. 'The place is crawling with slugs,' he said. The highly venomous molluscs were spilling their slime all over the vegetation, causing it to shine.

Haron was leaning over the side of his horse and Anwar shouted at him angrily, 'What's the problem now?'

'Sorry, sir—something slimy has gotten into my boot.'

'Take that boot off and wash away the slime.'

Haron tried to do as commanded, before encountering a problem. 'I don't have enough water,' he eventually said.

Anwar passed his container to Farouk, who passed it down the line. 'You'd better give him your container too, Farouk—and tell Osmin to do the same. He must get rid of the slime before it's too late.'

After several minutes, Haron sat upright. 'Done,' he called out cheerfully.

Anwar glanced at Farouk, who shook his head. 'Not warrior material, I fear, sir,' he said.

'No, he's a damned fool,' Anwar said. 'We can't afford these silly incidents. They all mount up—and before you know it, the two slaves will have got away.'

Anwar sighed. 'Now, listen to me,' he growled, sufficiently loud enough that they could all hear him above the noise of the insects. 'Make sure that none of that slime comes into contact with your horses. Hack the leaves away if you must, but make sure that none of it touches your skin.'

'I hear Aashif can be a formidable fighter. What will you do when we catch him?' Farouk asked Anwar.

'Well, that all depends on his actions,' the older man replied.

Chapter 38

When word reached the Bomoh that Aashif and Fatima had dared to pass through the graveyard of the unknown warriors, he was able to work out the way they were travelling. Over the past few days, he had spent many hours standing more or less in the same spot, training his brahminy kite. A short distance behind him were two human-sized figures moulded out of soil. He crushed coal into dust and used it to coat one of the figures.

He stepped to the side, blew a tin whistle that pierced the air and he stood with his arm outstretched, protected by a thick leather sleeve. Before long, the bird appeared above the treetops and swooped down to rest on its master's arm. It carried in its beak a small parcel: rice wrapped in banana leaf. When the bird had landed, the Bomoh strolled across to the dust-covered figure and waited for it to drop the parcel. He would have to replenish the stock of fish in the cauldron in front of the figures soon, he thought—the bird was allowed one as a reward each time it successfully completed a task.

* * *

Since the day that the spears had rained on Aashif and Fatima, they had followed the route of the river, but the sun had taken its toll, and they lay resting on a patch of grass by the riverbank.

Fatima's eyes were shut tight against the sun's glare while Aashif rested on his elbow, staring at her. He wondered what might be going through her head. Since they had first made love, they had repeated the act each night. He would have liked to lie with her now, but he did not want to disturb her.

He spotted her eyes flickering, 'Are you awake?'

'It's so peaceful here,' she said, staring up at the sky.

She rolled around and faced him, her eyes sparkling, 'What are you thinking?'

'I was daydreaming.'

'Anything interesting?'

'So many memories have come back to me since the day before we left.' She sat up, suddenly serious.

'I was thinking about when I was a young boy. My mother was chasing after me, threatening to throw me into the water. I was laughing hysterically. Then my father joined us and pretended to protect me from my mother.'

'You've never had these memories before?'

'No—they only began when I saw you in your green baju.' He gazed at her.

'Do you think your father would like me?'

Aashif laughed clumsily, 'Like you? He'd worship you.'

Fatima broke his reverie. 'I'm hungry,' she said. 'What I wouldn't give for a bowl of rice, some rendang ayam, and some purple jantung pisang.'

'And maybe then we could share some of Suraya's coconut cakes,' he teased.

He pushed himself up and picked up his bag. 'Maybe I'll try and catch a wild chicken—we could roast it on a fire.'

'Would that be safe?' Fatima asked.

'We'll see,' he said.

'Well, at least we can enjoy the jantung pisang.'

They had only progressed a few feet from the clearing when they discovered themselves on the side of the mountain, with a view of a vista of trees. Aashif stood and mapped their route with his hand. 'See that?' he said, pointing. 'Smoke.'

Fatima followed his gaze but could only see treetops. She ran her eyes along the line of his outstretched arm but still failed to spot the smoke.

'Could it be a search party?' she asked, suddenly tense.

'No—that would mean they were ahead of us.'

'Maybe it's a small kampung,' she suggested.

'If it is, I'll tell them we're slaves from Mecca and returning home.'

They said little on the way down, but then Fatima spotted something.

'Look at that,' she said, pointing out a brahminy kite gliding over the trees.

'There,' Aashif said. 'See the smoke, where the bird is circling?'

She shook her head, 'All I can see are the trees.'

'Let's keep moving.'

'Is it safe?'

'I think so. If it was a large village, there would be more smoke.'

When they finally reached the place where Aashif calculated a fire had been burning, it was mid-afternoon. They zigzagged through the trees, keeping as close to the river as they could. Then, without warning, they came upon a small pemburu pondok.

'What is it?' Fatima asked.

The sun was bursting through the trees as Aashif glanced at Fatima. 'It reminds me of the shack where that poor girl died—except this one is on stilts.'

They approached the hut slowly. In front of it was a small cauldron of rice over a smouldering fire. He guessed from the aroma that it had been mixed with banana leaves. He peered about, expecting someone to appear. He called out, but there was no response. He walked up the steps to the entrance, with Fatima following close behind. As they entered the hut, their ears were filled by the call of a bird. Fatima looked at the sky and noticed a soaring brahminy kite.

The ground outside the hut had been cleared of foliage. The cauldron sat in the centre, and under the hut there was a pile of earth.

'What does it all mean?' Fatima asked.

'It's common to find shacks like this dotted throughout the jungle. Some of them have a cauldron nearby where hunters can cook.' He continued examining their surroundings, 'Something must have disturbed whoever was cooking.'

'What about the earth under the hut?'

'Many people believe that earth spirits live directly underneath villages. The spirits are thought to guard homes from storms, and clay is placed under huts to protect the spirits.'

Fatima tugged at the sleeve of her baju. 'Doesn't the idea of spirits frighten you?'

'No,' Aashif scoffed. 'There's no truth to it—it's just hocus pocus. According to Hisham, it's just a ploy to discourage people from using the huts.' He looked around and saw that it was getting dark, 'We should stay here for the night.'

'But won't the owner come back for his rice?'

'It's getting late. Besides, there's nothing else here—whoever it was clearly took off in a hurry.'

They approached the cauldron and Fatima's eyes widened at the sight of the rice. 'I'm starving,' she admitted.

'Let me forage for something to eat with it.'

'Don't leave me,' she pleaded.

'Come and stand by the edge of the trees. If you lose sight of me, shout.'

Fatima felt agitated as she glanced between the cauldron and Aashif moving among the trees. A couple of minutes later he returned, carrying two coconuts, a handful of leafy *kalian*, and a couple of large banana leaves.

She sat silently as he prepared the food when a shiver passed through her.

'Something's upsetting the trees,' she said, not wanting to show her fear.

'There are lots of pockets of wind in the jungle,' he said nonchalantly.

She watched as he chopped the tops off the coconuts, poured their milk into a container, opened the shells, and worked the flesh free, before stirring it into the rice. He added the vegetables into the pot and stirred. Then he scooped a portion of the mixture with his axe on to a banana leaf and handed it to Fatima.

'At your service,' he said, and watched her eat.

'Good?' he asked, with a smile of encouragement.

'Wonderful,' she managed, through a mouthful of food, while Aashif looked on.

After a while, he noticed her studying their surroundings.

'I need to pee,' she said.

'Go behind the hut.'

'No,' she said, worried at what she might meet there. 'I'll go here.'

She stepped away from Aashif and crouched down. As she was facing the hut, a terrible dread swamped her at the prospect of spending the night there. She quivered violently at the tragic plight of the slave girl, who had suffered in a similar setting. Despite Aashif's attempts to reassure her, she found herself spooked every time she noticed a movement among the trees.

In the distance, the threat of a storm grew, and Aashif jumped to his feet. 'We're lucky to have found this place. We'll be well protected if a storm comes.'

As they strolled back up the steps, Fatima felt like her sanity was being violated—she couldn't stop thinking about the terror the slave girl must have faced. In the confined space, she imagined the walls being torn open to accommodate her small bed. She stared at the floor sceptically, refusing to allow herself to think about what might be underneath it, when a vision of Toh came to her. She remembered the princess tucking her in when they slept apart and allowed herself to be comforted by the memory.

Chapter 39

It had taken Shafie three days to reach the village, and he was into his second day of waiting. Upon his arrival, he had been told that the chief had left just an hour before. Nobody knew where he had gone, and he had not returned the previous day, as expected.

He stood alone on the top of the hill and gazed out over the trees below. The chief's house dominated the scene, standing apart from the longhouses that formed the kampung. He refused to think about what might go on in there, recalling the sight of the young girl who had stepped on to the terrace when they had first arrived at the village. She hadn't looked older than fifteen, the same age as the eldest of his three sons.

He decided to kill some time by slowly descending towards the village. When he was halfway down, he caught sight of the chief and a handful of men returning, and his mood lifted. Among the group, he spotted a man with his arms tied behind his back and started to walk more quickly. When he reached the village, he was disgusted to see two young girls stepping from the *rumah* on to the terrace.

Shafie was joined by his warriors, and they marched up to the chief while he tried to hide his contempt. A snarl formed on the chief's face, 'Where's your commander?'

'My colleague,' Shafie replied, 'is engaged on another assignment.'

The chief glared at Shafie, narrowing his stare, but Shafie was in no mood to appease a man who seemed to find pleasure in abusing young girls. He walked up to the man who had his arms bound behind his back, 'Who is this man?'

'My prisoner,' growled the chief.

'And his offence?'

'Abduction. I have yet to conclude my interrogation of him.'

Shafie's grabbed the chief's arm and snarled, 'My colleague is on duty at the Raja's behest, and so am I.' He tightened his grip. 'My men and I have been here for two days, waiting to interview you. You would do well to cooperate, otherwise I'll take you to the Raja and you can explain yourself in person. Which is it to be?'

The chief glanced around and noticed that the whole village was watching, before forcing a smile, 'A misunderstanding. He's your prisoner now.'

Shafie released his grip. 'Splendid—I'm glad that we understand each other.' He looked up at the two young girls standing on the terrace. 'I'll use your rumah for a short period to question the prisoner.'

'Of course.' The chief ushered the two girls away, telling them to return only when he called for them.

Shafie ordered two of his men to wait on the steps, while he led the four other warriors into the house, followed by the prisoner.

Shafie was struck by the neatness of the chief's home until he noticed the bed, which was covered in a messy pile of sheets and rumpled pillows. He ordered his men to stand guard by the windows and door and sat the prisoner on a stool in the centre of the room. The man looked dazed.

In an effort to absolve himself of any blame for the dead slave's murder, the chief had told Shafie that the prisoner was her chief and had accompanied the girl to her death.

Shafie bent low before the man and leant into his face. 'Who did you meet at that shack?'

The prisoner stared back at Shafie, who tapped him gently on the head. 'Who?' he repeated through gritted teeth.

'He was wearing a mask. I met him as I was leaving and handed him the key. He identified himself by showing his badge. I only locked her in, and then I left,' he whimpered.

'Why was she left there?'

'She was to lie with that chief,' he stuttered.

'The kampung chief who's outside?'

'Yes, but she refused.'

'And then what happened?'

'The chief ordered me to arrange for her to be taken to the shack and punished.'

'So, you punished her?'

'No. The chief told me to say I did, but I didn't.' He began to tremble violently, 'He told me that if I did not lie to you, my two young daughters would be taken into slavery. I promised my wife I would save our girls—but all I did was lock her in the shack.'

'And you would not recognize the man who was wearing the mask?'

The prisoner shook his head. 'No.'

'Could it have been the chief himself?'

'No. As you've seen for yourself, he's a large man.'

* * *

Toh was so agitated that she struggled to speak clearly, 'Every morning, I wake up drained by this recurring nightmare, plagued by the memory of seeing Fatima's hand on my husband's manhood. It is as if my thoughts are controlling me. During the course of the day, I find myself greeted by the sound of Aashif's singing voice coming to me through my window, before it is broken by the call of a bird. I try so hard to keep these images in my mind, but something constantly seems to torture me for my actions. I am exhausted by the fear of losing her. Then the pain of missing her takes over, and by the time I'm ready to go to sleep, it is dawn and I'm still awake. Maybe it is the turmoil I've carried through the day that finally releases me. I constantly ask myself what I could have done differently. By far the worst thing is the image the Dato implanted in my mind of Fatima being raped—it's tearing me apart.'

Toh began to cry. Desperate to maintain her composure, she spoke tersely, 'Please, Bomoh, you must help me.'

The Bomoh stared at her as she continued, 'Has the rice been delivered?'

He gave her a curt nod, without looking at her.

'Then surely by now it has been eaten?'

At this, the Bomoh spoke:

'The spirits of the trees witness matters clear,
The rice is devoured, so there is nothing to fear.'

Toh glared at the shaman, full of despair. If only he would speak in a manner she could understand, she thought, she might be able to see past his ugliness. 'In that case, it should not be long before Aashif experiences a yearning for me. Correct?'

He nodded once again and suddenly sat up.

'The love spirit must now be provoked,
To ensure his powers are finally invoked.'

The Bomoh retreated into the dark, leaving Toh alone with the rats and bats. 'Where are you?' she called out to him.

When the Bomoh reappeared, she noticed that he was carrying a cane and was worried that he was about to strike her. Instead of returning to his seat, the Bomoh stood in the light, allowing his shadow to fall on the cave wall. He began chanting words she failed to decipher, before striking his shadow with the cane three times and waving for her to leave.

* * *

Anwar and Farouk snatched short periods of broken sleep, while Haron groaned throughout the night and Osmin snored serenely. Their major concern was the smell that was coming from Haron's wound. It would not be long, they feared, before it attracted the attention of the nearby animals.

'I wish I'd made sure he washed off that slime.'

'We aren't here to mother him,' Farouk said quietly.

'Perhaps, but I hate watching him suffer.' Anwar's expression turned to anguish at the sound of Haron's groans.

'I thought I knew all the dangers of the jungle,' Farouk said. 'I was watching the lad carefully—alas, he has not shown sufficient regard for the wild. There are a great many hidden dangers in our midst.' Farouk paused and then went on, 'I gather that Aashif is an expert on our terrain.'

'Yes, he has been well trained by Hisham, and there's no better teacher. But to be frank, I'm just as concerned by Osmin as I am, Haron. In hindsight, I should not have brought the both of them—they're a burden.'

Haron's wound was protected by dock leaves held in place by thin strips of knotted vine. Anwar edged across to him and carefully sliced the vines, letting the leaves fall away. Both men were shocked at the extent of the wound. 'His foot's rotting away,' Anwar said.

Haron hadn't flinched. 'The spirit inside him is dead,' Farouk whispered.

Anwar applied a fresh dressing to the wound, being careful not to come into contact with the soiled leaves.

'Clearly, he must be taken back to the palace,' Anwar said.

'But do you think he's fit to travel?'

'He'll have to be, and his wound will have to be treated regularly on the way.'

Anwar touched Haron's brow to check for a fever. 'There's a fire inside him.'

'We might have to tie him to his horse,' Farouk said.

'Wake that irritating man up,' Anwar said gruffly, pointing towards Osmin.

Farouk nudged Osmin with his foot until the man awoke. 'Osmin,' Anwar said sharply, 'Haron's condition has been deteriorating and he has to be taken back to the palace for treatment.'

Osmin brushed his hands over his face while Anwar explained the dilemma facing them.

'As soon as it is light, you must set back for the palace with Haron.'

Alarm spread across Osmin's face as he considered the task. 'What if he falls off his horse?'

Anwar turned to Farouk. 'You must go too, Farouk—you'll have to ride two to a horse. Take the reins from under Haron's arms so you can hold him up and change places regularly to counter tiredness.'

'What about you?' Farouk asked.

'I shall go on alone. All being well, I should be able to arrest Aashif and Fatima before they escape these lands.'

Anwar witnessed Osmin's relief at the prospect of being accompanied but said nothing. Instead, he walked over to Haron, withdrew his badge from his possessions, and tied it securely around his neck.

* * *

One of Shafie's guards came crashing into the chief's house. 'A great crowd of men have appeared,' he said.

Shafie turned to face the prisoner, 'Where's your wife?'

The prisoner stalled.

'Where is she?' Shafie shouted.

He hesitated, 'I sent her away.'

'And your daughters?'

The man stared at Shafie.

'Are they safe?'

The prisoner nodded.

'Good. You're coming with us—you'll be safer that way.'

Shafie and his men went outside, the prisoner following behind.

The chief was at the front of the crowd. Shafie called down to him, 'Have some of your men bring our horses.' When the chief failed to respond, Shafie snarled at him, 'I'm taking this prisoner to face the Raja—unless you'd prefer for me to fetch the Raja here?' When the chief remained silent, Shafie continued, 'This man has admitted his crime, and the Raja will determine his punishment.'

At this, the chief ordered the man beside him to fetch the horses, and the prisoner nudged his way through the warriors. When he reached the front of the crowd, a bolt whistled through the air and struck him on the forehead, causing him to crumple to the ground, dead.

'The Raja's work has been done for him, it would seem,' the chief said, smiling.

Chapter 40

Aashif woke to find himself alone. Noticing that Fatima's bag was gone, he leapt to his feet and dashed to the opening. Fatima was crouched on the ground outside and called up to him, 'Good morning.'

His heart soared at her presence. 'I'm so sorry. I must have fallen asleep straight away last night.'

'You did.'

'What are you doing?'

'I'm clearing up some spilt rice.'

She looked tired and he asked her if she had slept.

'Not much.'

'You should have woken me.'

'You were in a deep sleep; I didn't want to disturb you.'

'I wish you had.' He enjoyed sleeping next to her and was disappointed at the thought of what he had missed. 'I hope I didn't snore?'

'No more than an occasional moan or groan.'

'Fatima, I'm more accustomed to this jungle than you are. Please wake me next time. It's important that you get enough sleep—it will help you stay alert.'

The morning sun sprung out from behind a cloud and cast light on her face. 'For someone who hasn't slept much, you look good.'

'Then you must see me after a night in a comfortable bed.'

She leant towards him, and they embraced. Aashif eventually released her. 'Let me help you clear up,' he said. 'Then we'll have something to eat and be on our way.'

He noticed her looking at the gap between the hut and the ground. 'Did it trouble you, sleeping in the hut?'

'I prefer our own shelter—I feel safe knowing that it was built by you and that there are no spirits to annoy us.'

It was while they were washing by the stream that Aashif spoke, a little self-consciously, 'Did I shout in my sleep?'

'Yes, a couple of times.'

'I hope I didn't scare you.'

'You startled me, but I wasn't scared. It seemed like something was upsetting you.'

Aashif grimaced, 'I've been suffering from nightmares for a few years.'

'Your mother?'

'Yes. What did I do?'

'Aashif, anybody who suffered as you did would have nightmares.'

'How did you manage to pacify me?'

'I kissed you on the cheek and you fell back to sleep straight away.'

Aashif turned Fatima around, and they kissed. She remained in his arms and stood motionless, unable to stop looking at the foliage next to them. She managed to suppress a shiver. 'We'd better get dressed,' she said.

'Maybe we should speed up a little.'

'Do you think we'll be caught?'

'No, but the sooner we can escape the jungle, the less danger we'll face.'

* * *

It was as they were setting off that Fatima was suddenly struck by the thought of Princess Toh. They were walking side by side and Aashif turned to her, 'Do you think Princess Toh will be angry with you?'

Fatima looked at him, surprised, 'What brought Princess Toh into your head?'

Aashif shrugged.

'I'm sure she will. After all, we've been close all our lives, and I deserted her.'

'Maybe when she considers the situation carefully, she'll realize that she treated you wrongly.'

Fatima had been constantly worrying about Toh. 'Knowing her as I do, I'm sure she'll be regretting her actions.'

'She has always struck me as being a fair-minded person, which makes her behaviour towards you so much harder to understand.'

'You like her, don't you?' she asked.

'Yes, I suppose I do,' he said. 'She must be so unhappy with that dreadful man who screams and shouts at her all day long. It can't have been easy for you, living alongside them.'

Fatima had been trying to ease her hurt and talking about Toh seemed to help. A smile formed on her lips, 'For a long time, she and I were happy. I remember her insisting that we always dressed properly before we went for a stroll. It was important to her to present herself tidily.'

Aashif noticed that Fatima's attention had wandered, and he waited for her to continue.

'I used to love wandering around with her, without a care in the world.'

'I don't think I've ever actually spoken to her.'

'Well, she and I loved to listen to you sing.'

Aashif turned to Fatima with a jolt, 'What do you mean?'

'A couple of times, we heard you singing at night.'

Aashif flushed, 'Where?'

'Underneath one of the palace windows.'

Aashif pulled a face.

'You have a beautiful singing voice.'

He was embarrassed and changed the subject, 'Someone should stop the Dato from shouting at her. The slaves were always talking about how violent he was.'

'She decided that she liked you when she saw you being interrogated by her brother. She said he was too harsh on you.'

'I didn't enjoy being questioned by him. Maybe if I'd known she liked me, I might have done better.'

'She was going to invite you to sing for us.'

Aashif's face lit up, 'I doubt I'd have had the nerve.'

'Not even for me?' she teased.

'You're different.'

Fatima spoke quietly, suddenly concerned, 'Aashif, someone's watching us.'

'I've noticed. It's a dusky leaf monkey. They're quite dark, with huge eyes. Don't worry—they're such docile animals.'

'That's a relief.'

'Maybe Princess Toh could train one to screech at the Dato every time he shouts at her?'

* * *

'Not again,' Fatima muttered to herself. In the past few days, she'd taken to drinking less water to stop her from having to empty her bladder so often. She was thoroughly miserable at the thought of having to hide behind yet another tree. She especially hated having to go when Aashif was standing nearby. She focused her attention on a tall tree ahead and struggled to hide her annoyance when she admitted to Aashif that she needed to pee again.

'You go on,' he said, 'and give me a call when you're ready.'

She hurried forward, stepped behind the tree, and hitched up her clothes, nearly losing her footing on the uneven surface in her haste. She guessed that the leaves under her feet were covering loose twigs and stones.

Once she had relieved herself, she was tidying her clothes when she stumbled forward and stubbed her toe, 'Ouch.'

She kicked her foot and her heart seemed to stop beating—her foot was embedded in a human skull, where the mouth would have been. Shrieking, she tried to shake her foot free.

Aashif caught up with Fatima in time to watch her crash to the ground, disturbing a pile of human bones in the process. He prised the skull lose from her foot and flung it to the ground, before leading her away from the tree and holding her in his arms. She was trembling and he tightened his embrace.

Her voice thickened, 'What happened?'

As Aashif looked up at the tree, it dawned on him what a terrible mistake he had made allowing her to go anywhere near it. It was an *Ipoh* tree and poisonous.

'I'm so sorry—I should never have allowed you to go anywhere near this tree. The sap can kill if it gets under the skin.'

Fatima stared into his face, close to tears.

'It drops its lower branches as it grows, meaning that it has a completely bare trunk,' he explained. 'Criminals who are condemned to death are offered the chance to live if they are able to climb the tree.' He grimaced, 'But those who fail fall to their death and are left to rot. I should have remembered,' he said, taking her in his arms.

Fatima stiffened, 'Not now.'

The atmosphere between them remained cold until they entered a plateau similar to the one where they had first rested on their way up the mountain.

'We should stop here for a while,' he said, gazing down at the valley below and turning to her. 'Will you be all right on your own while I do some foraging?'

Small tears trickled down Fatima's face. 'I'm so sorry,' she stuttered. 'I got such a fright.'

'I promised to keep you safe. I should have been more attentive.'

* * *

When they had eaten some coconut and a few figs, Aashif attended to the mosquito repellent. Fatima hated the stickiness of it on her skin, but she did not complain—the mosquitos were far more bothersome. Nonetheless, it was messy, and the strain of not being able to keep herself clean was beginning to annoy her. On top of that stress, she was unable to stop thinking about Toh.

They had reached a thicket of trees, and Aashif advised Fatima to go ahead, while keeping a close watch on her.

It was when they were making careful progress through the trees that Aashif identified some freshly broken branches. As he peered around furtively, his attention was suddenly captured by large tracks on the ground. He bent low for a closer look; he could tell from the prints' appearance that they were fresh. Stooping lower still, he noticed that one of the animal's paws was much smaller than the others. Alarmed, he sprang to his feet—it was a weretiger, according to Hisham, the most dangerous threat in the Malayan jungle.

Aashif made his way towards Fatima, who had stepped from the jungle and into a clearing. As she turned around to speak to him, she caught the sound of her name being whispered, 'Fa-ti-ma, Fa-ti-ma.' She stood terrified as all around her, the leaves quivered ferociously.

Chapter 41

Shafie was thinking about how he might return to the village with reinforcements to arrest the chief. At Anwar's earlier command, they were on the way to the palace. When they reached the river and the location of the slave girl's murder, they diverged from the path, eventually arriving at the kampung where the villager Zainuddin lived.

At their arrival, the chief and his villagers appeared and greeted them with great enthusiasm. Shafie and the chief introduced themselves to each other, and before long they were sitting among the villagers, enjoying a hearty meal.

'I'd like to meet Zainuddin and explain our plan.'

'I see no reason why not, but on one condition. You promise not to unsettle him?'

'I can assure you that I won't.'

'Then follow me.'

The chief rose, and Shafie followed, along with two of his warriors.

'We've moved him and his family into the centre of the village for their own protection,' the chief explained.

Children were playing noisily, but they fell silent at the sight of Shafie and his men when they approached. As he took in the serious stares of the children who now stood to attention, Shafie was reminded of his own sons. The chief climbed the steps to the property and disappeared for a moment, before emerging with a tense-looking woman and a man with cloud-white hair.

The chief led Zainuddin down the steps and introduced him to Shafie, while his wife watched on anxiously. 'He's a pale gentleman, as you can see,' the chief explained to Shafie.

Shafie made a show of greeting Zainuddin, both to demonstrate to his wife that there was nothing to fear and to put him at ease. Taking Zainuddin's hand, he gazed into his frightened eyes.

'I'm here on behalf of the Raja. Your chief told us about your recent encounter in the jungle.'

A wild expression appeared on Zainuddin face and Shafie smiled at him reassuringly. 'You have a handsome family,' he said, 'and one that we will protect.' He withdrew a folded sheet of paper from his pocket. 'This is a valuable drawing,' he explained, opening it and turning to the chief, while ensuring he had Zainuddin's attention. 'It is a diagram of an amulet, drawn for us by an elderly lady of considerable skill,' he went on, thinking of Suraya.

He looked at the chief, 'Do you have a Bomoh in the village?'

'We don't, but there's one not far from here.'

'Splendid. We must ask your most skilful craftsman to make as many amulets as possible and take them to a Bomoh, who will grant them the power to frighten any pontianak that dares to come this way again. Do you have such a craftsman?'

'We do.' The chief turned to the tallest child, 'Zaharah, find Latif and bring him here.'

The girl rushed off and returned accompanied by an old, wrinkled man. Shafie was about to show him the diagram when Latif snatched it from him and studied it closely, a knowing look on his face. He then gave Shafie the ghost of a smile and a wink.

'Can you make two or three amulets for each family?' Shafie asked.

'It will take time,' Latif said.

'Of course,' replied Shafie. 'I plan for a Bomoh to cast a spell over them and give them the necessary mystical powers.'

'I'll attend to that.'

Shafie took hold of Zainuddin's arms, 'You're safe now. Get yourself well.'

* * *

Toh sat by the window of the throne room, looking out at the gardens. She could not get the image of a new-born Fatima suckling on her wet nurse out of her head. She recalled how impatiently she had waited for Fatima to grow up, desperate that they should play together. The first time she took the girl outside, she had been like a proud swan protecting its cygnet. The calls of the birds outside reminded her of Aashif's melodious voice. It was, she thought, the sound of a man who knew how to express his love.

She was in turmoil, unable to decide which emotion to yield to—sadness, loneliness, anger, or rage. All she knew was that she would surrender everything she had to be reunited with Fatima.

A nearby commotion brought her back to the present but she struggled to identify its source. Abdul hurried into the room, and she sat upright with a jolt. 'Two of Anwar's men have returned, Your Highness,' he called.

She stared at him. 'Where are they now?'

'In the kitchen.'

'I'll go there immediately,' she said.

'I'll accompany you, Your Highness.'

They walked at a brisk pace and Toh asked Abdul for the warriors' names. 'Osmin and Farouk, Your Highness.'

When they entered the kitchen, everyone stood up.

'Osmin and Farouk, stay. Everybody else, leave us,' Abdul ordered.

The kitchen quickly cleared, and Abdul walked Toh to the table where Osmin and Farouk stood.

'Sit down, please,' Toh said. 'What happened? Where is Anwar?'

'One of us didn't make it,' Farouk said. 'Haron.'

Toh frowned, 'And Anwar?'

'He went on alone,' Farouk said.

'Explain yourself,' Toh said, glaring at Osmin.

'We were making our way through thick jungle when poisonous slime spilled over Haron's foot. By the next morning, it was rotting away. Anwar ordered us to return to the palace with him, but he died that night.'

'How many days ago was that?'

'The day before yesterday.'

'And where's his body?'

'We had to bury it.'

'What?' the princess shrieked.

'We were worried that the puss might rub on to his horse.'

'And you couldn't build a stretcher and carry his body back on it?'

'We wanted to,' Farouk said, 'but the jungle was too dense.'

'Am I right that you wanted to build a stretcher, Farouk, but you didn't agree, Osmin?'

'I was worried about the horse,' Osmin insisted.

While listening to the two men, Toh had the sense that some facts were being held from her. Anwar would get the truth out of them when he returned, she decided.

'One final question, for now. After you buried the body, why did you not re-join Anwar?'

'Anwar said he'd be quicker if he went on alone,' Farouk said.

'Go,' Fatima said to the two warriors. 'Abdul, stay here.'

As soon as Osmin and Farouk were out of earshot, Toh addressed Abdul. 'There's something about their story I'm not happy with. Who is this Haron?'

'He's a young recruit who had recently joined us.'

'How young is he?'

'Sixteen, perhaps.'

'Where is his family?'

'They live in a kampung not far from the grounds of the old palace.'

'As I say, I'm unhappy with the situation. Place Farouk and Osmin under arrest. I'll ask Anwar to interrogate them on his return.'

'Yes, Your Highness.'

'Thank you, Abdul,' she said. 'You may return to your duties.'

* * *

Suraya joined Toh in the kitchen and could tell from the princess's expression that she was stressed. She took her hand, 'How are you, dear?'

Toh smiled weakly. 'I'm at my wits' end, Auntie. The Dato keeps insisting that it was Aashif who murdered that young slave girl and he's suggesting that he'll do the same to Fatima.'

'How dare he,' Suraya growled. 'Listen to me, princess. Aashif is an upstanding young man who does not have such violence in him.'

Toh stared at Suraya. 'I miss her so much, Auntie.'

'Of course, you do—you've spent most of your lives together. She'll be missing you just as much.'

'Do you think so, Auntie?' Before Suraya could respond, Toh continued. 'I sometimes find myself feeling so angry with her.'

'Don't worry yourself over such feelings. As you have discovered, your heart knows how to forgive.'

'I keep finding myself trying to show the people that I'm strong enough to defend these lands in my brother's absence. I don't want there to be any rift that might cause him to return home. I only wish Aashif and Fatima had told me that they wanted to be together.'

'They want more than that, dear; they want their freedom,' Suraya said calmly.

Toh's face crumpled as Suraya continued, 'You know from your own feelings for Fatima, how strong love can be, but sometimes love alone is not enough. Often it needs a friend to protect it.'

Toh sighed, 'And now I must worry for Anwar, too. I rely on him so much—I hope he'll be safe on his own. How will he sleep at night? At least Aashif and Fatima can take it in turns.'

'Anwar is too experienced for you to worry about him, princess,' Suraya said.

'I wish the Dato would leave. He's not happy, and neither am I. He must understand that I'm not able to leave here.'

* * *

Dato Hamidi despised his wife. If she had not provoked him into shouting, he would never have lost his voice. He stood by the throne room window and watched Toh and Abdul scamper across to the kitchen. 'How dare you humiliate me by telling that man to explain my movements?' he said to the empty room. 'In doing that, you signed your death warrant.'

He climbed the steps to the stage and strolled across to the throne. It was at such moments that he remembered how he had felt when Fatima touched him. A shiver ran down his spine, as it always did when he recalled the incident. He had guided her hand, of course, but he could tell it was what she'd wanted to do.

He thought about Suzanariahin and sighed in pleasure. If only they could be together again, he would have no need of Fatima at all.

Driving his thoughts was a determination to retain his title. How would Suzanariahin react when he was no longer the Dato? No, it was either him or Toh—and he was damned if it was going to be him. An accident of some sort—that was what was needed. Here, in this throne room maybe. And then, what if something should happen to the Raja?

Chapter 42

'Please, Aashif. It was not your voice I heard.'

'But there's no one else around.' Aashif was getting exasperated. 'I shouted your name, but my voice must have been muffled by the trees.' He scrutinized her face and realized that she was annoyed with him. The strain of events seemed to be beginning to take its toll.

'Why won't you believe me? I know what I heard.' There was a long silence before she spoke again, 'Anyway, why weren't you close behind me?'

'I'm sorry. I'd got my baju caught in some branches, and it took forever to work myself free.'

'I have a horrible feeling that something is staring at us from within the jungle. I know I've said it before, but the feeling is so strong this time.'

Anxious not to make her any more frightened, he whittled away at the top of his pole until it formed into a sharper point.

'What are you doing?'

'Preparing to defend us against anything that might leap out at us.'

Fatima's eyes were wide. 'You think we'll need that?' she asked.

Aashif was running out of ways to appease her. 'You never know.'

Aashif had never been so confused. All he knew was that he had to protect Fatima. He swapped poles with her and began sharpening hers.

'This amulet may be a little uncomfortable, but you should wear it, for extra peace of mind.'

'There's something in the jungle, isn't there? Something you're not telling me.'

Aashif dropped the pole and took hold of Fatima's arms. 'Fatima, my love. If any harm came to you, it would break my heart. Everything we have been through so far would be meaningless if you weren't by my side, safe and happy.'

Fatima gazed at him longingly. 'I'm sorry, Aashif. I want that too; I simply hadn't envisaged the trials and tribulations we would face.'

They kissed. Fatima had wanted to say more, but she did not have the heart to admit that she was missing Toh desperately.

* * *

Fatima prayed that she had not upset Aashif. She kept stealing glances at him, and at one point he smiled at her. A feeling of love soared through her, and she was about to embrace him when she caught sight of a scene of extraordinary beauty. Below them, in a small clearing shaded by trees, were oleander plants with clusters of white, red, pink, and pale-blue flowers.

'I've never seen such a mass of flowers before,' Fatima said. 'I bet Hisham would love to have them in his gardens.'

'I hate to spoil your enjoyment, but don't sniff or touch them—they're highly toxic.'

'Is there nothing pleasurable on this mountain?'

Aashif ignored her remark. 'Unfortunately, I'm going to have to hack a safe trail through the flowers.'

She watched as he pounded his pole into the ground, crushing any flowers in his path. He had soon created a route from one side to the other, scattering many colourful petals in the process.

When Fatima caught up with him, she turned back and looked at the destruction. 'It's like a battlefield of flowers.'

She stood up on tiptoes and kissed his cheek. When they looked in the other direction, they found themselves faced with a sheer drop. Trees were jutting out from the cliff, and it seemed that they would have no choice but to clamber down.

'I'm not sure I want to join the monkeys and gibbons,' Aashif said, trying to make light of the latest obstacle confronting them. 'We'll wander along the edge for a bit and look for an easier route.'

They eventually discovered a track that offered them a safer course. 'Whatever you do,' Aashif said, 'don't rush or you could fall all the way to the bottom. If you need to, dig the end of your pole into the ground for support. I'll be just ahead of you.'

Fatima battled to keep her fear in check as she watched Aashif set off at a pace so slow that reaching the bottom would take them forever. Soon, however, the slope of the track became less severe, and they were able to increase their speed. It was as they were following a bend in the trail that Aashif fell to the ground and waved for Fatima to do the same. He held a finger to his lips. 'Voices,' he whispered.

Fatima crouched down and carefully crawled towards him.

'Look down there,' he whispered, and she peered over his shoulder and down the mountainside. She watched from afar as hundreds of men scurried about. 'What are they doing?'

'Working—it's a tin mine.'

Fatima's heart was pounding as the voices grew louder.

'We're going to have to wait until there are fewer men around,' Aashif said.

They sat down behind a thick hedge and looked down at what was going on.

Fatima sniffed. 'Can you smell that? It's making me hungry.'

'Me too.'

Fatima spotted plumes of smoke and saw a large group of men surrounding a fire. She pointed to the group. 'They must be cooking something,' Aashif said. 'We can move on when they've finished eating.'

Aashif was looking at the men more closely and noticed that they were all Chinese.

* * *

They set off again, though the fear that they might be taken hostage weighed heavily on Aashif's mind. Their progress caused him to worry about the amount of dust they were creating. At one point, a cloud billowed into the air, making Fatima cough.

They had nearly reached the bottom when Aashif spotted a handful of men looking up in their direction and pointing. His heart skipped a beat. 'Get down,' he whispered urgently to Fatima and they cowered behind some foliage. His fear eased when he looked up and saw a hornbill swooping overhead, crowing loudly; he guessed that it was the bird that had grabbed their attention.

Aashif stared at the endless expanse of trees below them. He was eager to enter the jungle again—they urgently needed more food. He glanced at Fatima, wondering how much more she could take and smiled cheerfully at her in an attempt to raise her morale.

Fatima took hold of his arm. 'There's something strange in the air. It seems cleaner somehow.'

'Yes, I noticed that too. It is less humid.'

'How far do you think we've travelled?'

Aashif had failed to count the days that had passed since they left the palace and had to admit that he didn't know. He looked down and saw that the men had disappeared. Glancing at Fatima, he shuddered at the thought of what might happen to her if they were captured.

'I'm thirsty—do we have any water left?'

He passed her his container. 'Finish this. I don't need any now. When we reach the bottom of the valley we should find some more. Maybe there'll be a waterfall.'

'It would be wonderful to wash again.'

As they approached the bottom, the trail fell away steeply, and Aashif lost his footing. He fell forward and slid down on his backside, causing more dust to swirl up. Having gotten to his feet, he noticed Fatima staring down at him in shock. He held both hands up, indicating that she should wait.

'Throw down your pole,' he called out as loudly as he dared.

She tossed it towards him, and he told her to chuck down her bag. 'Is that everything?'

She nodded.

'Come down at your own pace. I'll catch you.'

He was relieved that she had the sense to grab hold of a sapling and when she landed, they held each other.

'Aashif,' Fatima said, alarmed.

Suddenly alert, he followed her line of vision and saw a Chinese man standing nearby, gaping at them.

* * *

'It's the sea.'

'What?'

'The sea—that's what's beyond this stretch of jungle. That explains why the air is less humid.'

Fatima was still thinking about the Chinaman and his baffled expression as they had scampered into the jungle. Instead of being elated at the thought that their journey was coming to an end, she was in mental turmoil. She kept asking herself if this was what she wanted. She loved Aashif and wanted to help him fulfil his dreams, but she missed Toh desperately.

Aashif gazed at her, excited and bewildered, and she gave him a vacant smile. The more she thought of the princess, the quieter she became.

Chapter 43

The Bomoh's mood was much improved. That morning, he had been in a foul humour, having learned the night before that the tree spirits had lost the two slaves—again. He called out to them, 'You indolent fools, sucking nourishment from each other instead of keeping an eye on the two slaves. Well, let's see how you behave when you have a wild huntsman and a weretiger among you.'

Ever since dawn, he had been sending out whistles for Berani and Kuat, his two fearless hornbills, to return to him. He let his signals float on the wind, confident that the two birds would eventually pick them up and fly to his side. He heard their calls in the distance. As the sun burst from behind the clouds, he spotted the two birds swooping down and smiled wickedly.

As the birds approached, his heart bled for them—he could never tell how much humanness was left in them. The history of the species was at the forefront of his mind. According to his great-grandfather, mortal hornbills had been created by a poor man who had once lived in the jungle with his wife and daughter. A young man had claimed the hand of the daughter, but he was idle and did little other than sleep. Not long after, the married couple began quarrelling with the parents, and the young man threatened to chop down the stilts that held up his father-in-law's house. 'If you do that, I will curse you so that you become birds,' the man had said. The younger man ignored the warning and whacked away at the stilts, causing the house to crash to the ground. Then and there, the young couple were turned into hornbills.

The Bomoh had no idea if Berani and Kuat's progeny had ever mated with other hornbills or if they were the pure blood of their ancestors. Although their voices were failing them these days, they could respond easily to simple questions with a nod or shake of their head.

He could not decide whether he loved Berani and Kuat more than his faithful kite. As they swooped down towards him, he covered the food offering on the table next to the cave's entrance—that was for the wild huntsman, believed to be the soul of the dead. On another table, next to the two clay figures, was a feast for the hornbills—bananas, papayas, snakes, and rats.

He had laid out the preparations after the news had reached him the previous evening that the warriors had returned without the two slaves. But at least their leader was still on the hunt.

While the hornbills gorged themselves on the food, he remembered how Princess Toh had stood naked before him. What troubled him about the incident was the memory it stirred up of how he had been when he was in his prime. It had taken him many years to accept that he had no choice but to surrender to his duties and give up the woman he loved.

He shook himself free of his reverie and got on with the task at hand: instructing Berani and Kuat to find Fatima and Aashif. As for the wild huntsman and the weretiger, he had a plan for them that had been stoked by Dato Hamidi's behaviour towards Fatima.

* * *

Toh simply could not abide being in her husband's presence. Their relationship had soured to the point where he was irrelevant to her.

A full moon was providing her and Abdul with enough light to make their way across to the kitchen. As Toh trudged along the pathway, with Abdul keeping in step with her, she glanced across the gardens into the darkness and shuddered. How could Fatima possibly withstand such a terrifying environment?

Despite her despondency, she allowed herself to think about Aashif and all that he was doing to protect Fatima. She didn't care if he had his arms wrapped around her all night, as long as Fatima was safe.

'It must be frightening out there at night,' she said.

'It can be, Your Highness.'

As they approached the kitchen, Toh watched three stragglers leaving and hoped it would be quiet.

'I'll wait by the entrance, Your Highness.'

'Thank you, Abdul.'

She was relieved to find Suraya on her own when she entered. She needed a friend, someone she could confide in, and Suraya fit the bill.

The moment Suraya spotted Toh, she rushed forward. 'Hello, my dear.'

'You're not closing, are you?'

'No, dear—I'm clearing up.'

Toh looked at Suraya. 'Would you mind some company, Auntie?'

Suraya smiled warmly, which set Toh at ease. 'Come and sit,' Suraya directed her to a table.

'I'm at my wits' end worrying about Fatima, Auntie.'

'Of course—you must be missing her dreadfully.'

'I feel so alone. I love her so much. I've never held such feelings for any of my husbands.'

'And I'm sure she loves you too, dear.'

'Were you ever in love, Auntie?'

'Yes, dear, but a long time ago.' A smile formed on her face. 'You and Fatima are like two saplings planted together; she recently asked me the same question.'

'She never told me.'

'She was probably too preoccupied with her own feelings.'

Suraya's eyes glazed over. 'He was a fine man, and tall. He had a wonderful imagination, too—how he made me laugh.'

'What happened? Or should I not ask?'

The older lady's mood became sombre. 'The passion we held for one another was so deep that it could not be shared.' She glowed. 'I'm lucky that I have many joyous memories to entertain me.'

Toh sat up. 'I hope Anwar and Fatima return soon.'

Suraya flinched, 'What about Aashif?'

* * *

Dato Hamidi was tested by the presence of Fatima in his mind. She could deny it all she wanted, but he remained convinced that she'd flaunted herself in front of him. When she returned, he thought to himself, he would take her as and when he desired. After all, what did she expect, wandering around in her tight baju? She's a slave, which means I own her, he thought.

He sat on the throne, enjoying the sense of power it gave him as he reflected on where his wife had gone. She had taken to wandering around the compound seeking to assert herself, but she was making a complete fool of herself. What in hell did she expect to achieve? He was sure everyone was laughing at her behind her back.

He thought about who he could approach to help him eliminate her and allow him to get on with his life. Not Shaz, that was for sure. That servant was now in Toh's pocket, but not for long—he'd pay for his treachery.

He turned his attention back to the plan, which was well formed in his head, before taking respite from his scheming and allowing his mind to turn to the memory of Suzanariahin and the pleasures she always gave him. He smiled as he remembered her voluptuous curves and grew excited. Though she was many miles away, he vowed to visit her once his plan had been implemented.

He looked around the room yet again. This time, he calculated that the angle between a looking glass on the rear wall and the site he had planned for the accident required a slight adjustment. Disgruntled by the number of times he had to make an adjustment, he wondered whether he would ever get it right.

He looked at the floor and re-counted the number of dowels. By his latest reckoning, he would have to remove two more, which meant he would have to create two extra identical heads. Then, when he provoked Toh to charge at him, she would crash through the floor to her death.

He shivered with pleasure at the thought of Toh catching her breath in horror as she fell. He sat forward and rubbed his hands with glee, before striding across to a mirror and carefully adjusting its position.

* * *

The Bomoh would leave no stone unturned. The tree spirits had failed to keep watch on the two slaves, but it wouldn't happen again. He stared at Berani and Kuat soaring into the air. Unwilling to take any more chances, he made the final preparations for the wild huntsman's feast.

The huntsman, claimed to be the *raja hantu*, the king of the spirits, and an avatar of the storm god who hunted in rivers, pools, and lakes. Together with the two hornbills, he would surely be able to help him guide the weretiger to the slaves.

The Bomoh had killed and cooked a black fowl and a goat; he placed them both on the altar by the cave entrance, along with a raw egg. He expected the demon to arrive carrying a spear and perhaps be accompanied by a hound, but his message had stated clearly that his presence was all that was required.

He was about to enter his cave when his world fell silent. With the moon as still as a restful Buddha, the Bomoh turned around sharply and noticed a shadow descending.

'Not before time,' he muttered, aware that the huntsman would be keener to attack his feast than to pay attention to the Bomoh's instructions.

The Bomoh stepped inside the cave and returned with a crystal ball. He was preparing to perform an invocation, only to discover that the huntsman's head was turned upwards and that there was a tree shoot growing from his neck.

Chapter 44

It was morning, and Fatima and Aashif were resuming their journey. Ever since the hideous pontianak had made its appearance, Fatima had been scared that it would return. She had insisted on leading and had stopped to readjust her baju when Aashif noticed a sudden movement above her. Coiled around a stout branch was a giant python, its black and brown scales providing camouflage as it inched down the tree.

'Move!' Aashif roared. 'Now!'

Fatima sprinted forward, too scared to check what had prompted Aashif's order.

'A python—above you,' Aashif cried out, chasing after her. It took her several moments to spot the snake. 'Not venomous, but it's highly dangerous.' He smiled at her benignly, but she suddenly found his grin irritating.

'Let me lead,' he said. She stepped aside, her nerves on edge as she reflected on how she had rejected Aashif's advances the previous night.

'Do you think we have far to go before we reach the sea?' she asked, her enthusiasm ringing hollow.

'Maybe a day or two.'

'As long as that?'

'The air feels fresher, which is a good sign,' he said.

She shrugged. 'I keep thinking about what the sea will be like—we'll be able to wash until every speck of dirt and drop of sweat is gone.'

A sudden noise drew their attention skywards. Two hornbills were swooping about playfully and whooping to one another. Fatima and Aashif glanced at each other and broke out laughing.

'Come,' Fatima said, her mood improving. 'Let's see if we can follow them.'

Before Aashif could tell her to be careful, Fatima was in pursuit. Aashif did not protest—the birds were heading west—but he soon fell behind due to his injury. Until then, he had managed to conceal the impact of his fall from Fatima, but her pace caught him by surprise, and he limped along clumsily. It was only when she turned that she noticed his discomfort.

'What's wrong?' she asked, staring at him in alarm.

'I hurt myself coming down the mountain. I suspect there's a bit of bruising, but I'll be fine.'

'Do you want me to have a look at it?'

'Not now. Let's wait till we've reached a clearing.'

* * *

They kept on going and there was soon a significant distance between them. In an effort to keep up, Aashif broke into a sweat as he battled to overcome the pain.

'Come back,' he shouted loudly, causing the jungle to judder from the flight of frightened birds. 'Wait—don't move!'

He limped to her as quickly as he could. 'Moths,' he explained, struggling to catch his breath.

'What?'

'Poisonous tiger moths—they're everywhere.'

She turned around, and he stopped her. 'Wait. Come to me slowly.'

As she approached him, he explained that the moths could cause a rash that sometimes resulted in dangerous swelling. 'Walk behind me,' he said, his voice serious.

He noticed her mood change with this latest obstacle to confront them.

'What's it going to be next, Aashif?' she asked, her voice strained.

'Shush.' They stood in silence. 'I can hear water.'

Fatima's face lit up as Aashif carefully guided them through the moth-infested area. When they were clear he turned to her, 'Can you hear the water?'

'Yes—now I can.'

As they kept moving forward, the sound of water drowned out the hornbills' calls. Moments later, they were confronted by a tangle of dense vegetation.

'I'm going to have to hack through this,' he said. 'Can you take the coconut oil from my bag? We'll have to cover ourselves in it to avoid getting bitten.' He turned his back on her so she could remove the container from his bag.

They stood and slathered the substance over their exposed flesh. 'Ready?' Aashif asked.

He began to hack away at the foliage with his axe, causing swarms of insects to burst free. He passed Fatima a banana leaf, 'As we move forward, can you swat away the insects with this?'

Though the undergrowth initially seemed never-ending, they eventually broke through the bracken to find themselves next to a fast-flowing river.

'If we follow the river, we'll reach a pool where we can bathe.'

She looked at him earnestly. 'Do you want me to check your wound?'

'I'm fine,' he lied and allowed Fatima to lead so that she would not notice his discomfort.

Fatima gazed up at the sky. 'Those two hornbills seem to know every step we're taking.'

After an hour or so, they came upon a pool of water deep enough for them to stand up in. Without uttering a word, Fatima stripped. Aashif did the same and Fatima spoke. 'Let me look at your injury.' She stepped behind him and gasped. His left buttock was bloodied raw. 'You've peeled your skin—no wonder you've been limping.'

'Once I've washed it, I can dab some lime on it to help it heal.'

Fatima retrieved her bar of soap from her bag and plunged into the pool. He jumped in after her and landed in her arms.

* * *

With the tension between them growing, Aashif smiled at her before releasing her and washing himself. She was struggling to soap her own back and was pleased when he took the bar from her. He then rinsed the soap from her skin and began massaging her neck and shoulders.

'Pass me the soap and I'll wash your back.'

He did as she asked and turned away from her. She ran her hands over his smooth, dark flesh, working the soap into a lather before rinsing it off.

'Lean over the riverbank and let me wash your wound.'

Words came from his mouth in a rush. 'I can manage it,' he said.

'But you won't be able to see if it's clean,' she replied. 'You don't want it to get infected.'

He rested on his elbows on the riverbank and floated on the surface of the water. She took the soap and carefully massaged his wound. Aashif tensed at her touch but allowed her to clean him before she splashed water to wash the soap away.

When he began to move, she spoke, 'Wait.'

While he floated, she caressed him to arousal with her hands. He put his feet down and turned towards her. Her expression eager, she took hold of his hands and placed them on her breasts, before throwing her arms around his neck and kissing him passionately. His arousal grew against her legs, and his hands roamed over her body.

Longing for him to enter her, she spread her legs and guided him into her, her breath coming to her in short bursts.

* * *

As Fatima rested on the ground, Aashif built their shelter for the night and realized that he was reinvigorated. By contrast, her own energy was sapped, and she found herself barely able to speak. All she wanted to do was sleep, but she could not stop thinking about Toh. Watching Aashif putting the finishing touches to the structure, her emotions were mixed up and she struggled to resolve any of them.

Night was closing in, but the brilliance of the moon offered some comfort. 'Madam, your home awaits.'

She rose slowly and looked at their sleeping arrangements. 'It's your best effort yet,' she said good-humouredly.

Aashif gestured for her to enter the shelter. As soon as they lay together, Fatima gazed at him pleadingly. 'I'm so tired, Aashif,' she said. 'Sing to me?'

'Here? You want me to sing to you here?'

'Yes—the song that Toh and I heard you singing from our window. It was so beautiful.'

He paused and then began, his voice soft:

> The lamburi tree is tall, tall
> Its branches sweep the sky
> My search is vain, and o'er is all
> Like a mate-lorn dove am I.

To Fatima's ear, it was as if the whole of the jungle was joining in.

'Is it a song for the warriors?' she asked softly.

'No, it's a love song.'

'Please sing some more.'

> Clear is the moon, with stars agleam
> The raven wastes in the paddy field
> O my beloved, when false I seem
> Open my breast, my heart is relieved.

Unknown to Aashif, his voice was acting as a lullaby. He listened to Fatima breathing quietly and allowed the words to fade away.

> The waves are white on the Kataun shore
> And day and night they beat
> The garden has white . . .

Chapter 45

Anwar tapped his breast pocket to check that he still had Princess Toh's letter to Fatima. Next, he untied two bundles of wooden poles from either side of his horse and began to construct a shelter for the night. He filled in the gaps with branches hacked from the surrounding jungle and made a roof from palm, banana, and elephant leaves.

In a little over an hour, he was satisfied that he could settle down for the night, though the weather made him fear the worst. It was as if the thunder and lightning were trying to outdo one other, flashing and roaring like brutal warriors overhead.

After tethering his horse, he entered the shelter, just in time to avoid getting soaked. He stood and listened to the rain flogging the jungle, before closing the entrance and settling down for the night. He wondered how skilled Aashif was at surviving in the jungle; his major concern was the difference in their ages. Aashif was likely to be an agile fighter whereas he was a much older man. Of late, he had been contemplating following Hisham into gardening.

He fell asleep as soon as his head touched the ground. The following morning, he woke to the lingering hiss of the rain. As happened whenever he was troubled, his head was flooded with thoughts concerning his baby sister. The memory of her brutal death fuelled his determination to ensure that Fatima was returned safe and well.

He rose, left the shelter, and watched the light break through the clouds, convinced that by this point he should have picked up some sign of Aashif and Fatima's presence. He decided to cut across the mountainside towards the sea and was soon approaching level ground.

He had checked at the few kampungs he had passed on his journey, but there had been no sighting of the two slaves. At the last one, he had thought about the task he had set Shafie, and he hoped that his colleague's investigations had resulted in an arrest. His desperation to catch Aashif and Fatima was matched by his single-mindedness to secure justice for the murdered slave.

When least he expected it, his horse stepped away from the mountain and he found himself next to a tin mine, a site that was swarming with Chinese workers. He guessed them to be Hakka Chinese, a race who had traditionally mined for tin in Perak.

He greeted the first man who reacted to him in the Hakka dialect. When the man nodded agreeably, Anwar explained that he was looking for two travellers and described Aashif and Fatima. The miner called to one of his colleagues who proceeded to join them, before telling Anwar what he was hoping to hear.

* * *

Escorted by eighty men, Shafie stared down at the kampung, recalling how hostile the villagers had been on his previous visit. As had been arranged, he split his men into two groups and sent a party in each direction. After giving his men time to surround the kampung, he made his move. He descended with four warriors from the hilltop, wary that they could find themselves fenced in at any moment.

It was only when the village children became alert to their presence that the place came to life. All around them, doors opened, and Shafie and his men acknowledged the villagers. The chief strolled on to his terrace, as if he didn't have a care in the world. He merely stared at Shafie, who offered him a lively greeting.

'What do you want?' the chief growled and looked around at the gathering crowd.

'I've come to invite you to meet the Raja.'

'I have no wish to visit him,' the chief replied.

Shafie smiled. 'That may be the case, but he has a burning wish to meet you.'

The chief sighed in exasperation, 'He knows where to find me. Let me know when he'd like to visit, and I'll be ready. In fact,' he added, a smirk forming on his face, 'I'll arrange for all the villages around here to greet him.'

'I fear you misunderstand—he only wishes to meet you.'

'Perhaps, but I am answerable to many people here and cannot simply abandon them,' he said, looking around confidently.

Shafie squeezed his horse with his legs and jerked at the reins causing the animal to rear up and neigh loudly—a signal to his men. A great roar filled the air, and they charged through the jungle, their weapons drawn.

Shafie looked back at the chief. 'As I was saying, the Raja wishes to meet you.' He dismounted and climbed the steps to the chief's rumah. Having given him a curt bow, he turned to the villagers, 'Many of you will recognize me from my previous visit; I'm one of the Raja's senior officers, and the men behind you are his warriors. The Raja asked me to bring your chief to his palace, so they may discuss matters greatly troubling him. The death of your neighbour, killed by a bolt shot from the jungle behind you, was most distressing to him.' He paused. 'You need not worry that it might happen again; more warriors are close at hand, dotted throughout the jungle to ensure your safety. However, each warrior is under the Raja's orders to bring down any who oppose us.' He turned to the chief, 'My men will not hesitate to follow the Raja's decree.'

The chief slumped, unsure of where to look, while Shafie stretched a hand towards the steps, indicating that he should follow Shafie down. 'Let us have no more of your folly.'

The chief staggered down the steps where two warriors met him and tied a lengthy rope around his midriff.

'To stop you from getting lost in the jungle,' Shafie said. 'It is for your own safety.'

The chief called for his horse, but Shafie interrupted, 'You won't need your horse. For the most part, the journey will be on foot.'

* * *

Dato Hamidi wandered into the throne room and found his wife writing. When she carried on as if he wasn't there, he glared at her furiously. Irritated by a dampness in his right ear, he pulled a handkerchief from his pocket and dabbed at it. Small spots of blood showed on the cloth.

He had begun having trouble retaining his balance, but he was determined not to show Toh this. He walked carefully towards the stage and climbed the stairs before gazing at the throne. He paced back and forth across the stage, thinking about how Toh would meet her death. As he glanced in her direction, his contempt for her was obvious. 'Your day is near, woman,' he muttered to himself, his mood dominated by a desire to witness her demise. He caught her looking at him, but since he couldn't hear anything she might say, he chose not to acknowledge her. Intermittently, he stopped pacing and rested against the back of the throne, taking pleasure in the fact that she was becoming riled by him. He decided to provoke her further by sitting on one of the throne's armrests. When she jumped to her feet, he turned away and resumed his pacing, stopping only when she rose, strolled across to the window, and leant out towards the yard below.

His attention was drawn to the reflection of Abdul approaching in one of the looking glasses. The guard stood to attention before speaking to Toh at length; after a while, they left the room together and hurried down the stairs.

He walked to the window and looked out at the courtyard to see a huge crowd of dishevelled warriors milling around. He expected to find the Raja somewhere among the men, but he was nowhere to be seen. Then he spotted Toh and Abdul approaching Shafie. He had never talked to the man but he'd often overheard Anwar praising him.

Their discussion seemed to go on forever, and he grew enraged, frustrated that his lack of hearing prevented him from joining their conversation.

Then, all of a sudden, Toh stopped and appeared to go rigid, before turning to face whatever it was that had seized her attention. At this, the Dato stretched further out of the window and saw the chief step into view.

* * *

Dato Hamidi had little choice but to seek the help of Shaz, who in exchange for a gold coin told him everything he needed to know. The chief had admitted to recruiting the murderer, but to punish the slave rather than to kill her. The villain's face had been masked, he claimed, but he was a man who wore fine clothes, and the chief would be able to recognize his voice instantly. At this news, Dato handed over the payment to Shaz, more determined than ever to eliminate Toh and set his life on a new course.

Chapter 46

Later that day, Toh rose from the table in the throne room and walked to the window. As she stood watching people milling around outside, she remembered the chats that she and Fatima had enjoyed as they strolled around the grounds.

After a while, she went back to the table and tried to return to the task at hand, but she found herself falling forward and dropping her face into her hands. 'Please come back, Fatima. Please.'

At the sound of Dato Hamidi shuffling into the room, she sat upright with a jolt. At that moment, all she wanted was to be left alone—she could not bear to be in his presence. She half expected him to walk up to the throne and do something to tease her, but to her relief, he left the room. She sighed and returned to the window, before trying to remember the route she and Fatima had always enjoyed when they went for a walk. Fatima had loved to gather flowers ever since she was a girl, and Toh pictured her now, sniffing them as she walked back to the palace.

She stepped back from the window and tried to imagine the effect the Bomoh's spell would be having on Aashif, but then her eyes shot open—she hadn't for a minute considered what would happen if Aashif loved her instead of Fatima.

As if the memory of making Fatima sleep in the dormitory wasn't mortifying enough, she shook violently at what she had now done. Aashif was a fine man, strong and gentle and surely in love with Fatima—why else would he have run off with her?

She lurched back to the table and forced herself to complete her report.

* * *

The Bomoh and the Jinn were sitting outside the Bomoh's cave, enjoying a moment of tranquillity.

'I cannot get over the madness of those two,' the Jinn said. 'You say that she believes that the graves are guarded, but he clearly does not. They are two lucky people: Any one of those spears could have brought them down.'

The Bomoh stared at him, relieved that Fatima had not been struck—after all, he had been tasked with sending her back to Toh.

'My role is limited,' the Jinn went on. 'I am simply the guardian of the graves. You must use your powers to make them forget their journey through the cemetery. If that cannot be done, you must eliminate him—after all, if he is dead, no one will be able to confirm her claims.'

The Bomoh nodded slowly as he continued to watch the sky for news. The moment he heard the call of a hornbill, he spoke abruptly, 'It's time for you to leave.'

The Jinn sprung to his feet and left without comment. As soon as the Bomoh spotted the bird swooping over the treetops, he could tell it was Berani. His father had once told him that his birds' great-grandparents had spoken in clear, crisp voices, but whenever Berani or Kuat spoke, the Bomoh had to strain to catch their words.

The Bomoh was now about to learn where Aashif and Fatima were. He had left a meal on the table behind him for Berani and the bird filled its belly while the shaman asked his questions.

'The tree spirits have awoken,' Berani whispered. 'They guided us toward the two, who are under close watch.'

The bird took another helping of food while the Bomoh waited. Then, between mouthfuls, Berani spoke, 'We have yet to spot the wild huntsman, but the arduous journey is making Fatima more agitated.'

The Bomoh's face was stern. 'And the young man?'

'He's fearless.'

'More foolish than fearless,' the Bomoh snarled.

'She tried to pass an amulet to him, but he rejected it,' Berani murmured.

The Bomoh paused. 'Describe it to me,' he insisted.

When the bird had finished describing the piece of jewellery, the Bomoh burst out laughing. He had thought the amulet was lost, and now he knew that it had been stolen from him. How cunning she was, he thought.

His heart pounded at the news that Aashif was unprotected. It no longer mattered whether Aashif loved the princess—he couldn't possibly survive the weretiger's presence. Fatima, on the other hand, would be safe as long as the amulet was in her possession. The way matters were progressing, the warriors' presence would hardly be required. 'Nearly got them,' he said jubilantly.

He watched the hornbill eat the remains of the meal before addressing it again.

'Tell the tree spirits to create as much aggravation as they can to keep the runaways uneasy—particularly Fatima.'

The Bomoh watched as Berani flapped its great wings and sailed into the sky. 'Be warned,' he called out. 'Do not let me down.'

* * *

Toh was hoping that the kitchen would be empty at this late hour. Accompanied by Abdul, who waited outside, she entered the building; sure enough, Suraya was alone.

'Good evening, Auntie.'

As Toh wandered across to join the cook, she was unable to hide her misery.

Suraya rose and waved a hand towards the seat beside her. Toh slumped on to it and gazed at Suraya sorrowfully. 'I'm sick with worry, Auntie.'

'Of course, you are, my dear.'

'I thought I was doing the right thing, but the more I reflect, the more I understand my mistakes. I keep asking myself why I didn't arrange for Fatima to sleep in the staff's quarters instead of insisting that she join the other slaves. I thought she would feel more at ease among the other women, but I was wrong. I should have talked it through with her and left her to make the decision. Auntie, I didn't even let her grow her hair long.'

'I fear her move from the palace was a step too far. But had the women reacted more favourably to her, everything might have been different,' Suraya said.

'I'm so troubled by the pain I caused her.'

Suraya stared at Toh, an enigmatic expression on her face. 'I think you're more distressed by other events unless I'm mistaken.'

Suraya watched as Toh's eyes filled with tears. After checking that they were still alone, Toh lowered her voice, 'I did something stupid, Auntie.'

The gravity of Toh's voice unsettled Suraya and she became uneasy.

'She's my baby sister, Auntie. I'm so frightened for her. She's not safe in the jungle.'

Toh peered at Suraya and pulled a face, 'I got the Bomoh to pass them blood from my menses.'

Suraya struggled to remain composed and waited for the princess to continue.

'I thought that if they drank it, they would fall in love with me.'

'But Fatima already loves you, Toh,' Suraya said.

'I believe so, but I couldn't ask the Bomoh to deliver it to Aashif alone. I thought that would be impossible, and I didn't want to rile him.'

Toh fell silent, wondering if Suraya understood the magnitude of what she had done. 'Now Fatima and Aashif will return, and Aashif will love me, which will make everything worse. What have I done, Auntie?'

Suraya remained still for a moment and then took hold of Toh's hand. 'Do you know how the Bomoh plans to deliver your blood?'

'I allowed a drop to fall into a portion of rice.'

* * *

Suraya was trying to raise Princess Toh's spirits but found her mind wandering to the painful separation from the love of her life. In those days, she had been regarded as a true beauty who would cause men's heads to turn. 'We all do things we regret,' she said. 'I was once terribly mean to the man I loved. I stole some things from him, only to learn later that he had spent days searching for them.'

'What were they?' Toh asked.

'Oh, they were harmless charms, but they meant a lot to me,' she said, a wayward expression on her face.

'What was he like?'

'Young, handsome, virile,' she said, a hint of excitement in her voice.

The two women fell silent until Toh spoke, 'I must visit the Bomoh and ask him to reverse the love spell.' She stared at Suraya. 'Come with me, Auntie?'

'I won't be able to make a journey like that,' Suraya said hurriedly. 'He frightens me sometimes, and he offers advice in rhymes that I struggle to follow.'

'What does he say?'

'I wrote down the rhymes he used towards Dato Hamidi, lest I forget them.'

'Read them to me.'

Toh went back to the palace and returned shortly afterwards. 'Can you make sense of what he said, Auntie?'

Suraya listened intently as Toh read the Bomoh's couplets and a strange warmth entered her body. She fought back tears of joy at the knowledge that he still loved her after all these years—The Last Great Love Song told her that.

Chapter 47

It was early morning, and Aashif and Fatima were tracking their way through the jungle once more.

Fatima had no idea why she was being so obstinate—it felt like a devil was inside her, controlling her mind. She loved Aashif, yet this morning she was finding it impossible to keep the promise she had made to herself not to upset him. She had never experienced such mood swings before and found herself battling her emotions trying to understand what was going on.

While she was in a state of confusion, a piercing screech came from up ahead and she trembled, terrified as the leaves about them began to shake uncontrollably. Fatima could tell Aashif was tense by the way he gripped his axe. She grabbed her amulet, a source of comfort to her ever since their encounter with the pontianak.

What Suraya had said about the weight of the amulet was true—it was a heavy object, but Fatima had taken to wearing it because it settled her mind.

'As long as you keep it close by you, you should be safe,' Aashif said reassuringly.

'It's really cumbersome,' she complained.

After a lengthy pause, the calls of the two hornbills echoed through the trees.

'Our friends are back,' Aashif said. 'Half the time I find myself wondering whether they're following or leading us.'

As they resumed their journey, the frightening screech played on Fatima's mind. She was terrified at the thought of what could be coming next. When a squall of wind whipped through the trees, Fatima threw herself at Aashif and he held her tight. Once the gust had passed, Aashif retained his hold on her and kissed her brow.

When they came upon a small papaya grove, Aashif warned Fatima of the need for caution. The fruit was her favourite, and she was ready to devour the first one she found.

'We should only eat the hanging fruit,' he insisted, spotting a bunch of papayas dangling from a branch above their heads. 'The ones on the ground have probably been contaminated by rats.'

While Aashif cut down the bunch, Fatima, tired of the weight of the amulet, removed it and dropped it into a pocket of her baju. To her delight, they soon came upon a shallow stream and decided to rest. 'At least we can wash,' she said. She stripped naked as Aashif dug his water container from his bag and handed it to her. 'Use this to collect the water and pour it over you.'

* * *

Aashif reminded himself that while he had been roaming the jungle for years, Fatima had no experience in these matters. As he watched her dousing water over her body, he wondered how he could cheer her up. He contemplated what sort of shelter he should build for the night. He sensed that it should be more secure than the single-beam structure he tended to construct. Something to reassure Fatima, he decided.

Conscious of the slow-moving trickle of the stream, he also decided to boil their water. On the mountainside, the water had been fast-flowing, but this time he would light a fire. He sat hunched over his knees, reluctant to leave Fatima unattended.

'Is it cold?' he called out to her.

'Yes, but nice too.'

Aashif was remembering the first time they'd made love when Fatima turned round. 'You can help me dry my back now.'

He pushed himself up and wandered across to her, keen to look nonchalant. He picked up the cloth they use to dry themselves and began to assist her.

'Your turn now,' she eventually said.

'I thought I'd chop down some wood for our shelter first.'

'All right,' she said, clearly disappointed. 'So, we're resting here?'

'I think we might as well—although we shouldn't be too close to the stream at night because it will attract animals.'

Suddenly huffy, Fatima snatched at her baju and hurriedly dressed.

They re-entered the jungle in silence and Aashif was relieved to find the trees thinning out. Soon they came upon a wide clearing. 'Here's perfect,' he said.

The construction of the shelter took him longer than he envisaged, but once it was done, he stood back and admired his handiwork. 'What do you think?'

'Is this a special occasion?' She fiddled with the amulet before burying it in her bag.

He shrugged, 'I thought it would give us a little more comfort.'

As they walked back to the stream, Aashif was concerned that the insects seemed to have fallen silent, but he said nothing to Fatima. He stepped aside and chopped down several bamboo poles before stuffing leaves into the end of each of them and filling them with water. 'I'll hang these over a fire to boil; then it will be safe to drink.'

On their way back to the shelter, Aashif was in the process of cutting down two coconuts and some bananas to eat with the papaya they had found, when he heard rustling in the foliage. He gestured at Fatima to stand still and peered into the undergrowth but was startled when a wild fowl stared back at him. He flung his axe at the bird and chased after it. 'Our dinner,' he said when he reappeared, a broad smile on his face as he held the bird aloft. Fatima smiled back at him and rubbed her hands in glee.

Later that night, with their meal over, Aashif lay down beside Fatima and started to talk about his hopes and dreams for the future, but when he turned to her, she was asleep.

* * *

Fatima woke up thinking about Toh. The memory of the princess berating her husband reminded Fatima of how much she missed her, and she suddenly found herself having to fight back tears. Guilt-ridden at having abandoned Toh in her hour of need, she stared at the dying embers outside the shelter.

She glanced at Aashif, who was fast asleep, and wondered how he would respond if she were to ask him to take her back to the palace. Her feelings for him had not changed, but her remorse for what she had done to Toh felt overwhelming. She imagined how the princess would be struggling to shoulder the responsibilities of running the palace.

She gazed up at the same moon and stars that were shining down on Toh. She smiled at the memory of the night before Toh's wedding to the Dato.

They had both been certain that Toh's marriage was going to cast aside the sadness she'd endured at the hands of her first two husbands.

Her gaze returned to Aashif. She was tempted to curl up against him, but she did not want to risk waking him. He was breathing easily, and his expression suggested that he was in a contented place.

She resumed the conversation she'd been having all day in her head. 'I promise you Toh, once you get to know him, you'll like him—he's so sensitive and strong. I'm sure he'd take me back if I asked him.'

* * *

Suraya and Hisham strolled around the inner gardens of the palace, the moon shedding a golden glow. Suraya could not stop thinking about the sad memories in Toh's unhappy past. 'She asked me to accompany her to meet the Bomoh, and I had to pretend that I was too old to make the journey,' she said, her voice wistful and troubled.

Hisham knew all about the love affair between Suraya and the Bomoh and nodded. He could remember the pain Suraya had gone through when the relationship ended. 'Duty before pleasure,' he recalled the Bomoh explaining.

'I keep waking up to the sound of Fatima's laughter. Goodness, how I miss her.'

Hisham grimaced, fully aware of Suraya's suffering—he was missing the youngsters too, but he was not prepared to admit it. Nor would he reveal the prayers he offered for Aashif's wellbeing, convinced that as long as Aashif was unharmed, Fatima would be safe.

'Where do you think they are now?'

'It depends on the route they took, but getting close to the coast, I'd say.'

'And Anwar?'

'He'll be closing in on them, I fear.'

'I hope they make it.'

'Anwar is a good man,' he said. 'I only pray that Aashif doesn't become hot-headed. If he does, I dread to think what might happen.'

* * *

The wild huntsman was accustomed to the winds of the jungle but riding on the back of the weretiger was a new experience. He had to keep his head low so the branch jutting out from his neck didn't catch any of the overhead branches and dislodge him from the creature's back. But the regular calls of the Bomoh's hornbills kept him on course, and he was excited about his imminent rendezvous.

Chapter 48

'You must reverse the spell,' Princess Toh pleaded, 'Aashif cannot want me instead of Fatima. It would break her heart.'

The Bomoh said nothing but reflected on the chant he had sung after he'd collected the drop of blood from her. He stared at her silently for several minutes, thinking about her naked body and leaving her tearful and shaking.

Through her tears, Toh reminded the Bomoh just how greatly her husband had distressed Fatima. She explained that it was imperative that her marriage remained intact until her brother returned—once he resumed control of the palace and its people, she would end the marriage.

In a series of rhyming couplets, he told Toh that he would frighten Fatima into ending her journey and returning to the palace. He would capture Aashif's soul, his roh, when he was asleep and pass it to a weretiger. He explained that such a creature was already racing through the jungle to confront the two slaves.

He was delighted at the sight of Toh's shocked face until she became angry and ordered him not to execute such a plan.

'How would Fatima feel if Aashif's roh failed to return to him?' she shouted, suddenly panicked.

In response, the Bomoh cast a shape-shifting spell to ensure that Aashif's roh would return to his body and stared at the princess with an expression so cold that she shivered. Then he began another chant, calling on the spirits of the jungle to answer his invocation. 'I offer you, in exchange, the life of another,' he mumbled, careful that Toh could not decipher his words.

After she'd sat there for more than an hour, Princess Toh watched alarmed as the Bomoh began to sway from side to side. When he fell to the floor in a heap, she rushed to his aid. At this, the Bomoh was incandescent. He lashed out at her and rose slowly, afraid that she might break his spell.

* * *

Anwar was intrigued by the presence of a pair of hornbills that he had regularly seen in the sky over the preceding days and had become convinced that they were leading him to his destination. The fact that one of them kept on disappearing, suggested to him that they were keeping an eye on someone else.

He sat on the ground next to his shelter and watched the female circling overhead, unsure whether the bird was protecting him or leading him into danger.

The moon, glowing pink in the sky, warned him that it would not be long before nightfall. He retired under his shelter and felt excited at the prospect of confronting both slaves. He tried to imagine how Aashif would react when he was challenged. Ever since he had set off on his journey, he had been struck by Aashif's daring, and he felt increasingly wary about the young man.

His mind returned to Haron, and he compared his conduct with Aashif's behaviour. Haron, he had long ago concluded, was a petulant fool and no match for the young slave. A young man like him had no place in the Raja's army, while Aashif was a perfect fit for the role of a warrior. He was also troubled by what Osmin had done by potentially leading Haron astray with his irresponsible chatter. He was typical, he thought, of many people who empowered themselves by befriending weaker men. Osmin, he decided, was not fit to continue as one of the Raja's warriors if he continued to lead young men astray.

The issue bothering Anwar most, however, was the role that Hisham had played in Aashif's young life. Hisham had been a surrogate father to the young slave from the day he had arrived in the palace and had trained him well. It was clear that Aashif would be a formidable opponent.

That night, he twisted and turned like a warrior in battle, until he finally fell asleep. The next morning, he emerged from the shelter and stretched life back into his limbs, convinced that he was facing the day of reckoning.

When he recommenced his journey, he checked that he still had the letter from Princess Toh on his person, wedged inside his jerkin. As he thought about what lay ahead, he began to feel disconcerted. He knew that he had all the guile of a fighting man, but would he have Aashif's speed and agility? He would simply have to outmanoeuvre him, he thought. His one great hope was that after a journey of undoubted challenges, something would distract Aashif in a fight to the death.

* * *

Fatima was pining for Toh in a way that she had never done before. She had spent the day struggling to find the necessary courage to tell Aashif that she wanted to return to the palace. The problem was that she would never be able to return on her own—she would never find her way. Nor could she cause him to abandon his quest for freedom.

She was finding the hornbills increasingly irritating, and she wished they would fly away and find another source of entertainment.

'Let's stay here for another day,' she said, keen to delay their journey. 'After all, you went to so much trouble to build our shelter last night. Maybe you could catch another fowl and we could have another cooked meal?'

While she was washing, Aashif whispered to her. 'Don't move—I think there's something in the foliage.'

Her gaze was drawn to the spot where Aashif had caught the bird, the previous day. An unexpected wind suddenly blew through the trees, and the youngsters stared at each other, motionless.

'What's happening?' Fatima asked.

'I don't know.'

Fatima threw on her baju and ran to him, clinging on to his arm.

'Why isn't there any sound, Aashif?'

'I don't understand what's happening.'

The wind died as quickly as it had started. 'Where's your bag?' Aashif asked.

'In the shelter.'

'What about the amulet?'

Holding hands, they ran back to the shelter. Much to Aashif's relief, the bag was still there. Fatima rummaged through it and nodded her head when she found the amulet inside.

As the night drew in, they said little to each other. 'I wish we had some rice to accompany this meat,' Fatima remarked as she pulled the remaining fowl meat from the bones.

Aashif stared at her and remembered the rice they had discovered in the cauldron outside the hut. Despite his hunger, he had only eaten the vegetables and was glad that he had left all the rice to Fatima.

* * *

Aashif was saddened by the thought that he no longer seemed to make Fatima happy, and he was also frightened—might he be on the verge of losing her? His thoughts kept returning to their first meeting, and he reflected on everything that had happened since then. Despite them often making love, he recognized that their relationship had been tense for several days. He was relieved to settle down for the night and claim some sleep, Fatima resting quietly against him.

* * *

Fatima was only able to sleep intermittently, her mind was in such disarray. The moon and the stars cast so much light that she could see the edge of the jungle clearly. She sat clutching her knees and glanced down at the sleeping Aashif. She was peering into the darkness when another silence invaded her world, and a shiver ran down her spine. She was paralysed by fear and thought about waking Aashif, but she was too scared to move. Ashen-faced, she shut her eyes tightly; when she opened them, she was sure she could see a shadow passing over Aashif and leaving their shelter.

She eventually managed to doze off again, only to wake with a jerk, moments later. Staring at the surrounding trees, she strained her eyes, trying to penetrate the darkness; fear wrestling in the pit of her stomach. The incessant buzzing of insects and the croaking of frogs were getting on her nerves. Her throat felt parched as the darkness closed in on her. She was convinced that she was being watched and attempted to call out, but her words got trapped in her throat. She turned to Aashif for help, but it was as if he had sunk into the ground.

A horrible snarl came out of the darkness, and she sensed a large figure approaching her. 'Go away,' she shrieked.

A figure came gradually into view; their eyes met, and she gasped and backed further into the shelter. The tiger loomed over her, and she called out again, desperately pushing herself further back and knocking over her bag, spilling the contents in the process. She sensed something familiar that she couldn't quite identify, and as she squinted at the creature's face, Aashif's features appeared before her eyes. A deep sigh filled the night and Fatima began to weep uncontrollably.

Chapter 49

'Have you ever heard the stories of the weretigers, Abdul?'

'Of course, Your Highness.'

'Are they true, do you think?'

Abdul hesitated. 'I believe so, Your Highness, yes.'

They were standing at the top of the staircase in the palace.

'For someone to be turned into a weretiger must surely be a worse punishment than banishment,' Toh said.

'I suppose so, Your Highness,' Abdul answered.

'Have you seen my husband anywhere?'

'No, Your Highness.'

Princess Toh wandered along the corridor, observing the growing number of looking glasses wherever she looked. Whichever way she turned, she found herself confronted by a sheet of glass; she could not imagine that the Raja would tolerate such unsightliness. She decided to remove them—if Dato Hamidi didn't like it, he could leave the palace.

She entered the throne room, her head lowered. It was only when Dato Hamidi cleared his throat that she became aware of his presence. She looked up and her expression hardened when she realized that he was sitting on the throne. Inflamed, she forgot about his deafness and roared at him to get out of the chair. But Dato Hamidi just brought his hands to his ears and shrugged, reminding her that he couldn't hear her. She stormed towards him, but he just sat there eating a piece of bread.

'Found your slaves yet?'

She seethed at his failure to get up from the throne while he chewed loudly. 'Aren't you worried that he's having his way with her?'

Toh was unable to suppress her contempt. She stared fiercely at the floor to demand that he step away from the throne. But Dato Hamidi just smirked and shrugged again.

'She's obviously enjoying being pawed by that filthy slave—otherwise she'd have returned to the palace long ago. You misjudged the situation once again.'

Toh was tempted to grab her husband by his hair and drag him from the throne. Instead, she continued to glare at him and pointed at the floor.

'It's pointless trying to communicate with me—I can't understand what you're trying to tell me.'

Toh watched as he inspected the floor in front of him, trying to understand what he could possibly be looking at. She turned away from him, marched to her table, and picked up a jug of water, returning to the stage and drenching his lap.

He brushed away the water as if it was nothing. 'Tell me, is there something wrong with the floor?' he mocked. 'Perhaps Fatima could teach you a thing or two about how to please a man—you certainly have a lot to learn on that topic.' When she didn't respond, he continued. 'Mind you, you'd have thought that after two marriages you'd be ready for a third, instead of leaving me to find entertainment elsewhere.'

Toh stared at him with disgust.

'Why I've got to go back to my old mistress is a question for you to consider,' he snarled. 'Remember this, woman: Just as I intend to occupy this throne as often as I choose, I'm entitled to take that brat as often as I want—she's nothing more than a slave. And when she gets back, I will have her, whether you like it or not.'

Toh was clearly disgusted but refused to react, gaining strength from the fact that remaining silent riled him even more.

'You and your brat have sought to humiliate me; well, no more,' he growled.

Thoughts of Fatima's distress at the Dato's hands flashed through her mind, and she promised herself that never again would she place Fatima in such danger. She glared at him before storming back to the table. Snatching a sheet of writing paper, she scrawled a message: 'Unless you step away from that throne, I'll have you dragged from there by the guards, and the whole community will know about it.' She marched to the stage clutching her message, before screwing the paper into a ball and flinging it at him.

Dato Hamidi's pallor darkened when he read her note. 'It's about time everybody knew their place,' he shouted at her. 'From now on, I'm going to exercise my rights openly, just as I did with that damned slave.'

At the sight of Toh's shock, Dato Hamidi continued, 'And if that little brat had behaved herself instead of attacking me, she might still be alive today.'

As Toh reeled in horror, an odd expression came over the Dato, as if he realized that he had gone too far, but he continued, 'She was like a wild animal. If I hadn't been armed, she'd have torn my eyes out.'

At the back of the stage, a new sheet of looking glass caught Toh's attention. She turned away from him and he shouted out, spittle flying from his mouth, 'What the hell was I supposed to do—let her kill me?'

* * *

Dato Hamidi realized that he had said too much. His anger had gotten the better of him. He sat in suspense, terrified that Toh would call the guards and tell them what he had revealed. His thoughts raced around in his head as he considered what lie to tell. He would say that his wife and her slave were two scheming witches who had paid Aashif to murder that girl before blaming him. The two slaves, he would say, had made their escape because they were frightened of what the Raja would do to them.

He was terrified at what Toh would do and knew that he had no choice but to draw her forward so that she fell through the floor to her death. He gripped the armrests of the throne and watched her standing there, staring at him.

As the seconds passed by, he accepted that there was no way he could retract his words. He had to rile her enough to charge at him.

'If only that slave had behaved herself, I could have given her so much more pleasure,' he dared. 'It was nearly as pleasurable as when Fatima stroked me. Yes, your innocent little slave, toying with me—and enjoying it, too.'

He watched her snap; he was unable to hear what she was saying, but he could tell that he was needling her. 'That young girl would have made a worthy wife,' he jeered. 'She certainly gave me more pleasure than you ever did.' He watched as the princess clenched her fists and could tell that she was losing her self-control. 'Don't even think of offering yourself to me. You're no match for her—or Fatima, come to that.'

He sat back in the throne and folded his arms, daring her to attack him. She began to glance from side to side between the many sheets of looking glass at this point, and he wondered what was going through her head. Her gaze eventually settled on the mirror at the back of the stage.

She turned away from him and walked slowly back to her desk. He thought she was going to write him another note, but instead, she picked up a solid marble paperweight and felt its weight in her hand. She wandered up to a cabinet that was made of highly polished wood, with a glass frontage. Inside, was a gilded ceremonial axe. She tossed the paperweight in her hand several times before flinging it through the glass.

Dato Hamidi stared at his wife in horror, aware that he was unarmed. 'What are you going to do with that—chop my head off?' he asked nervously.

* * *

Toh was surprised by the weight of the axe but determined to strike at the Dato in the way that would do him most harm. She slowly walked up to the nearest looking glass, her breathing laboured. Turning to face her husband, she swung the axe at the glass and watched as it shattered. Looking closely at his reaction, a sense of satisfaction came over her as she saw just how baffled he was by what she had done.

The sound of footsteps filled her ears—she suspected that Abdul was rushing to discover what was going on, but she could not stop now. She turned to the next sheet of glass and whacked the axe against it. It too, shattered into shards that covered the floor.

Dato Hamidi bellowed at her to stop, but Toh took no notice and swung the axe at a third mirror. As yet more shards of glass crashed to the floor, she twisted her head towards him, the hatred within her rushing free. She turned to the next mirror before hitting it with such force that she almost toppled over and moved towards the next pane. This was the first that the Dato had installed and the most precious to him because it gave him a view of the corridor below.

Dato Hamidi screeched as she raised the axe, springing to his feet and pushing himself forward with a horrific scream. Toh froze, unable to understand the sudden terror on Dato Hamidi's face.

It happened as if in slow motion. A violent shriek from the Dato caused the hair on the back of Abdul's neck to stand upright. Toh gasped as her husband fell through the floor. Abdul rushed past her and up the short flight of stairs before staring aghast, through the hole in the floor, at the motionless body below.

Chapter 50

Fatima's throat was tight as she screamed Aashif's name. Terror washed over her in waves, and she grew hysterical as the weretiger burrowed its head between her legs. 'Please,' she pleaded, 'please.'

She sensed that the beast was taking in her scent and tried to kick out, but the weight of the creature's head held her still. It cast a long stare at her and gave a low purr.

'Get away from me!' she screeched. In the weak light, she spotted a glint in the creature's yellow eyes, and she shrieked at the top of her voice, beating the ground in a desperate attempt to wake Aashif. 'Wake up,' she roared, desperate for him to come to her aid.

At this, the beast raised its head and moved it towards Aashif. She tried to push it off her, and it drew back and stared deep into her eyes. She continued to see Aashif's features in its own and she began to shake uncontrollably. She retreated from the beast until it gave a roar that startled all the nocturnal animals in the jungle.

As she attempted to push herself even deeper into the shelter and away from the beast, its flaming eyes bore into her, and she screamed again. At this, it lifted its head skywards, opened its jaws and roared in rage. As she felt the sensation of the beast's tail on her feet, she stiffened in terror.

The creature gave an angry, grumbling sound and Fatima tensed; by this point, her face was soaked with tears. The animal pushed itself up on to its haunches and Fatima curled herself into a tight ball, drawing her knees to her chest with her arms locked around them, and prayed loudly. Suddenly, the beast raised its head to the skies and let free a mighty bellow. Fatima screamed again, but then, out of nowhere, a dark shadow burst through the roof of the shelter.

* * *

Anwar was drawn to the scene by Fatima's screams, filled with a desire to defend and protect her. His heart was pounding when he threw himself at the weretiger and wrapped his arms around its neck, his fingers interlocked.

The beast quickly fled from the shelter and began jumping around in a frenzy, trying to shake Anwar off, but the man hung on for dear life, retaining his grip as the creature sprang from side to side. The weretiger's howls and the sounds of the jungle combined to make a noise so chilling that it was as if hell had opened.

Anwar knew he would be torn apart by branches if the beast left the clearing and entered the jungle—he had to keep it in the open. Each time he sensed that the monster was preparing to jump into the air, he tightened his fingers around its neck.

In a frenzy, the beast sprang one way then another, jumping around in circles as it struggled to rid itself of Anwar, who clung on perilously. It noticed a gnarled branch on the edge of the jungle and attempted to rub up against it, but Anwar spotted the danger in time and swung his body away. He knew that it was only a matter of time before he lost his hold, leaving him at the mercy of the beast's claws. He also knew that he did not have the strength to bring the beast down. He bellowed at Fatima, 'Wake Aashif up.'

Menaced, the weretiger rose on its hind legs and resumed its effort to shake Anwar off. As much as the warrior tried to tighten his grip, he became aware that his strength was failing—he had to bring this battle to an end before the beast threw him off and pounced on him.

The creature stopped abruptly and shook its head while growling furiously. Instinctively, Anwar tried to prepare himself for another explosion of rage and what he knew would be a battle to the death.

He considered trying to grab the two daggers that were strapped across his shoulders, but he feared that if he did, he would lose his grip on the creature's neck. Out of the corner of his eye, he spotted Fatima scrambling to her feet, and he screamed at her again to wake Aashif.

'He won't wake up,' she shouted.

The weretiger turned towards Fatima and Anwar watched, dismayed, as the girl fell to her knees. The weretiger whimpered at first, but then began to hiss contemptuously in her direction. Anwar realized that he had no more options left—he could only pray that if he held on for long enough, the beast would wear itself out.

* * *

Lying on the ground, Fatima stretched her hand out until she touched Aashif. She was unable to comprehend what was happening to him. Trembling with fear, she stared through the dark and saw that the weretiger was glaring at her. Remembering the amulet, she began to crawl on the ground, searching for her bag. She swept her arms in desperate circles, until one hand touched something familiar. She pounced on the bag, but it was empty. 'No!' she cried.

She resumed the search but kept grabbing her bajus and shoes. It was when she was pushing herself up with her hands that she cried out in pain—one of the amulet's spikes had punctured the tip of her thumb.

Using her uninjured hand, she grabbed the amulet and stepped out from the covering. She was so nervous that she gasped for breath, but she stepped forward and squared up to the weretiger. 'Here,' she shouted and held up the amulet.

Bewildered, the beast stopped completely and looked around, confused. Fatima stepped forward gingerly and held the amulet even higher. At the same time, Anwar loosened his grip on the beast, vaulted over the creature, and landed beside Fatima just as she was pressing the amulet towards the weretiger's face.

The beast's hostile features faded in a pathetic gesture of fear, and it retreated towards the jungle, its eyes lifeless, leaving behind a trail of broken branches.

Anwar stood facing Fatima, who stood in stunned silence before falling against him, limp in his arms. While he was holding her he thought he detected some sort of movement—a blurred shadow, almost like a cloud-like substance—enter the shelter.

'It was Aashif, Anwar. I could see him in the creature's face.'

A groan came from the shelter, and they stared at each other.

Aashif sat upright and tried to take in his surroundings, before leaping to his feet in alarm. He raced from the shelter but the sight of Fatima embracing Anwar stopped him in his tracks. 'What's happened?'

'A weretiger,' Fatima said.

'A weretiger?' Aashif stood open-mouthed. 'What about the shelter?'

'That was me,' Anwar said, and he told Aashif what had happened.

'The amulet—it frightened the beast off,' Fatima said, holding it aloft.

* * *

The three sat around a fire, each trying to distract their companions.

'The weretigers are believed to have their own town deep in the jungle,' Anwar said. 'They are demons, the deadliest of all beasts.'

Fatima no longer knew what she was thinking. Anwar's presence caused her to think of Toh, and she pined for her deeply. At the same time, she yearned to feel Aashif's arms around her.

When Aashif rested a hand on the ground and Fatima's fingers touched his, his spirits soared. He knew that Anwar was there to take them back to the palace, which meant that he was going to have to fight the warrior if they were to gain their freedom. He sensed that the older man was putting off the inevitable moment when he would tell them that they had to return with him.

Fatima cuddled up to Aashif, and she was asleep within minutes.

'This is as good a time as any,' Anwar said, 'for me to tell you why I'm here.' He spoke softly so as not to wake Fatima.

'I know why you're here, sir,' Aashif replied. 'But we're not coming back to the palace with you.'

'I was scared you might say that. You realize that I'm obliged to persuade you otherwise—by whatever means possible?

Aashif nodded.

'Then at least show me the courtesy of listening to what I have to say.'

'I'm listening.'

'Tell me, what route did you take?'

'Across the mountains—through the warriors' graves.'

'I suppose you'd like to know what goes on up there?'

Aashif nodded; his eyes wide. 'Yes, I'm curious.'

Anwar nodded. 'Some years ago, when the late Raja was on his deathbed, he confided in me. He made me promise to keep his secret, and I've kept my word until now. You're right that there are no dead warriors up there—it was the late Raja who started that rumour, in order to assuage his worries about how he might defend the lands. To make the story work, he embellished it to the extent that today's warriors are scared to go near the place. I'm sure you're wondering about the spears that doubtless rained down on you both. Several machines designed to fire projectiles have been modified to shoot spears at the enemy.'

'We were lucky.'

'Yes, you were, but what troubles me is the stress that you must have put that young woman through. Have you considered how she will manage crossing vast seas, and travelling through countries confronted by strange, often dangerous, people? Are you willing to put her through all that?'

* * *

It was daylight when Fatima woke to find that the two men were still in conversation.

'Young woman, I have a message for you from Princess Toh,' Anwar passed her the sealed dispatch Toh had entrusted to him.

Chapter 51

Fatima's hands were shaking as she prised open the letter from Princess Toh. She held the folded piece of paper firmly, aware that Aashif and Anwar were watching her closely. As she started reading, a ball of tension was in the pit of her stomach.

Dearest Fatima,

You may be worried that I'm about to scold you, but I am not. You may fear that I'm angry with you, but I am not. I am angry, but my anger is towards Dato Hamidi—and myself. I failed you. I should have evicted Dato Hamidi, which I now intend to do, rather than sent you from your home.

Fatima, I miss you dreadfully. You are like my baby sister, and I love you deeply. You are also my greatest friend, yet I failed you in so many ways. In recent times, I was so preoccupied with my responsibilities and proving my worth to the Raja that I overlooked your importance to me completely.

Please come back. I miss you so much, and there are so many dreams I want us to fulfil together. In this message, I'm doing something that I should have done a long time ago—I'm freeing you from slavery. Yes, Fatima, by the power granted to me as representative of the Raja, from this day forth, you are a free woman. Please come home and we can live as equals.

I have learned of your love for Aashif, and the message inside is for him. It confirms that I am freeing him too—he is worthy of standing tall as a free man.

Toh

Fatima unfolded Aashif's message, scarcely able to believe what she had read. She passed it to him and studied his reaction.

Aashif,

I'm disappointed that you've taken Fatima from me and embarked on such a perilous journey. Nevertheless, many matters have been brought to my attention since then, and I'm pleased to write this message to you.

So that you may fulfil your Haj unencumbered, I free you from slavery, as I do Fatima. I declare that from this day forth you are a free man, just as Fatima is a free woman.

Princess Toh

Aashif stared at the letter in silence. He gazed at Fatima, stunned. He was not able to speak, such was the elation and sadness that was rushing through him. He was unaware of what Toh had written to Fatima in her letter, but he could guess, and that was the reason for his sadness—he knew she would accompany Anwar back to the palace.

His heart was pounding when he raised his arm, pretending to shade his eyes from the morning light—in truth, he was covering his sadness as he passed the letter back to Fatima.

Aashif and Fatima sat in silence for a long time. Finally, they passed the letters to Anwar. After he read them, he addressed them both. 'You two clearly have a lot to discuss. I'll leave you to talk about what you want to do. Of course, as free people, I have no claims over you, and you are at liberty to go wherever you choose.'

The youngsters watched as Anwar rose and stepped away to tend his horse. They sat in silence for a couple of minutes before their eyes finally met. 'I'm going back, Aashif,' Fatima said.

'I know,' he said, his voice faltering.

After a pause, Fatima spoke again, her lips trembling, 'When we first left the palace, I was driven by a desire to spend the rest of my life with you, to help you achieve your dream of finding your father while becoming a free woman myself.' She paused to catch her breath, before continuing, 'What I hadn't considered was how much I would miss Toh.'

* * *

After the youngsters had washed and dressed, they sat together, Fatima holding on to Aashif's arm. She was troubled by a strange feeling of discomfort that had lingered for days and she struggled to know what to say to him. She couldn't stop thinking about the one memory that continued to dominate her thoughts—the moment when she had first given her body to him. She finally plucked up the courage to speak, her voice quiet, 'After the journey we've been through, far greater challenges surely lie ahead, and I'll only be a burden to you. You must complete your Haj on your own and then try and find your father.'

She bit her lower lip and lapsed into silence, before eventually finding the courage to continue, 'I ask only one thing of you. Promise me you'll do everything in your power to return?'

'I promise,' he said.

They silently made their way back to the clearing where the battle with the weretiger had taken place, but they were surprised to find that Anwar was nowhere to be seen. They both shouted his name, to no avail, and then Aashif discovered that his horse was gone.

'He can't have gone,' Fatima said, before hurrying to the shelter. Their meagre possessions were still there, but there was no sign of Anwar. It was as they were stringing their bags across their backs and preparing to set off, that a tremendous noise shattered the peace. Moments later, Anwar came crashing through the foliage on his horse.

'Up there and beyond,' he said, nodding to his left, 'is the sea. Because we're far below the level of the hilltop and in the dense trees, you can't hear the waves, but we're very close to the shore.'

Fatima whispered to Aashif, 'I need to pee.' He smiled and directed her behind the shelter. Once she had left them, Aashif turned to Anwar, 'I've been hoping to talk to you on your own. Please take care of her until I get back.'

'When will that be?'

'A year or so.'

'Yes, I'll keep an eye on her.'

'Thank you.' Aashif paused. 'One final thing. The young slave girl who was murdered; was she buried in the graveyard of the unknown warriors?'

'Yes,' Anwar said. 'I buried her there so that her grave would be left in peace.'

'I thought as much—we came across her grave. Now that I know it's hers, I'll be able to direct my prayers to where she lies.'

'Are we ready?' Anwar asked when Fatima returned.

Aashif nodded at Fatima. 'Ready,' she said.

As Anwar walked ahead of the two, all Aashif and Fatima could do was cast occasional glances at one another. Once they'd reached the top of the ridge, they stared at a vast expanse of sparkling sea, open-mouthed. Aashif spotted a peninsula out at sea and drew Fatima's attention to it. 'In a year or two, I'll come sailing around that point.' Fatima took hold of his hand and squeezed it, as she tried not to cry.

Anwar turned away when Aashif stepped up to Fatima, 'Promise you'll be here when I return?'

They kissed and Fatima's tears spilled on to his face. 'I love you,' he said, before walking away. Only when he had reached the tip of the peninsula did he turn back, and his heart soared when he saw her waving at him.

* * *

Fatima knew she'd been irritable in the days before Aashif's departure, but she could not understand how she could have treated him so badly. It was as if her body had been infiltrated by some strange spirit. If only she had displayed her true feelings for him throughout those days, she thought, she would not be so angry with herself now.

She was exhausted from having to share Anwar's horse, and by the time they arrived back at the palace, she was desperate for a hot bath. Anwar helped her from the horse, but as she walked towards the building, she suddenly felt like a bundle of nerves.

'Remember,' Anwar whispered, 'broken love can always be repaired.' He smiled at her. 'I promised Aashif that I would watch over you, so please come to me if you are in difficulty.'

The guard at the foot of the stairs greeted her and she climbed the stairs, where an overexcited Abdul threw his arms around her. Fatima was startled and unsure how to respond, but gave in to his embrace. 'You're about to make a sad lady extremely happy,' he said.

At the sound of footsteps running across the throne room floor and rushing down the stairs, Abdul released her and left the hall to give both women some privacy.

'Fatima!' Toh shouted, sprinting along the corridor. She kissed the girl's cheeks and then her nose. She broke away and gazed into Fatima's eyes, before tweaking her own nose, 'You need a bath.'

'Where's Dato Hamidi?' Fatima asked anxiously.

'He's dead, Fatima,' Toh replied quietly.

Fatima was stunned.

'He fell through the floor in the throne room.'

Fatima stared at the princess in shock.

'It was horrible,' she said. 'Come—I'll tell you all about it.'

They went to their washroom and Fatima stepped out from her baju and wrapped a towel around herself, before waiting for hot water to fill the bath. When it was ready, she slipped into the water. Toh gazed at her, 'I don't know if Dato Hamidi was trying to kill me, but it was such a shock when he fell. If I'm honest, I was glad. He'd just admitted to murdering that tragic young slave girl.'

* * *

The following morning, Anwar entered the jail where the chief was being held, along with Shafie and four other warriors. The chief was crouched on the floor and struggled to get up. The terror on his face had completely replaced his arrogance.

'Get up,' Anwar snarled at him. 'Before you had the local chief executed, he revealed to Shafie here, the truth behind that young girl's murder. You may not have struck the fatal blow, but you deemed her unworthy to live.'

Then Shafie spoke, revealing to the chief what the local chief had admitted.

'He lied,' the chief shouted.

'That may be, but we're choosing to believe him,' Anwar growled. 'Especially after you had the man assassinated.' He turned to the chief, 'On the orders of Princess Toh, you'll be taken from here and led into the jungle where you will be cut and left to fend for yourself—which is more of a chance than you gave that girl.'

'Please allow me to have a weapon?' the chief snivelled.

'No,' Anwar snapped.

* * *

When Osmin walked into the room, he was surprised to be confronted not just by Anwar, but by Shafie and four warriors.

Seated, Anwar gazed up at him threateningly. 'You were tasked by me to return Haron to the palace. Why did you not do so?'

'He was dead,' Osmin snapped.

'So, you buried him in the jungle?'

'Yes.'

'Farouk wanted to bring his body back.'

'I didn't want the muck that was seeping from his wound to come into contact with the horses.'

'Why didn't you build a stretcher and drag him through the jungle? Then, at least, his parents could have buried him properly.'

Osmin stared at Anwar, 'I made the decision I took.'

'And have you explained that to his parents?'

Osmin stalled, 'No.'

'Why?'

'The boy was dead. What more could I have done?'

'Your decision protected yourself, first and foremost. You are unfit to represent the Raja's name. On the orders of Princess Toh, I'll have your badge.' Anwar rose sharply and stretched out his hand. 'You will leave here instantly, never to return, on pain of death.'

Epilogue

Four years later, the scene before Fatima was familiar to her. Anwar stood next to her, the sea stretching to the horizon. Waiting at the bottom of the ridge were a small number of people, including a handful of warriors.

A pleasant breeze carried a strong smell of salt. Fatima recalled how she had felt the first year, when she had stood in exactly the same spot. On that day, she had waited until dusk before turning away broken-hearted, the knowledge that she would have to endure another year resting heavy on her mind.

Had it not been for Hisham, by the second year she might have forgotten what Aashif looked like altogether. She cast her mind back to his departure, recalling the year that followed as one of great sadness. 'If not after a year, then after two years, that's what he promised,' she had insisted to Anwar.

Her stomach churned all day as she sat on the ridge and gazed out at the horizon. This time, she fought to keep her attention on the skyline and tried to avoid making eye contact with Anwar. She stared at the tip of the peninsula as she struggled to control her mounting disappointment.

She glanced down at the small group of people and wished she had come alone—she did not want the others to witness the misery she'd endured for the past four years. Her heart pounded in her chest as the time for her to turn away approached and it felt like she'd lost Aashif forever.

She noticed Anwar staring at her, and she hoped he would remain silent—she had nothing to say to him.

They stood up and turned away from the sea. Anwar took Fatima's hand, and they began their descent from the top of the ridge. It was as they were manoeuvring the first few steps that Fatima tightened her grip on Anwar's hand and stopped. She swung round to Anwar. 'What's that sound? Listen.'

Anwar stared at her.

'Someone's singing. Can't you hear it?'

While Anwar strained to hear, Fatima scampered back to the top of the ridge, excitement filling her whole body. Then, when she was at the summit, she spotted a small rowing boat crashing through the waves. The voice was being carried on the wind, and she struggled to make out the words:

> Deeper yet the water grows
> Nor the mountain rain is stilled
> My heart more longing knows
> And its hope is unfulfilled.

She recognized it instantly – it was The Last Great Love Song. She leapt up and down and waved frantically, overcome with happiness, as the rowing boat disappeared behind the trees blocking her view. She couldn't decide whether to rush down to the beach or wait.

Anwar took her arm. 'Don't go injuring yourself now,' he cautioned.

Fatima was peering through the trees when Aashif suddenly appeared, a bundle on his back. He put down his load and Fatima stood agape at the sight of an old man struggling on his feet.

Anwar left Fatima alone, and she walked down the slope, her long hair flowing in the breeze. Aashif moved forward, and Fatima called out his name as she ran to him. They fell into each other's arms. 'I'm sorry,' he said. 'I should have returned two years ago.'

Fatima gazed into his eyes but was distracted by the old man. Aashif turned and smiled at him before speaking a language she couldn't understand. 'My father,' he said, smiling.

In a rush of words, he told Fatima that he'd been reunited with his father after he'd found him begging in the market at Jeddah. He had been sold into an Arab family and when his health failed, he was left on the street to fend for himself. 'It was a miracle, Fatima,' he said. 'By doing my Haj, I was rewarded.' He paused. 'He knows I have you to thank for my return.'

The old man spoke, and Aashif translated. 'He says he understands now why I was so desperate to return—you are very beautiful.'

Fatima laughed.

'I told him all about you, and Anwar, and Hisham, and Suraya, and Princess Toh.'

Fatima's eyes glazed over. 'Aashif, Hisham died nearly four years ago.'

Aashif stared mournfully at Fatima, but at that moment Anwar appeared carrying a small boy. He handed the child to Fatima, his mother, when the boy stretched his arms out to her. She took him gladly and held him out to Aashif, 'I named him Hisham.' Aashif stood open-mouthed as he tried to come to terms with what she was telling him. 'Aashif, hold your son,' she said, her voice shaking with pride.

Acknowledgements

I had the privilege of visiting the Royal Palace of Perak, situated in Kuala Kangsar, the royal town of Perak, Malaysia, on many occasions. Today, the building is under the protection of the Perak Royal Museum. Although built one hundred years after the setting of *The Last Great Love Song*, it was nevertheless the inspiration for the palace depicted in this book. I would urge any visitors to Perak to pay the palace a visit.

Although I was to become familiar with Malaysia's topography, I was helped enormously in describing the terrain, as well as the wildlife, in my story by a wonderful site to be found on Facebook, *Kinta Heritage*, administered by Yvonne Blake. The site is dedicated to the preservation, transmission and promotion of the history, heritage and identity of the Kinta Valley, Perak, Malaysia.

Whereas Fern mountain stands alone in Perak, I was inspired to draw it into my story because of its sheer beauty, and so placed it at the beginning of the mountain range I wrote of. To this end, I claim poetic licence.

I drew inspiration from *An Analysis of Malay Magic* by K.M. Endicotte, *Malay Poisons and Charm Cures* by John D. Gimlette and *Malay Magic – Being an Introduction to the Folklore and Popular Religion of the Malay Peninsula* by Walter W. Skeat, as well as Wikipidia and the Internet. I must mention Eka Kurniawan and his wonderful book, *Man Tiger*, a worthy read on the topic of weretigers.

Thanks to Nora Nazerene Abu Bakar, Thatchaayanie Renganathan, Ishani Bhattacharya and Divya Vijayak for all the help and support they have given in the publication of the story. As for any errors subsequently discovered, I claim total responsibility.